Women of Algiers in Their Apartment

Women of Algiers in

Their Apartment

By ASSIA DJEBAR

Translated by Marjolijn de Jager

Afterword by Clarisse Zimra

CARAF BOOKS

University of Virginia Press

CHARLOTTESVILLE AND LONDON

This is a title in the CARAF BOOKS Series

UNIVERSITY OF VIRGINIA PRESS

Originally published as *Femmes d'Alger dans leur appartement*
© des femmes, 1980
This translation and edition copyright, © 1992
by the Rector and Visitors of the University of Virginia

First published 1992
First paperback printing 1999
ISBN 978-0-8139-1880-8 (paper)

3 5 7 9 8 6 4

The preparation of this volume was made possible in part by a grant from the
National Endowment for the Humanities, an independent federal agency.

The Library of Congress has cataloged the hardcover edition as follows:

Djebar, Assia, 1936–
 [Femmes d'Alger dans leur appartement. English]
 Women of Algiers in their apartment / by Assia Djebar ; translated
by Marjolijn de Jager ; afterword by Clarisse Zimra.
  p. cm. – (CARAF books)
 Translation of: Femmes d'Alger dans leur appartement.
 ISBN 0-8139-1402-7
 I. Title. II. Series.
PQ3989.2.D57F413 1992
843–dc20
                                              92-16856
                                                   CIP

Printed in the United States of America on acid-free paper

Contents

Women of Algiers in Their Apartment

Overture

These stories, a few frames of reference on a journey of listening, from 1958 to 1978.

Fragmented, remembered, reconstituted conversations . . . Fictitious accounts, faces and murmurings of a nearby imaginary, of a past-present that rebels against the intrusion of a new abstraction.

I could say: "stories translated from . . . ," but from which language? From the Arabic? From colloquial Arabic or from feminine Arabic; one might just as well call it underground Arabic.

I could have listened to these voices in no matter what language, nonwritten, nonrecorded, transmitted only by chains of echoes and sighs.

Arabic sounds—Iranian, Afghan, Berber, or Bengali—and why not, but always in feminine tones, uttered from lips beneath a mask.

An excoriated language, from never having appeared in the sunlight, from having sometimes been intoned, declaimed, howled, dramatized, but always mouth and eyes in the dark.

Today, how do I, as water dowser, craft words out of so many tones of voice still suspended in the silences of yesterday's seraglio? Words of the veiled body, language that in turn has taken the veil for so long a time.

Here, then, is a listening in, by means of which I try to grasp the traces of some ruptures that have reached their term. Where all that I could come close to were such voices as are groping with the challenge of beginning solitudes.

*

*   *

Women of Algiers in Their Apartment

Once I used to think that going from colloquial Arabic to French would bring a loss of all that was truly alive, of the play of colors. All I wanted to remember then was a sweetness, a nostalgia of words. . . .

Do women live despite this padded sound? This constraint of the veil drawn over bodies and sounds rarefies the very oxygen of fictitious characters. They are barely getting close to the light of their truth when they find themselves once again with ankles shackled because of the sexual taboos of reality.

For at least ten years—as a result, no doubt, of my own Arabic woman's silence, by fits and starts—I have been affected by the extent to which speaking on this ground has become, in one way or another, a transgression (except for spokespeople and "specialists").

Don't claim to "speak for" or, worse, to "speak on," barely speaking next to, and if possible very close to: these are the first of the solidarities to be taken on by the few Arabic women who obtain or acquire freedom of movement, of body and of mind. And don't forget that those who are incarcerated, no matter what their age or class, may have imprisoned bodies, but have souls that move more freely than ever before.

*

* *

New women of Algiers, who have been allowed to move about in the streets just these last few years, have been momentarily blinded by the sun as they cross the threshold, do they free themselves—do we free ourselves—altogether from the relationship with their own bodies, a relationship lived in the shadows until now, as they have done throughout the centuries?

Are they really speaking in truth as they dance, and not thinking how they'll always have to whisper because of the eye through the peephole?

Assia Djebar, 1979

Today

Women of Algiers in their Apartment

to Sakina, my sister
in Abu Dhabi

I

A young woman's head, blindfolded, neck thrown backward, hair pulled back—the fog in the narrow room prevents one from seeing its color—either light chestnut, auburn rather, might it be Sarah? no, not black . . . The skin seems transparent, a droplet of sweat on one temple . . . The drop is going to fall. That noseline, the lower lip with its bright pink edge: I do know it, I recognize it! And the profile pitches sharply; to the right, to the left. A light rocking without the lullaby voice of the wet nurse who would keep us warm together in the tall and somber bed of childhood. It pitches down to the right, to the left, without the weeping of gentle sorrow, the droplet of sweat has become a tear, a second tear. Smoke rising in spirals. The left half of the blindfolded face (white bandage, not black, she is not condemned, she must have put it on herself, she's going to rip it off, she's going to burst out laughing, explode with life in front of me, she . . .), the left half streaming wet all over in the silence, rather in the severed sound, the gasps stuck in her throat like a fishbone; the other part of the face, profile of stone, distant statue that's going to float backward, always backward. Sound severed . . . Sarah . . . Call her, quavering in the call to prevent the sacrifice, what sacrifice . . .

At last, noises in the opaque room: bare-chested men, nurses' masks over their mouths (no, not "my" nurses: these are athletic, well fed, unruffled . . .), they come, they go, I can't count them. At last, noises, what respite: the countryside should be there, very close by, through the open skylight, some douar. The bleating of a goat; followed by an entire henhouse of piccolo music . . . No birds, children crying in the distance in light-hearted tones, a fairly high fountain, more of a spring really, the water splashing the budding grass . . . Very close by, the head nurse is fiddling with a motor, gets it to start, but the water of the fountain submerges everything in floods nourished by deliverance, the goat bleats all alone toward the blue sky, no more children who sing or moan, which is the same . . .

The young woman's still mask has fallen aside, neckless perhaps, and at last the table becomes visible with bottles suspended on either side, and tubes, just like kitchen equipment? . . . "My" table, "my" room, no, I am not operating for I am not there, inside, similarly surrounded, I watch but I'm not with them, will Sarah wake up, the anesthesia, beginning or end of the operation, and the nearby douar without women's or children's voices, without calls on the horizon, only the goat, a white goat with a neck stretched out, the skylight has grown wider, a pure white sky, as if painted, a new sky, silent too, growing larger above the male nurses, no, the technicians, sky that will annihilate them. Again a child whimpers nearby, or could it be Sarah, blindfolded, holes where eyes should be . . . The motor begins to run dangerously, the "gene"—generator— is wired, place of torture . . .

Ali jumped out of bed.

The room, flooded with sunlight, the balcony looking out over a corner of the city and leaning toward the boats in dock. Quiet vessels.

Sarah, coming and going in the kitchen, was using the toaster. Leaning briefly against the casing of the window that opened onto the balcony, Ali slowly began to wake up. Blinking his eyes against the morning's iridescence, he stepped back inside, heading for the bathroom. "Water," he thought, "I need fresh water!" He'd splash himself with it and that would pull him fully from the edginess of his sleep.

The telephone. Sarah rushes into the hallway.

She bends over, waits: the milk on the stove might burn.

"It's me!" Anne begins. "Can you come over? I'm not well . . ." (suspense; Sarah calls, whispering) . . . "Not well at all," the detached voice in the distance begins again.

Sarah, coming back into the kitchen, abandons the breakfast

preparations, puts on her shoes in the bedroom where Ali is now doing his exercises, takes the car keys.

"And Nazim, still out?" . . . (behind her the man's voice grumbles). "We might need him here, now that . . ."

The door slams in the breeze. Sarah drives through narrow streets that climb, descend, turning more and more into sliding dreamlike corridors. Streets piled high with garbage. Sarah suddenly observes: "Third day of the work stoppage by the garbage collectors." Throughout the drive, an uneasiness persists inside her.

"Is it only with Ali, is it with all of them? . . . When others talk to me, their words aren't connected. . . . They float around before they reach me! . . . Is it the same when I talk, if I talk? My voice doesn't reach them. It stays inside."

Yet, Anne, on the phone: with her first word it was as if a flash of anguish had shaken the instrument.

The car parked, Sarah opens the door of a hallway covered with mosaic tile. For two days, Anne has been cloistered inside this old building.

Sarah's precise, efficient gestures in the bathroom of green-colored marble: with the faucet wide open, Anne over the bathtub vomiting at length. Sarah brings over what is needed: bucket of water, wet mop, sponge; so much havoc to clean up.

She sees herself in the mirror above the sink: standing behind the Frenchwoman whose hair is too long. Sarah pulls back the black mass. Anne bends over, splashes her cheeks, her forehead, her whole face. Lets out some fitful groans. Without moving, Sarah braids her hair; with one hand she takes a bottle of cologne, opens it, pours some on the neck of her friend, moves back. She splashes herself with it too. Get rid of the smell of vomit . . . She isn't listening to Anne, who moans: "I'm sorry . . . really, I'm so sorry!"

In the wide, low room wrapped in semidarkness, where the transient one had slept, Sarah straightens out the mattress, fluffs up the pillows, shakes out the mat of dry reeds. . . .

"It pays to be living with a surgeon. Before, I would stupidly have called emergency. Too many pills all at once: just make her vomit, it's quite simple!"

Anne is pacing around, drawing stubborn circles in the middle of the bare room. Sarah sits down in a corner, on the marble floor. Marble kills all odors: odors of sickness, of despair.

"A fit of the blues!..." Anne snickers. "A real soap opera: a mature and abandoned woman in distress, unsuccessful suicide attempt!... There's only one unknown factor: why come from so far all the way here for this?"

The choppy motion of her arm, pointing at the cushions and the mattress, now neat again.

"I should've told you yesterday when you were waiting for me at the harbor" (she sighs... finds her gentleness back again), "Sarah, I've come here to die!"

Sarah, far away, crouched in the gloomiest corner, suddenly wishes she could melt away in the darkness.

"I understood it yesterday at dawn, as I came out on deck: the boat was coming in to shore. Everyone was looking at the white city, its arcades almost diving into the water, its leaning terraces. Facing this long-awaited scene, I was crying without even knowing it, and when I did realize it, the only words that came to me—despite the splendor out there—were: 'My God, I've come here to die!' It all seemed so obvious to me: this city where I apparently was born, which I had forgotten, even when yesterday's newspapers were talking about it all the time, I come back here for the end...."

Then Anne chronologically pours out a story, a predictable one. "Her" story; the husband, the three children, fifteen years of a strange life contained in one hour of words: Is it trite? It's trite.

Finally, Sarah gets up with stiff knees, goes to the bay window, does what she's been wanting to do since the story began: with a quick movement, she pulls open the enormous curtain of red-striped linen.

"No!" the other cries out, blinded.

Sarah turns halfway around: the braid on her shoulder, Anne has retreated to the white wall in the back, both hands over her eyes as if to blindfold them convulsively, her raised elbows

Women of Algiers in Their Apartment

still shuddering. Later, a little later, she sobs: "I can't bear the light!"

Sarah, once again crouched on the mat, takes her in her arms, rocks her rhythmically while she continues to come apart, to put herself back together in a different kind of weariness.

*

*   *

INTERLUDE

In the house next door in this section of badly whitewashed little homes, the *hazab* has ten daughters. The *hazab* is the reader of the Koran in the mosque. That does not prevent him from continuing his craft, from going to his shoemaker's stall between the hours of prayer, a shop that's a meeting place for scholars of Islamic law. He is an old man, dressed in a white toga, a clean one every day, that floats nobly around his gnarled body. He now goes around encircled by the visible respect of the neighborhood.

More than thirty years earlier, during the riots of 8 May 1945, he had been condemned to death for having tried to blow up the arsenal of a small seaside town. Pardoned three years later, he married, came to live in the capital, had four daughters, then spent five years in Barberousse prison (from the very onset of the "events" in Algeria, with the first suspicion of underground activity, he had quite naturally been arrested).

His wife had raised her first brood in utter poverty, for it was her primordial concern to fill the weekly baskets for the prison. She had again picked up the regular rhythm of giving birth "the day after independence" (many far nobler tales still begin with this oratorical expression . . .). In her fortieth year and with her twelfth pregnancy, one of which had been a miscarriage, Allah, may he be praised, at last granted her the son she'd been dreaming of.

The *hazab*'s heir was just beginning his sixth year. They were about to celebrate the boy's circumcision, the first family celebration.

Three of the daughters from "before independence" (the fourth, the most unobtrusive one, had just become engaged to a bank teller) caused some problems. The eldest, twenty-four years old, had been practicing judo since her teens, and furthermore insisted on going out only in slacks (the only explanation, incidentally, for the persistent lack of serious marriage proposals). The second one, at twenty-two, was at the university, finishing a bachelor's degree in the natural sciences (and the father, strolling around outside, was making an attempt at understanding the relationship between the natural sciences and a female brain but dared not speak of it; as he grew older, he had become shy with his daughters and was suffering all the more because he had to hide it). The third one, finally, Sonia, twenty years old—the teller of this minichronicle—was spending all her free time in athletic training. She had recently decided to become a physical education teacher. "Oh, just to live in a stadium!" she'd add with fervor.

This very morning, Sarah entered the *hazab*'s house, devoted a good bit of time to calmly reeling off the proper formulas of politeness in a tiny courtyard where the mother, seated with her legs widely spread in front of a brazier, was grilling green peppers and tomatoes, while two of her daughters were sliding barefoot in the water and arguing in little bursts of laughter. Unfortunately, Sonia was training: Sarah asked that, upon her return from the stadium, she be sent to keep Anne company.

At the door, the visitor met the *hazab*. She kissed his right shoulder. He spoke to her for a few moments to apologize for the garbage that lay strewn all over; he told her he'd managed to obtain the neighbors' promise to keep their trash cans covered. Sarah listened to him, then went back to the car, which she maneuvered through the alley under the watchful eye of the *hazab* and some children rooted in the doorways.

Two hours later, young Sonia entered Anne's place. From the narrow orchard where all the girls would gather, there was a connection, through a door, with the building where Anne was staying in a studio that overlooked the surrounding terraces. And so Sonia slipped in, lightly dressed, slippers on her feet. Opening the door for her, Anne was fleetingly touched by the svelte and dark-olive beauty of the young girl.

"I am the promised neighbor!" Sonia said.

Without further ado, she prepared some tea, went back to the orchard to pick a handful of jasmine blossoms, which she put in the sugar bowl, and then announced that she'd like to get better acquainted.

At first playful with the Frenchwoman, she soon turned into a fine family chronicler.

*

*   *

II

"Your father has a vesicle to remove, and he should be out in twenty minutes," remarked the secretary, impeccably made up, glasses in hand. Through the glass partition in the door, Nazim briefly watched Ali's gestures on the screen of an interior television that hung over the operating table.

The room seemed narrow. In a corner, Nazim noticed the motionless anesthesiologist, face frozen. Another aide was standing behind a geometric figure of bottles and tubes that came out of the enormous oxygenation machine.

The atmosphere of the semilighted place seemed tragically unreal in its confinement. Ali's masked face imprinted itself once more on the television screen . . .

As he turned around, Nazim bumped into the secretary.

"Go wait in his office!" she suggested. "There's even some coffee in the thermos."

She followed the adolescent with her eyes as he walked away down the hall.

He didn't take the elevator, crossed a crowded waiting area that opened into two consultation rooms where interns were seeing patients. An old peasant woman upbraided him in Berber. Nazim stopped. Half veiled, a gaudy dress covering her buxom body, the woman was railing at him as she showed him a dozing baby in the hollow of a black shawl that cut into her chest.

The young man made a helpless gesture, turned around to look for a bilingual nurse. The old woman started her speech again, now to Aïcha, the secretary, who answered in the same rough accent. Relieved, Nazim left them.

In the air-conditioned office with its shiny brown teak furniture, he turned on another television monitor: on the screen the surgeon, who was about to finish, made one or two curt and commanding motions to his aides, then his eyes staring boldly out, like those of a veiled city woman, focused for a rather long time in close-up.

The adolescent took a blank sheet of paper, a pencil, and from right to left, right across the page, he furiously wrote several slanted lines in Arabic characters.

He went out as his father's face was disappearing from the screen to make place for the fluttering whiteness of the void.

Ali used only colloquial Arabic: the work load of the Department of General Surgery, one of the most modern in the country, hadn't allowed him to retrain himself in the national language during the past few years.

He phoned the Cytology Department, close by, had them call a laboratory assistant who came from the same village as he.

"Daughter of the Aurès mountains," he said to her in a somewhat forced grumble, "I need your help again in translating, this time for some family literature."

She came right away. In her voice, diligent—as was her whole person, round and fresh—she read: "You have been, you say, among those who spat on your submissive fathers in order to run up into the hills to 'light the fire of the revolution' . . ." ("Arabic is always so full of imagery," she noted, as if she were apologizing).

"Is that all?" Ali cut in.

"Wait, he goes on to say: 'Sons no longer spit on their fathers in order to venture out . . . I'm leaving, I don't know where . . . If I come back later, it will be only to kiss Sarah's hand.'"

Silence.

"That's all," Baya finally said, as she began to fiddle with a button on her white blouse.

"We've spoiled him too much, I must have said so a hundred times, we've been much too permissive!" Ali murmured gruffly as he got up.

He had always been rather massive, but now he was growing even heavier. Standing in front of the bay window, his wide back hid the view over the harbor. Some forty ships at least, motionless and waiting for days on end for a less crowded dock, looked as if they were forming the fragile figures of a ballet between sky and water. Anchored motionless, despite themselves, they became almost unreal as they faced the invisible gaze of the terraces . . . Abruptly Ali thought of freedom: that word, it hollowed out a large, furtive gap in the light flooding in from outside. It made him shiver. He turned around, his face hardening once again.

"I'll leave it to you to phone Sarah!" He hesitated: "Do what you want: either read her the message or ask her to stop by . . . I'm going back to the O.R., a liver operation, it'll keep me busy for at least three hours!"

He left the room, a cup of coffee in his hand: in the doorway, Aïcha was observing the young woman as she would have an intruder.

"He's worried," Baya murmured, frowning. "A teenager running away from home . . . At fifteen, that's normal!"

She had often felt close to Nazim. To her, he was above all a cousin with whom she could laugh. On his last birthday, she'd even introduced him to one or two new dances.

Slowly Baya went back to the Cytology Department and thanked her colleague for having kept an eye on her cultures while she was gone. That very day, a whole family from the south was anxiously waiting for the verdict of the chromosomic chart: their child, whom they'd been raising as a girl until now, seemed to be of questionable sex. Baya delved back into the elucidation of the charts her "boss" would ask her for at the end of the morning.

Outside the hospital, Nazim tore down a staircase ramp, hoping to find somebody he knew so that he could give the speech he'd prepared about his father out loud: "What has he ever told me about his five years in the underground? . . . The way in which he opened the official ball at the Kremlin just before the sixties (there were five of them, the first "students-fellaghas" to have been allowed into the USSR through the help of the underground and "brother nations"). . . . And about his life in the underground, one single "wretched" detail: that, burrowed deep inside some caves, they would kill their lice in the winter! A comrade from that glorious period even added, in front of me, one day when he was pretty soused: 'We used to kill so many of them and we'd become such experts at it, that the lice made the sound of real machine guns as we crushed them between our nails.' . . . Then Sarah used to say to me (more than a stepmother, she behaves like any aggressive playmate): 'Why do you accuse him of remembering so little of the war? Would you like it better if Ali meticulously fabricated some convenient heroic aura for you to use, as so many fathers do?"

Nazim picked up the speech again as if he knew it by heart. Without seeing anything of the street, obsessed by his words, his vehemence, he arrived at the deserted old port, the harbor of the former "kings of Algiers." . . . He sat down on a parapet. A drunk, in Western clothes with a turban on his head—his face chiseled like those of earlier adventurers, drunk with pillaging and power—shouted an invitation. Nazim refused to drink with him: beer still made him sick. As the other one fell asleep, the young boy began to look around, a row of former fishermen's houses, clustered together under arched roofs, one after another, on a level below a bustling avenue: uprooted peasants were living there now as if in an underground tunnel. Undoubtedly the only ones in the city to permit their little girls and their wives to sit outside as they combed each other's long hair with the gracefulness of gypsies. From afar, some of them began to make fun of the young man and the old drunk, asleep in a ball at his feet, the turban over his reddened face.

"Not to go back to the hospital any more . . ." Nazim thought, then became numb with exhaustion as he faced the layered slopes of the city, whose noises were dissolving in a dusty haze of early morning mists.

At the hospital, among his assistants, Ali was getting prepped. "The most delicate of operations . . . A huge liver to be opened . . . very little chance this old, nationalist notable is going to make it . . ."

Three sons of the patient, eminent civil servants, rigid more with their own importance than with grief, were waiting in the surgeon's office. The fourth one, an industrialist of recent fame and garishly dressed, joined them a little later while Aïcha was serving them coffee in silence.

Ali was operating in a second room: a smaller one, a full corner narrowed into a triangle. Just before, the very moment he entered masked and gloved, he'd hesitated for just a second:

this was the exact spot, he remembered in a flash, where his dream of the preceding nights had taken place.

A hot day. And so, driving the old Peugeot was more wearing on Sarah than usual.

In the laboratory of the institute of musicology, she took off her jacket, rolled up the sleeves of her shirt. As she straightened her hair, she passed her hand over her forehead, took the time to massage her neck once or twice: the first moments of physical well-being since . . . She stopped her memory short—since what pleasure, since which night? She forced herself to figure out how to make up for these two lost hours.

Sitting down, she worked the usual tape recorder, got the headphones ready, took a tape out of its box. Irma, the sound engineer in charge of the laboratory, effusively began to recount the last Moslem weekend, which she always spent with her husband and three boys in an old-fashioned little town in the interior of the country.

"From now on, the law is in effect: pigs will no longer be raised anywhere. Until now we used to stop on the road, at such a lovely independent farm on the plain, where they were raising about a hundred of them there! Whatever cold cuts we'll buy from now on will be processed wild boar . . . There's a lot of wild boar in the woods now that the sharecroppers are leaving many of the garden plots in the foothills . . . They're even going to be exporting deep-frozen wild boar . . ."

Out of courtesy, Sarah kept the headphones on her shoulders. She took advantage of the silence to put them on her ears. With a motion of her finger she apologized and went back to studying the *haoufis* of Tlemcen, women's songs of times gone by.

She put down two sheets of paper in different colors, near the machine. On pink paper, she wrote nervously what pre-occupied her every day now while she ran around the streets of the city, whether on foot or by car, seemingly absentminded:

> How to put an entire city to music
> projected documentary

In the same wide handwriting she added, on white paper:

Women of Algiers in Their Apartment

Documentary on the streets of Algiers
time: to be determined, for a *haoufi*.

She hesitated over the last word; she remembered they used to call those songs of city women "songs of the swing," but hadn't those games of young girls on the terraces been over with a long time ago?

She started the machine. Almost without any accompaniment, two women were humming words, sometimes hesitant, as if their memory would momentarily falter. Nevertheless, Sarah recognized the melody: in her childhood, aunts, cousins, would suddenly start to clap their hands in some courtyard, right in the middle of the household chores. They'd intone these same songs, would childishly insist that one of them get up, make the hip movements in a slow and graceful rhythm. . . . Bit by bit Sarah began to translate:

> Greetings to my house and to the room up
> high . . .

Sarah stopped the tape for a moment, looking for an approximation of the Arabic formulas (is the *ghorfa* just the room up high?), then started the machine up again:

> oh, enemy of enemies
> oh, you, lover of young girls . . .
>   . . .
> The young girls have passed by and found you in
> the middle of your evening meal . . .

Sarah was transcribing the text more slowly than the Arabic verse lines progressed; sometimes, faintly, one of the singers would shriek with laughter as she recalled something:

> The vine full of grapes, the brook full of fish
>   . . .
> You, who climb the mountains,
> may salvation be yours
> may salvation be yours, oh my brother, my
>   mother's son . . .

The song went on. Sarah was no longer writing: the singers' voices were reciting shreds of verse lines in nostalgic fragments—the researcher broke in to announce that these were his mother and sister, recorded on such and such a date and year. . . . Clumsily, Sarah seemed to be following along on some path of sadness. A world of tenderness, with which these voices were filled, was coming to the surface again, like a water lily of oblivion. In earlier days, only the hope for an encounter of love on a terrace, a miracle . . . dwelled on the patios underneath the open sky.

Roughly, Sarah rewound the tape, started the same song again from the beginning, stopwatch in hand. She planned to get the exact timing of the first stanza.

Irma, a band of black hair braided just above her forehead, her body quiet, was standing, engrossed in the cards to be filed; some of them had all the references in Arabic only. She put them aside: they concerned funeral dirges by women of an oasis; but which one exactly, and what kinds of percussion were used? She needed to verify whether the names of the women reciting were mentioned or whether they had remained anonymous.

When she reached a stopping point, Sarah would agree to help her. Irma showed her the cards in silence; Sarah smiled, yes.

The phone. From the hospital, Baya read Nazim's message. Sarah put the receiver down slowly and remained motionless.

Irma came closer: she thought the young woman was going to faint.

"Bad news?" she asked, and her too thick German accent masked the concern in her voice.

Sarah forced herself to move, wanted to go back to her place then decided to take the cards in Arabic that Irma had put down; she began to copy the references:

> Funeral dirges of the women of Laghouat
> ceremony taped in the family X . . .
> the 2nd of the month of Moharrem.
> reel no. . . .

She left the numbers blank: Irma had learned to read Hindi numbers.

Once more in front of the tape recorder, Sarah put the headphones back on. On the pink paper she wrote:

Dance on balconies filled with clusters of children
children daydreaming
circular space.

She pondered these notations as if they concerned the beginning of a poem. On the front of the white sheet she transcribed a new women's song she heard:

Oh, Mother, my Queen . . .
I've met a handsome young man
I gave him the peach
He said to me: "oh my queen, I am ill,
Love has come into my house . . .

Repetitions included, the song lasted two minutes and twenty seconds. On the preceding sheet she noted: "very slow panoramic, from right to left—2:20."

"Nazim has split," she said to herself at last, emerging completely undone by the music, and she wondered, because of the headphones, if perhaps she'd said it out loud . . .

"Strange! You could imagine a world in which women—was I going to say "our" women?—would have been made deaf instead of invisible. They'd decide on an age of enthronement in the forbidden realm, on a ceremony, on an entire ritual: this would serve to equip their ears with enormous barriers, just as I'm wearing now, but then forever . . . They wouldn't listen to anyone anymore and it would be a crime of honor in case a male, whether he hailed from far away or from this very place, were to attempt to be heard by them. . . . All they'd make out would be their interior gurgling until such a time as they reached old age and could no longer bear children.

She dreamed on, started the magnetic tape to listen, in a new space of resonance, to a flute solo.

". . . an adolescent crisis" concluded Irma, who must have said several other things without Sarah having raised her head. She stared at Sarah with the embarrassed look of those who come to offer their condolences, picked up her Arabic cards, now translated, then left the lab with dignity.

In the operating room, a blindfolded head, a profile of stone overturned. The patient has died on the operating table. The anesthesiologist redoubles his efforts for a few more minutes. The oxygenation machine rumbles. Hollow silence among the six or seven white masks. Gestures of gloves in an unreal burst of speed. Irrevocably a corpse. Nervously, Ali orders them to sew up the body. He is the first to leave. The three high-placed civil servants were waiting, the industrialist having departed after a half hour of impatience.

"A cirrhosis in its last stages," Ali explained without further ado, once he had announced the fatal outcome . . . . "If you prefer to call it a form of 'generalized cancer' so that your devout wives will not be shocked, feel free to do so. . . . That's a family matter! . . ."

"Thank you, professor," gratefully replied the eldest, who took the concession as a favor done to his elevated position. And he looked his brothers up and down without a word.

Ali left the hospital. He knew how to forget a patient who'd died "on the table": he took his car, leaving the city by the western corniche, and stopped a little later at the house of the painter, his only friend. The latter lived comfortably, that is to say there was no lack of alcohol, in a humid villa.

In the huge, ramshackle garden tents were being set up: the master of the house appeared, disheveled, in shorts; to the new arrival he explained: "Fifteen Palestinians are settling in here . . . For two years now they've been trainees in hydrocarbons. . . . The institute is closed for the summer: the administration isn't even capable of making provisions for the brothers. . . . They've come to protest. Instead of going there to insult a bunch of civil servants, I'd rather they just stay here. The beach isn't far. . . ."

For the painter, more of a poet really (but it was his painting that he sold to the newly rich, while his daily invectives were sure to bring him innumerable hostilities), the national war had not lasted seven years, but was being prolonged by at least seventy more. And so he was still in the middle of it. Perhaps Palestinian friendship might succeed at last in . . .

"In what?"

"In pulling you out of your hatred!" Ali laughed mockingly as he sat down on a mattress inside, surrounded by portraits of gaunt mothers with accusing eyes, some of them in a blue sky, others with an almost black background.

"Hatred!" the painter hissed as he brought both tea and whisky. "We suckle it with the milk of our exploited mothers! They've understood nothing: it's not only colonialism that's at the root of our psychological problems, but it's the belly of our frustrated women! When we're just fetuses, we're already damned!"

"Feed me first," Ali groaned.

"I went to the madhouse this morning," the painter began after his first glass. "I draw for them. As if I had anything to teach them, just like you, professor," he snickered. "And going from one cell to another, whom do I find there, in isolation, locked up for four or five days now, but Leila! . . . Yes, the great Leila, the heroine. Do they give a damn if she's a drug addict; does she harm the others, those decorated together with her? Absolutely not! . . . 'What are you doing here?' I cried out. She wept when she saw me. I opened everything up, shoved everyone out of my way, and I took her with me right then and there. I cursed out the psychiatrists and the rest of their gang. . . . When they come to this lousy country, what do they know? about you, about me, about Leila? . . . She was depressed, she passed out . . . so what? Condemned to death at age twenty, after that years of imprisonment, and again they lock her up? What gall! . . . In the name of fucking science? I've brought her here, I'm going to cure her!"

After some thought, the painter confessed: "Since you're here, pal, I might as well tell you first, I've decided to marry her! . . . I'm the only male around here who refuses to lock a woman up on any account. . . . As long as she's with me, she can count on being able to take off safely. . . ." In one gulp he emptied another glass.

"Do you think she'll go along?" Ali replied.

"Your doubt pains me!" the painter wailed, slipping into the early stages of gentle drunkenness.

When Leila woke up, she put a record on: an old Jewish songstress who reminded her of her childhood and whom her uncle, a shopkeeper in the Casbah, used to have come to every family ceremony.

"What has become of my friend, the one who was with me?" Meriem Feki sang; her melancholy voice used to console the women languishing on the patios in earlier days.

On the bed, listening to the same record over and over again, Leila plunged back into the drifting images of her nightmare: the looks of women veiled in white or in black but their faces freed, who were weeping silently, as if behind a windowpane. And Leila was telling herself, her body in pain, that they, these disappeared aunts and grandmothers, were weeping over her, over her dismantled memory.

"Leave the city for good!" the heroine moaned. "Let them give me a newborn baby, my breasts will swell up with milk at last, and I'll be able to leave, barefoot, and take to the road . . . all the way to . . . to the Lalla Khedidja mountains!"

Sarah, her work done, wandered around outside for a bit, strolled around the "square of the horse" (the horse of General Bugeaud, whose statue had been knocked off its pedestal during the earlier rejoicing): prowlers brushed against her, but so did some children in splattered play. Over there, the line of housewives at the crowded bus stops. Further down, as if sheltered by the foliage, the tangle of masts in the harbor.

Sarah stared at a specific house, not far from the municipal theater, close to an arcaded street. An antiquated balcony, the only one without curtains and open. Every day at the same moment, around six in the afternoon, a woman in a long skirt, orange-petal bright, would appear, half lifting a four- or five-year-old child. Her arms sketch out a dance, the same one every day. She twirls around once, twice, then stands motionless, as if suspended, distant, half bent above the noisy square.

For three consecutive days, during her research for the sound

Women of Algiers in Their Apartment

images of the documentary, Sarah has been observing the little game before going back to her old car. She drives through the hubbub, can't manage to forget the unknown woman: Is she locked up that she thus takes revenge, by this gratuitous burst of frivolous dancing . . . or is it the child who demands space, freedom?

At the steering wheel, Sarah thinks about the teeming of children in rooms up high, on multiple balconies with shutters closed that line the front sides of the streets. She thinks about the cloistered women, not even in a courtyard, just in a kitchen where they sit on the floor, crushed by the overcrowding. . . . Water too regularly cut off, smell of children's urine, scoldings, sighs. . . . No more terraces, no more openings of sky above a feeble fountain, not even the soothing freshness of worn-down mosaics . . .

The only free women in the city go out in single white files before dawn, to do three or four hours of cleaning in the glass offices of low-, middle-, and high-level civil servants who will arrive later on. They burst out laughing in the stairwells, clean up the clutter, with their heads still held high, slowly lifting their headdresses, and all the while they exchange ironic comments on the respective floor managers, those who protectively ask them about their children's studies, and those who don't talk because one doesn't speak to women, whether they work outside the house or are, like their own wives, objects of representation. . . . The free women of the city go home and, with a cup of coffee in front of them, dream of the oldest son who will grow up, who will surely also become one of those floor managers: they will finally be able to close their door and in their turn supervise the young girls in order to keep them sheltered between their walls.

*

*   *

INTERLUDE

In the orchard, near the four orange trees and the lemon tree, heavily laden with fruit, the daughters of the *hazab* were dancing. The voice of the "Old Man"—as the most popular singer of Algiers was called, at least among the confused adolescents and the uprooted intellectuals—jumped as if he had the hiccups: the Andalusian song, unchangeable when others sang it, was charged with a half-ironic, half-despairing mockery when he sang. Broken folklore, its echo would haunt the terraces. At first, the lute would support the singer in slow rhythm; it was the "Old Man" himself—irregular and whimsical in his breaks—who would beat the acceleration of the time at his own choosing. A chorus of senile voices would follow him with difficulty.

As the orchestra resumed, a group of very young girls, slowly dancing, had formed under the lemon tree. Round or thin hips were visible through the foliage and its fruit, despite the semi-darkness; then a candlestick was brought out and put on the flagstone. End of a piece. Laughter crisscrosses between the dancers in the back.

Anne is sitting in the doorway of the low rooms, near Sonia's mother and an old turbaned woman who are decorating diamond-shaped pastries, fat with almonds, with multicolored spangles. Her knees spread, her arms extended, as if she's let a weight fall off, Anne is listening to the calls and exclamations of young voices without understanding them, holds on to the crystalline sound of a laugh, the guttural quaver of a sentence.

A little girl, about ten, barged in: baggy pants too wide for her skinny legs, the father's fez half covering her frizzy hair. Armed with a stick, she threw herself into a Turkish farce, a cruel shaking: a master of the house beating his four wives. Deep in the back of the orchard, the game switched to obscene gestures and shouting.

The mother, fat and jovial, a fine tattoo between her eyes, turned to Baya, who'd come directly from the hospital. She asked her to tell the Frenchwoman what a pleasure it was for her to be hostess to Anne and to welcome her and to tell her also: "This evening, the eve of the circumcision of our youngest—may God preserve him for us! For his protection and his future happiness, we'll put a bit of henna on his hands."

Baya elaborated on this return to folklore: a small spot of red in the palms of his hands, whereas in earlier days, she explained, it used to be an entire ceremony, hands up to the wrists, feet up to the ankles, swaddled throughout the night in the flaming red paste of Paradise.

"Folklore, thus preserved within the family as jam would be, reassures us . . . ," Sonia intervened as she loosened her hair.

The "Old Man" started a new composition after an overture of guitar and lute. The prelude had seemed to scatter the darkness everywhere. Someone had turned off the lights in the rooms on the second floor, no doubt a male cousin who'd come to watch the girls dancing in the dark.

"So they're the ones who hide!" suggested one girl laughing.

"Impudent, aren't you!" another protested. "It's so nice and quiet, far away from the men."

Baya regarded Anne as a true foreigner. Anne happened to mention she'd just come from Lyons, and right away the girl began to reminisce effusively and with obvious pleasure about a study period she'd spent in Lyons, two or three years earlier. It was there that she'd started cytology as the first woman in her country, together with three young men; and Professor Monod, "Nobel Prize Laureate" she specified, who was visiting the department, had personally lavished encouraging words on her.

"We explain to the parents that of the forty-six chromosomes in the blood cell, the last two, XX or XY, are those that determine the child's sex. Our department, the only one in the country, examines the abnormal ones (she was explaining this good-naturedly, as if she were handing out recipes for pastries). What we do is to establish the karyotype, solely on the basis of peripheral blood cells, not on samples of bone marrow as yet . . ."

"What is the abnormality of the day?" Sonia's sister, the one who practiced judo, asked; every time Baya came to visit, it was she who'd suggest they should calm the father by telling him a lie: after all, why should his last chromosome not be a Y instead of an X?

"Just change one letter," she'd sigh emphatically, "and for us everything here would change, really everything!"

"Today," Baya whispered, "it's a twelve-year-old boy who was brought in from the remote hills of the Constantine district. He can't walk, can hardly stand up. His poor mother, totally distraught, can't keep the horrible secret any longer!"

The mother and the old woman in the turban had gone back upstairs, carrying the tray with cakes. The smell of the mint they were preparing for the tea was permeating the air as the lights were turned on again on the second floor.

"My abnormality for today," Baya began anew, as she slid her fingers through her black hair and slowly pulled at it, "well, he had an enormous sex organ. . . . Really! the genitals of an elephant!"

"The light is attracting the mosquitoes," two or three dancers' voices were objecting in the background.

The "Old Man" on the record nasally started his verse again, for the third time, without following the traditional modulation but rather hurling it like a taunt, clearly out of tune with the rhythm:

> I said to her: "my love, my habit, my Meriem,
> Let me be reborn into happiness from your look
>   full of promises!"

"After tea," decided the mother, coming back to put the low table down next to Anne and Baya, "you will see my son in his gandoura: beautiful as an angel, my only one!"

Baya translated and pointed out that the henna wouldn't soften on her palms before midnight.

Sonia had stopped dancing. She came closer; her shoulders bare, laughing, she was munching on a lemon as big as a grapefruit. She handed one to Anne, who declined.

The "Old Man" was still unfurling his plaintive song on the lute. As he listened to it, the *hazab* was trying to sleep on another floor of the house. Every night, despite the music and the smell of the pastries, he didn't feel quite at home somehow in his own house. . . . He blamed his discomfort on his recent disappointment: he had to resign himself to the fact that his son would be circumcised by a doctor and not by the ceremonial sacrificer of earlier days, generally the man with the quickest knife in the village or the district. During certain summers, those able men of yesteryear wouldn't know which way to turn; ten, fifteen, or twenty little boys would have to be stained with blood in just one afternoon, amidst the ritual ululations of the women, as the foreskins were tossed into towels filled with jasmine flowers. Days of celebration that have disappeared! The *hazab* sighed.

That same night Sarah had turned down her friends' invitation. Lying next to Ali in the dark, she saw their bedroom as a temple, deep and empty. "How could I have spent time with them while the child . . . where is he sleeping right now?"

She thought of a Turkish bath, of the heads of peasants piled together under blankets . . . or perhaps a corner in the cellar of an apartment building. There were stories about young girls, often just high-school girls, who'd run away from home if the father suspected some crush. Sarah dreamed of a sacred friendship between adolescents in revolt, and those winding streets of the districts she so loved during the day now seemed to her to be threatening passageways . . . Nazim and his tall, bony silhouette, his gaze that had become so restless, his tic: the index finger rubbing a spot behind his right ear. He should have gone through puberty with quiet circumspection. For six months now he'd been refusing to go to school, sometimes giving away his personal belongings; sometimes he'd be walking around in old rags.

"When I saw him for the first time, he was five years old, five years and three months; he looked at me gravely, a look that was much too serious then. He must have been thinking something like 'Will you know how to love me?' Ten years later, I still haven't managed to close the distance between father and son . . ."

When it came to marrying Ali, she had hesitated for a long time; not because Ali, a widower, had a child to raise, no, very simply because of the marriage itself. . . . After having spent her adolescence in prison—rooms full of murmurs, full of whispering comrades—she had prolonged her years at the university beyond limits.

"What is it you do?" Ali, introduced to her in the hallway of the hospital, had asked her politely.

"I walk all day," she'd answered. "I never get tired, you know, of walking around outside."

She turned over in her bed toward the sleeping man: his sunken eyes, his badly shaven beard and his alcohol breath, exceptional behavior, tonight.

She had married him. Her daytime wanderings had maintained their vaguely circular design, improvised in the vibrant space of inexhaustible light. But from now on they would always return to the same point of departure: this double bed, this man's body.

"In the past he used to move me, asleep like this. And yet, I'd sense him as if he were closed off, as if he were hiding secrets beyond my suspicion. Sleep closed in on itself. His body doesn't even quiver. If he were dead it would be just the same. Opaque, a man always remains opaque."

Very early in the morning she opened the shutters. In the kitchen she listened to some music. Made a few light exercise movements in front of a sun-filled window. She came back into the bedroom with a tray. Ali was beginning to wake up.

"I'm bringing you breakfast. The radio has just announced that the city will be cleaned up: despite the harbor's congestion, the garbage trucks, the gigantic ones we've been waiting for, have been delivered. The sanitation people have been working for at least four hours."

Outside, the sloping streets were streaming with fresh water. In front of their building Ali and Sarah noticed that the stink from the dovecotes of a neighboring house had disappeared. Its garden would be fragrant this evening when they came home. A flowering jasmine encircled its wire fence.

Sarah left Ali near the hospital. It was only then that she realized she'd been talking ever since she got up in the first glow of a persistent cheerfulness.

*

*   *

III

In this working-class district the public baths were open to women every day except Fridays—the day of prayer at the Great Mosque—and Mondays, because the children were not in school and the mothers, saddled with their brood, would really waste too much water. And the owner, a pious and thrifty woman in her sixties, didn't care to raise the prices, so that she wouldn't have to make the necessary renovations. That would be up to her only son when he returned from Europe . . . if he was going to return.

In addition to the problem of the urgent need for repair work, the old lady's obsession was that she might one day find herself with a European daughter-in-law. And so, with a look of suspicious condescension, she scrutinized Anne as she came in with Baya, and preceded by Sonia, who frequented the place.

While she was undressing, Anne decided to go in wearing a two-piece bathing suit. Baya and Sonia were wearing their usual pagnes with the conspicuous stripes, which brightened up the semidarkness of the steam room.

There were few women at this hour: four or five on the other side of the marble slab. One of them, not visible, was humming a sad ballad in a contralto voice.

Very quickly Anne freed from the black jersey fabric her heavy breasts—which sometimes weighed her down. Sonia opened the faucets, rinsed out two small bowls under the streaming water, and took out a set of copper-colored cups in different sizes. Baya, made more beautiful by the luster of her plump, white skin in the translucent steam, began in a motherly fashion to pour tepid water over Anne's hair, which, as it fanned out, covered her entire back.

"Sarah is late," Sonia remarked.

"She rarely comes to the baths," Baya answered, while she smeared Anne's scalp with a greenish paste.

Drowsy from the heat, Anne offered no resistance and looked around. A skylight in the widely vaulted ceiling: an ancient vault that could have been an abbey. Who might hide there at night? Who would mix her sobs of silence with the seeping water? The mystery of a universe of subterranean water.

The bather who was singing near the marble slab continued her somber threnody.

"What is she singing?" Anne asked under her breath.

"It's just one word she keeps repeating. . . . A lament she's modulating," Sonia said after a minute. "She's improvising."

"It's more that she's consoling herself," Baya added. "Many women can only go out to the baths. . . . We'll see her soon in the cooling room. We can talk to her then."

The unknown woman stopped short, as if she'd guessed they were wondering about her, then in a raucous voice asked the water carrier for a basin.

"Boiling! I want boiling hot water!" Whispering, Baya translated for Anne, while she was rubbing her breasts with her hands; it was then that the Frenchwoman stopped asking questions, looking at the wasted bodies around her in fascination. Arms of a masseuse, standing straight up on the marble slab, then kneeling down, encircling the body of a bather whose face, belly, and breasts were crushed against the stone, her hair a reddish mass, her shoulders dripping with trails of watery henna.

The masseuse opened her lips halfway, showing golden teeth that shimmered; her long, pendulous breasts were crisscrossed with little veins all the way to the tips. Under the light that came down in oblique rays from the skylight, her villager's face, aged before its time, was turning into the mask of an oriental sorceress. The silver pendants she was wearing made a clanging sound every time her shoulders and knotted arms came sliding down on the neck and further down to the breasts of the bather, now falling asleep. Almost black, peaceful, working rhythmically, the masseuse seemed herself to be relaxing. Stopping to catch her breath, then slowly pouring a cup of hot water over the naked bronze back, while hoarse sighs were exhaled below her.

While little by little mothers with sleeping children and whimpering infants began to fill the steam room, the couple formed by the two women on the marble slab high above the other bathers, became entwined again in panting rhythm, taking on a strange shape, that of a slow, well-balanced tree whose roots plunged down into the persistent streaming of the water on the grey stone.

"Allah is great and generous!"

Women of Algiers in Their Apartment

"There'll be a pilgrimage for you yet this year, mother!"

Blessings were being reeled off in the direction of the masseuse, whose services several groups were now requesting. As she came down from the marble slab, solemn as an old idol, she allowed a wrinkled belly full of spots to show as her pagne slid down.

"Nowadays, pilgrimages to Mecca are for just anyone," she exclaimed haughtily. "May the Prophet forgive me, but even if I were to find myself covered with gold, I've lost the desire to go all the way to his tomb. . . . Unless I could be sure it was to go and die there, to leave this life of hard labor!" she grumbled.

She was addressing Baya and Sonia while she took a good look at Anne, who was huddling bare-breasted, trying to find a stable spot in this place of humidity and hollow sounds. By the manner in which she sat on the stool that was too low for her and the way in which her nudity burdened her, the old woman sensed she was a foreigner, despite her black hair and particularly her somewhat weary smile, her resignation, which made her look like a woman of this city.

Baya asked to be massaged. She was questioning the masseuse, then would relay the answers to Anne, who suddenly was beginning to have trouble breathing. "Too much heat all at once for you," Sonia concluded and pushed her toward the exit into the cold room.

At the other end of the steam room they were leaving, amid thick clouds of steam strongly smelling of sulfur, Anne noticed two or three bathers who were meticulously shaving their pubic areas, having moved their children out of the way first.

Now the coolness of the second room with steps of stone all around on which to sit. Leaning against the cracked wall. . . . In a corner a kind of blackish alcove, where the women, coming out of the steam room one after the other, rinsed themselves at length, each furtively taking off her pagne, each with her own secret sense of modesty. Then sitting down, all of them rosy, looking alike, they were getting ready to be more lighthearted: conversations or monologues unrolled in gentle, trifling, worn-out words that slid off with the water, while the women laid down their everyday burdens, their weariness.

Sarah arrives at last, the pagne, clutched under her armpits, comes halfway down her thighs. A comb in her hand, a cup of fresh water to drink, she quietly sits down in the middle of a group. Very close to her, one bather is sprinkling her swollen feet with small splashes of tepid water, her head smeared with henna, her look distant. She immediately picks up the thread of her chronicle.

Sarah doesn't know her. But, while she moves toward Anne and offers to untangle her wet hair for her, she listens to the unknown woman with the absent eyes; in the back, a brouhaha of interwoven voices. The whispering about troubles continues once the pores of the skin are thoroughly open, and open too the shade of the cold stone. Other women, mute, stare at each other across the steam: they are the ones who are locked inside for months or years, except to go to the baths.

At the same time, Sarah remains attentive to the ever-present streaming of the water that here transforms nights into a liquid murmuring. . . . A door opens slightly: enough time for a deep sound to punctuate the air, basins colliding, the ether pierced by a laugh or a moan, constant whining of clean children being diapered and railed at by their mothers, who are tired of having to bring their burdens of flesh along too, of not being able to let themselves be enveloped just by heat, by forgetfulness.

Anne lets herself be combed. Sarah listens to voiceless music and words that seek each other out.

The unknown woman intervenes: "In a socialist village (and she cites her references: a daily paper in the national language that her little boy of ten reads to her every day), peasant women have broken the faucets so they can go to the fountain every day! . . . such ignorance!"

"Freedom!" replies Baya, coming out of the steam room. "How were the new houses built for them? Closed in, every one of them, locked in upon herself. . . . Is that how they live in the douar?"

"What wouldn't I break, inside of me or outside if need be, to get back with the others? To get back to the water that streams, that sings, that gets lost, that sets us all free, if only bit by bit." Sarah has stopped listening.

Anne braided her own hair, smiled with embarrassment when

a child, perched in the arms of a woman next to her, suddenly began to caress her naked chest.

"How many children has she nursed?" the woman asked, addressing Sarah, who jumped.

"Three," she answered without translating as Anne, now cold, got up to go back to the heat of the steam room.

Baya really wanted to talk, not to Sonia, whom she thought too young, but rather to Sarah, who would reassure her; that way, she might finally manage to strip bare her fears. Since the previous day they hadn't exchanged a single word about Nazim's letter, which Baya had read to her on the phone. Sarah daydreaming. Sarah silent. Whom is she concerned about, Baya thought, about the teenager who has disappeared or about the father? She so much wanted to hear her: the words Sarah would choose would give reality to this flight, would make it a catastrophe or a trivial incident.

"I continue to worry about getting married," Baya finally confided to Sarah, who asked no questions but did bend toward her in anticipation.

Her hands were mashing a paste of crushed herbs and oil. . . . She was listening: some of the virgins of the city would come to you with their emotions and anxieties, one might almost say with their hands outstretched. Their naïveté open as if it were a gift. If Sarah could, she'd weep with defeated tenderness in the semidarkness of the feminine voices. For nothing, for all of them. . . . Evolution, the small steps taken in complete myopia, when an ancient warmth at least kept the revolt from turning on itself in a ludicrous headspin.

"Do you remember the fiancé I told you about last year?"

Sarah hesitated, nodded that she did.

"Give me some water—no—cold!"

Baya, beginning to relax, went on: "In the end, my father in an uproar threw him out of the house. And yet we had set the date for our engagement, but his oldest sister, whom he respects and who lives elsewhere, had been the last to be notified. . . . She was furious and swore she wouldn't be there. So then he wanted to postpone the date, and my father . . . well, you know how men are in the village, they're so short-tempered . . ."

Sarah let the same child cling to her back. The mother, exasperated, let them be.

"I have no luck."

"Yes you do," Sarah protested, "it seems you've been given a promotion at the lab."

"Sure I have," Baya moaned, her eyes bright, "but you know how I am: I won't be happy if I don't get married."

A newcomer in her middle years, who understood French, commented. With short motions she was soaking an injured arm in a basin of hot water that stood between her feet.

"With your beauty!" she exclaimed, then added in Berber to confirm the girl's regional origin, "Gold coins don't need to go looking for takers. The master destiny has chosen for you will present himself."

Baya smiled flirtatiously. Sarah moved away from the conversation, also wanting to enter the steam room at last, where she couldn't stay more than fifteen minutes at a time because of the strain on her heart.

Sarah joined Anne, who, when Sarah kneeled and let her pagne slide off, noticed her friend's wide, blueish scar. "A burn?" she asked, touching it lightly all along her abdomen.

Sarah didn't respond. She ought to say, probably in a melodramatic tone of voice at that, "a war injury." Anne knew nothing about the city during the period of fire and murders just past: women outside under attack by submachine guns, white veils with bloodstained holes. . . . How had Sarah squandered her youth? Somewhere, this way, in these open streets, then in prison crammed together with other adolescent girls. Was she working on this ostensibly artistic project, a documentary of the city, in order to answer the interrogation that had begun to take possession of her these days? The city, its walls, its balconies, the shadow of empty prisons.

The year before, Sarah and Anne had bumped into each other in an airport: the emotion of having been to elementary school together, well before the war. Anne's father, a magistrate, had been transferred later to another colony. A flight of stairs leading down to the square. They used to walk it together, such different little girls, but every day they'd be full of laughter as their encounter was repeated. The scent of acacias embalmed the public garden, "you remember?" Anne wanted to know, Anne who'd ended up by dancing, weeping while she danced through the night they'd spent in the orchard. "The same rhythmic movement of shoulders, arms swaying under the heavy lemon tree, childhood laughter among so many women . . . is that what I came back for, too?"

The two women rinsed each other off. The masseuse offered her services with what seemed like banter: she was bringing towels, cold water for their feet in the last of the outer rooms, she had even put down mattresses in the coolness of the vestibule for the languid rest of the indolent, hoping as she always did for a good tip. It was then, after she'd maternally wrapped them both up, "like two young brides" as she put it, happy with the complicity this cliché never failed to provoke, it was then, as she moved with the copper cup in her hand, that she suddenly slid and fell, the back of her right hand hitting the edge of the marble slab.

Besides the two women who were leaving, there was a hefty bather, who abandoned her children to help carry the masseuse, now whimpering.

Outside, Sarah was the first to get dressed. She wrapped a fringed scarf around her hair, went out to phone from the corner grocery. The owner of the baths, usually riveted to the cash register, accompanied her to the vestibule, then began to throw a fit of hysterics as she thought of the disorganization she foresaw for the days to come: Where was she going to find women to carry the water now that the profession was disappearing?

"What she means is," the injured woman added, having come out of her first shock, "where will she, the *Hadja,* find someone like me, both a water carrier (and it's those buckets that have done me in, they're the bane of my existence) and a masseuse at the same time? It's a good thing that I do the massage for my own benefit!"

Anne was observing the hollow face, the eyes burning with helpless hatred. She wiped the woman's perspiring forehead.

Now fully dressed, she went back into the cold room and brought out a cup of water so that the injured woman could freshen her hands and face.

In the taxi, swaddled in a worn veil of wool, but its whiteness intact, the old woman dozed between Sarah and Anne.

At the hospital, Sarah asked to be taken to the emergency room. A young doctor recognized her. This reassured the masseuse.

"We'll examine your right hand again in an hour. . . . We're going to admit you to the hospital, mother."

The old woman checked the tranquilizers the young intern had given her suspiciously. Anne decided to stay by her bedside in a ward where other women were resting.

She was holding the hand, wrapped in bandages, like a life buoy: the other patients assumed she was an attentive daughter-in-law, and that surely the son would soon make his appearance.

Sarah came back accompanied by Ali, who was coming out of a class with some students.

After a long examination: "It's nothing to worry about, mother," he confirmed. "My colleague, a woman, will take care of you and will certainly be the one to operate on you."

"Operate! . . . I don't want to be put to sleep, it's against my beliefs!"

"What beliefs?" Ali retorted roughly. "So get up then and leave if you want, but you'll not be able to work again with your hand in that shape!"

The old woman didn't say another word, not even when Ali left. Anne, who'd understood, gave her a reassuring smile. "If only I could tell her that I feel a bond with her. . . . I must have had a wet nurse like that. . . . If I . . ."

"Sarah, what's her name?"

"Fatma," the old woman replied brightly. She suddenly showed her toothless mouth (wisely, she'd taken her denture of gold out in the taxi, thinking the hospital would charge her if she didn't). "Explain to her that in our country all *fatmas* are named Fatma!"

An hour later she fell asleep, overcome by fever.

Sarah told Anne she'd come back with the surgeon. The

only female surgeon in the city had specialized in hand operations as work-related accidents had made that a particularly
overcrowded area.

Remaining by the bedside of the water carrier, Anne scrutinized the other patients carefully. With her hand dangling in
the space in front of her like the arm of a drowned person going
under, the dozing old woman began to moan and seemed still
to be struggling under the weight of her basins.

When she was taken by ambulance to the surgical department
at the other end of the city, she barely woke up. Her dream,
punctuated by the siren of the ambulance trying to get through
the traffic, knotted and untied itself in halting words, like a too
ancient suffering.

*
*   *

For a diwan of the water carrier

*"Asleep, I am the one asleep and they are carrying me off, who
is carrying me off . . ."*

> heavy body, horizontal, in the screaming van that marks
> its trail across the low part of the city. A hiss, breathing
> that looks as if it comes out of the belly. . . . Navel, a re-
> opened eye, hands facing heaven, the right one turbanned
> in white, larger by far than a baker's board, and the
> other dwarfed by veins, wrinkles colored by old henna,
> the palm that massages—in second place—the flesh of
> bathers whimpering underneath the humid vaults . . .
> Oozing evaporated words, miasma after miasma under
> these same stones of shadow, floating in the corridors of
> water. Liberated words following my old sculptress body,
> making me a furrow in the ambulance as it tears along.
> Words in electrified harmony with the ululations of the
> harem, words transparent with vapors, with echoes. . . .

*"Asleep, I am the one asleep and they are carrying my body
off. . . ."*

... Every invocation to the Prophet or even to his widows turns leaden. . . .

Only words, prehistoric words, unformed words of strident white, words that oppress no longer while these hands, one white and the other reddened, slide, beat the rhythm that follows the panting of devout bathers, evanescent words that might illuminate the constant screaming of the ambulance racing along on my behalf—royal camel paying no attention to the roads climbing between cliffs of stairs from which only yesterday I still descended, veiled in worn wool. . . .

From here on in, naked like this, I circulate, I soar, and I will not be a mummy, I am a sovereign, horizontal empress of the gesture that runs the risk of amputation, but for now a gesture of offering. This is my only passage, a triumphant flowing (the ships in the dock down there are my motionless witnesses) for I circulate, I the woman, all the voices of the past are following me in music, uneven song, broken cries, words in any case unfamiliar, multiple words that bore through the city in metamorphosis at noon. . . .

"I am—am I—I am the unveiled one . . ."

From the depths, a geology of wasted words, fetus words, swallowed up forever, will they escape, black wing sheaths, will they awaken to splinter me when I no longer, never again, wear a mask on my face outside, or carry basins on my head inside, it's over, are they drowned, the layered pain, the second voice that has no tone, no vibration:

"I am—am I—I am the Excluded One. . . ."

A swarming of words from the abysses, surging up once more in the horizontal body moving forward, and the ambulance cuts its path: twisting streets that curve and bend between balconies on which the eyes of chiseled children grow wider. . . . Watercolor ships, the sea as an eternal barrier, right now the heights of the city are mauves stretched out in silence: is the hospital still far away, is the surgeon getting prepped, alone at last, covering up her mouth with white fabric? . . .

The murmurs come together in a knotted bundle, a sheaf of rumblings shaped above the belly at the bottom of the hollow chest. . . . The frayed stanzas are regrouping, where to determine the language Arabic women utter, long uninterrupted interior sobs that stream forth in sad accompaniment, blood-streaked losses of a rebirth of the menstrual cycle, gaping memories of harems of decapitated subservient janissaries, where white-washed walls rock with new sounds, lacerated words, all around me, the water carrier, creating my new space. . . .

An uncertain voice in pain, out of breath because it has to find itself:

"It is me—me?—It is me they have excluded, me whom they have barred
It is me—me?—me they have humiliated
Me whom they have caged in
Me whom they've sought to subdue, their fists on my head, to make me drown while standing straight, all the way down to the monkey-faced layer of evil, me within the marble halls of mute distress, me inside the rocks of silence of the white veil. . . ."

—and the water, in inexhaustible showers, the water that continued coming down in torrents all that time, a silk of burning shivers, black buckets on shoulders are poured out outside the steaming hole.

"Me, it is me they've been wanting to suffocate, to snatch away from stable ground into the maws of fire, me whom they thought of as having skin branded alive and gaping with open scars, me, is that me? . . ."

The brakes just barely squealing, the driver-nurse slides the ambulance into the hospital building of the upper city, the siren stopped for a moment, begins again in the room, a torture chamber for my sleeping body, which is being fully anesthetized, rustle of glass slides, of scalpels, of knife blades. . . . Minutes before the operation.

The singsong of the interval at last becoming the rhythm

of preparations under the long lashes and antimony-blackened eyes of the surgeon, the lower part of her face veiled.

"I was the one whom they claimed to marry in the dawn of the world . . ."

My Sahara stretched along the edge, my parents remembered that they'd been nomads and I, little barefoot girl, would run on top of the dune. . . . The rooms smelled of dung, my goat, I had a white goat, would stretch her neck toward the blue. . . . And so it stood, my father's farm that I used to think was opulent.

My father dressed in legionnaire's uniform; I remember that uniform, the red cloth of his coat. I used to rub my cheek against it, closely against it, when he'd hold me hugged closely between his knees. . . .

And I'd tremble. . . . He used to come home only every now and then. . . . My mother had died when I was born, clusters of my aunts would choke with spluttered laughter when I, dressed in the multiple garments of women, was presented to my father when he arrived—and I, I'd lower my eyes, would slide close against his voluminous, scarlet pants. . . .

On one leave, my father arrived with another soldier; my aunts were silent. They were going to take me away, a bride of the beginning of time. . . . For the son of the stranger, they said, the father had decided. The aunts wept, saying that if the grandmother were living, the father would never have dared. . . .

At thirteen years of age, my face was painted, my eyebrows plucked, they waxed the hair off my armpits and pubic area, put spangles on my forehead, on my cheekbones, and bought me embroidered slippers. My heart was beating for this, my first journey, I, the bride of all beginnings. . . .

The carriage went north,

"Asleep, I was the sleeping one and they are taking me away, I who . . ."

the carriage fled along, unknown women with cumbersome black veils touched me with their henna-reddened fingers, too much henna, palpated my breasts, shoulders, abdomen, then ululated with joy, threw out their rippling cries, while I was going up toward the plateaus of the north. Guttural cry, intermittently let out now by one, then by another (they were four, four sisters), that cry gave me chills, drove my childhood deep inside me, my running through the dune, the cascades of laughter. . . .

"I was, I was the bride of the dawn of the world. . . . Only to end up as a carrier, a water carrier, in holes steaming with vapor. . . ."

Thirteen, tall for my age and of the desired dark hair, hair down to my lower back, eyes blackened, palms made red. At thirteen, I had been full-breasted for a year or two, my heart was beating for this, my first journey, hope, then fear, then. . . . Suddenly it's black, today I am fifty, sixty years old, I don't even know my age, the blackness of time: no doubt it was a basin of water, too hot, sent by fate onto my thirteen-year-old shoulders. Since then I've always been fifty, sixty years old, what's the difference, the bathers still come and go, the children carry on in the steam of the bathhouse, the water never stops flowing down the stone, it weighs in black bronze on my shoulders and finally I massage, and . . .

"Carrier, I want water . . . boiling water! . . . Carrier, water carrier . . ."

Behind, the black and the smoke of the hole. . . . The wretchedness of that farm at the end of my first journey! Children on the floor with bloated bellies, flies in their eyes; not even a lamp in the rooms of dried mud, the jars on the floors taking up every inch of space. . . . The women with aged faces, their breasts out for nursing, their babies pulling at them, empty; a few men, their look feverish, sit around all day long; stretches of stone, further down a green, lush plain that the French had seized earlier, after the arrival of the men of law and the police. . . . As I stepped out of the carriage, the master welcomed me; he was wearing the same belt as my father and was eyeing me with interest, as if I were there for him. . . . That night, the husband, an adolescent whose hands groped over my cold body. The next day, the nagging of the women: "Get to work! Show us what you can do, princess!" . . . And a little later: "You, your father gave you up for two bottles of beer in a garrison town!"

Finished, I knew from their insults that it was all over! Two or three more months of misery.

The second voice begins to sing again, jarring, broken, with a little gasp:

"Me—is it really me?—they wanted to break me, they claimed they would plunge me headfirst into the blackish crust of monkey-faced evil . . ."

At last I ran. One night I fled without a veil, in a red gown and with these words inside me: "run straight . . . always straight ahead!" The south no longer existed, the north no longer existed, only space and the night, the long night of my life was beginning.

No more children with bloated bellies, no more sisters-in-law feeling me every morning "When is she planning to get knocked up, this girl?" Me, all alone in the opaque night, only these simple words alive inside me: "leave . . . run now . . . ahead . . . straight ahead!" Words, like fish bones, sometimes stick in your throat, shred your chest . . . words tear you apart, it's true, words tear at you. . . .

Run, I run across the night. Black. Follow the road, hurry, faster, faster still, faster than the antelope of my lost desert!

At dawn, a small town. In a market, some old men gossiping in a corner, steaming tea and its smell of mint. . . . "If only I had a burnoose, looked like a boy! . . . Amble along the streets, be someone else. . . . People, real people . . ."

A woman's whisper, her eyes lonely in the masked face: "What are you doing here, my girl?" An hour later, a haven, no, a place to work: two years of weaving carpets by day, of serving a madam by night. . . . In the end, back on the street: a flight this time, not on foot, not at night, another man to whom I am delivered at the end of the road, the capital. I'm a duly registered prostitute, I have a police card. I have clients. Five years, ten years, the years go by. . . . Independence celebrations: houses open, jubilant streets, I go out, I think I'm free. My face in a shop window: "old, I'm old . . . and I'm hungry!"

One or two years earlier, in the Casbah during a riot, a peasant arrives. They hide him. He speaks. He's from my village, he knows such and such a tribe, a certain political group. . . . My heart stops cold: "Do you know Amar, the legionnaire? He used to have a big farm. . . . that's a long time ago. . . . He must have retired since then. . . . I used to work there (and I lied) as a servant."

"He was one of the first collaborators they killed, right at the start of the war. . . . They found him in a ditch with his throat slit. . . . When his farm was sold, his people became beggars and wanderers. . . ."

"Thank you, brother," I said and refused him my bed, another one took my place in the room out of friendship. . . . Then came the proprietress of the hammam. The heat of the steam room, the baths, the basins. . . . One basin, one client . . . Why even count? Once again the same tune, outside the brothel, outside the hammam. . . . Yesterday in the street they were singing of hope, but me, I am invaded only by the lament:

"I am—who am I?—I am the excluded one. . . ."

*
* *

In front of Fatma's prostrate body the surgeon is fully focused; Anne sits rooted in the waiting room. At that same moment, Sarah stands in front of Leila's bed; Leila is delirious. The Jewish songstress on the record has stopped her wailing song of the thirties. . .

For a divan of the fire carriers

"Everywhere they've announced that I'd been tortured. . . . Tortured with electricity, you too know what that's all about! . . ."

Leila continued, and at the same time Sarah, clutching the bed's metal rim with her fingers, was remembering: "Where are you, you women who carry the bombs? They form a procession, in the palms of their hands grenades that blossom out in explosions of flames, faces illuminated by flashes of green. . . . Where are you, you fire carriers, you my sisters, who should have liberated the city. . . . Barbed wire no longer obstructs the alleys, now it decorates windows, balconies, anything at all that opens onto an outside space. . . .

In the streets they were taking pictures of your unclothed bodies, of your avenging arms in front of the tanks. . . . We suffered the pain of your legs torn apart by the rapist soldiers. And it is thus that the sanctioned poets evoked you in lyrical divans. Your turned-up eyes . . . no, worse. . . . Your bodies, used only in parts, bit by little bit. . . .

The lady patronesses went back to their collections of jewelry, . . . Turkish and Berber. Necklaces and pendants for your severed heads . . . chastity belts, silver and coral mounted for those who'd been held in isolation in the prisons. . . . They should make vast closeups for every triumphant Woman's Day: look at the fingers, ordinarily painted with henna, usually the active hands of the mothers who have survived (face aflame to make bread and to be burned), the same fingers without henna but with manicured nails carrying bombs as if they were oranges. Exploding every body we believed to be those of other's. . . . Tearing the enemy flesh to ribbons. And those who were still alive, or what passes for alive, behind iron prison bars, then behind the bars of memory, then . . . (she is weeping), then like me behind the delirium of fever (for you know, Sarah, I do have a fever, I shall always have a fever), were they really still alive? The bombs are still exploding . . . but over twenty years: close to our eyes, for we no longer see the outside, we see only the obscene looks, the bombs explode but against our bellies and I am—she screamed—I am every woman's sterile belly in one!"

Women of Algiers in Their Apartment

Sarah was weeping, sorrow constricting her chest.

"My darling, my sweet," her voice came through at last, she heard herself speak in her regionally accented Arabic, "be quiet, my darling, don't talk anymore! . . . Words, what good are words?"

"On the contrary," Leila attacked in French, "I've got to speak, Sarah! They are ashamed of me. I've dried up, I'm the shadow of my former self. . . . Perhaps because I've held forth too much in yesterday's tribunals, I've entered the public frenzy once too often, and when the brothers were applauding I thought . . . (she laughs). Were there ever really any brothers, Sarah . . . tell me, were there? . . . You . . . Even then, they already called you the silent one. . . . They never knew the carefully listed details of your own tortures. Afterwards they took care of you as they now do of me, they thought you were left with just a few scars, they never knew. . . ."

"I've always had a hard time with words," Sarah mused as she undid her blouse, her face still wet with tears. She uncovered the blue scar that started above one of her breasts and stretched down to her abdomen.

She approached the bed, embraced Leila. She ran her fingers over her forehead, the arches of her eyebrows, she would have liked to start licking that face and so weep over her, crush her emaciated body with warm vehemence, that body with its hunched shoulders, those scrawny arms, those childlike wrists, that head all angular and corpselike. . . . Sarah felt a purely sensual rush. . . . She looked for words, like a deaf-mute, words of love, informal words, but words in what language, like grottos or whirlwinds of tenderness. But she didn't move and became exasperated with herself when she slowly buttoned her blouse again.

Leila was still delirious when the painter came into the room. He came close to Sarah: "No use getting upset. It's a crisis. I'm used to drug addicts. I've been through this myself . . ."

And as Sarah was going to leave: "You'd better concern yourself with Ali's son. Only you can make him come back."

Sarah looked at him, distraught. She was wishing herself back in the car.

"What do you know about it?" she exclaimed heatedly, once

back in the street, and was herself surprised when she suddenly felt herself trembling. "Did you ever bother to ask yourself why he really left? After all, just think, the boy may have seen us fight one evening, his father and me. You, buried out here all by yourself, do you have any inkling of how couples spend their nights in the city?"

And she started the car. The painter remained standing for a long time in front of his gate after the car had disappeared.

"Maybe I should go to the old aunt's," Sarah said to herself, taking a long time to calm down. In the Casbah, where Nazim had found refuge these past few nights. Wait for him and with that in mind sleep on the terrace every night: in a patio below, as within a well, young girls are busy as bees under the inquisitive eye of the youngest brother. "Prince Charming," the young neighboring women think out loud, "will never be able to introduce himself at the door, but perhaps he can parachute right into the middle of the patio!" and they shriek with strident laughter . . .

Nazim—Sarah was driving through the overpopulated suburbs—Nazim would end up by coming back, his look peaceful at last. If not, if nobody came, where would the new children of the city be?

She stopped the car at the hospital entrance. Shortly thereafter, Anne told her that Fatma's hand would heal. In the lobby, where the nurses were taking a boisterous break, the surgeon had just removed her white mask and coat and, looking weary, smiled at them.

*

* *

IV

"I see no other way out for us except through an encounter like this: a woman speaking in front of another one who's watching; does the one who's speaking tell the story of the other one with the devouring eyes, with the black memories, or is she describing her own dark night with words like torches and with candles whose wax melts too fast? She who watches, is it by means of listening, of listening and remembering that she ends up seeing herself, with her own eyes, unveiled at last. . . ."

In the silence that had fallen once again, Sarah paced the dark room. She was smoking nervously, feeling herself come out of the tensions that had accumulated these past days in which nothing had actually happened, at least not to her.

"How will the transition be made for Arabic women?" Her head lowered, she approached Anne near the lamp, then raised her widened eyes toward her. "Isn't it too soon," she whispered, "to speak in the plural?" She resumed her restless pacing.

"Before," Anne began, questioning her friend for the first time, "how were things for you during your time in prison?"

Sarah faced her, took a moment before sitting down, a lost look in her eyes.

"The most difficult day," she mumbled, "the longest day in all those years of being locked up. . . . They came to tell me in the visiting room that my mother had died, had died quite suddenly. I didn't cry. I couldn't. I'll never forget what tore me apart later. . . . Perhaps because I learned of her death in that place?"

She stopped; Anne was waiting, not daring to move. Sarah, seated again, her legs folded, her face on her knees, more and more crumpled: "I believe I must have had the thought that I'd never leave the prison again. From that day on (I spent another year in Barberousse prison) it was as if, with every movement, my body ran into the walls. Silently I was shrieking. . . . The others noticed nothing but my silence. Leila said it only yesterday: I was a voiceless prisoner. A little like certain women of Algiers today, you see them going around outside without the ancestral veil, and yet, out of fear of the new and unexpected situations, they become entangled in other veils, invisible but very noticeable ones. . . . Me too: for years after Barberousse I was still carrying my own prison around inside me."

"Sarah," Anne sighed gently, "remember: when we were children together we were free, we used to play in that garden!"

"My mother," Sarah murmured. Suddenly she wept; tears were flowing in streams, abundantly, regularly, without changing the features of her face. Anne didn't show any sign of her compassion. Sarah was wiping the bottom of her cheeks with her hands, which she then rubbed dry against the fabric of her dress.

"I could imagine her sitting for centuries, her eyes staring into space, inconsolable! . . . I could talk about my mother for days and days on end!" she spoke again with a sharp gasp.

Finally, late in the night, she found her deliverance. . . . And Anne began to think: in this strange city, drunk with the sun but with prisons high up on every street, does every woman live first for herself or for the chain of women once locked in, generation after generation, while the same light, an unchangeable, rarely dimmed blue, continues to pour forth?

"My dead mother. . . . Her life in which nothing happened. One tragedy only: she had me, no other child, no son, no one else. She must have lived in fear of being repudiated then, I suppose. I didn't think of that until later, after she died, while my cell mates were trying to console me. . . . It was as if my mother, seated and motionless, had joined me in prison. Before, at home, in the big low house we had in the suburbs, she would be silent and work all day long. She never stopped. She'd scrub her kitchen; when everything was done, she'd soap down the flagstones, the walls, she'd air the mattresses, wash the blankets again. She'd polish and clean and scrub. . . . An obsession like any other, after all. Then when I learned of her death in that prison, I saw all her gestures again (she didn't talk to me, almost never, sometimes she'd kiss me, in agitation, when she thought I was asleep). I understood also why I had left home at sixteen, left high school (and my father was so proud: a daughter with a diploma, as if he'd had seven sons all at once!) But . . . (her voice jumped bitterly) the war of liberation at the time, here,"—she thought, hesitated—"we jumped on the bandwagon for freedom first, we had nothing but war afterwards."

Sarah's eyes gazing vacantly. After some silence, she began again, her voice flat, without bitterness but without passion: "Every evening when my father came home, my mother would arrive carrying a copper bowl full of hot water and she'd wash his feet. Meticulously. Sitting on one of the steps—I must have been seven or eight—I would watch her. I wasn't thinking anything! Never, never did I say anything, no matter what, even to myself. No doubt at the time I must have thought that scene was normal, perhaps I was present at the same ritual in other patios with jasmine and faded mosaics like ours. . . . I never once got up to overturn the bowl, to say to the couple, so calm and serene: 'Go to hell, you two!' And yet I knew that I would never in my life wash anything like that. In a way, you might say that the empty folklore of the copper bowl killed everything else. . . . Still, it was years later in that prison cell in Barberousse that a family scene like this one assailed me and wouldn't leave me alone. That's how my mother died: silently, following a simple chill. I understood then that she would never have her revenge. And I was truly unable to accept it."

Anne was listening. During the pauses she didn't say anything, was even careful not to budge. Was it only a few days or was it years earlier that she herself, in this very same studio, had unraveled the story of her own life in a rush of words?

"I really didn't think of it," Sarah started again, "as 'revenge on my father.' My father was thought of as a pretty good husband by his own family, I believe. When I came out of prison, as he was walking with me between two classes at the university, he announced in a rather embarrassed tone that he was marrying again; I wondered why he was so subdued about it. But my mother cast a shrunken yet stubborn shadow, she who'd never declared her fears out loud, or her joys, who'd never even moaned like so many other women I know, who'd never cursed anyone, nor noisily choked down any sounds, my mother, it was as if I couldn't manage to set her free! . . . I can go out all I want, lead my life one day at a time, improvising as I go and in whatever way I see fit really, try as I might to enjoy all my "freedom"—to call it by its true name—but one single question keeps plaguing me, this freedom, is it really mine? My mother died without even conceiving of the idea of a life like mine, with its twists and turns. . . . Anne, what should we do? Lock ourselves in again, begin to weep for her again, live again for her?"

She'd wiped her tears, but she was in pain, her fine face tight as she pursed her lips in helplessness. "For me it is my mother," she added more softly, a brief confidence, "for others there are different family ghosts."

The dawn began to rise on the studio's window shades.

"For Arabic women I see only one single way to unblock everything: talk, talk without stopping, about yesterday and today, talk among ourselves, in all the women's quarters, the traditional ones as well as those in the housing projects. Talk among ourselves and look. Look outside, look outside the walls and the prisons! . . . The Woman as look and the Woman as voice," she added somewhat obscurely, then snickered: "Not the voice of female vocalists whom they imprison in their sugar-sweet melodies. . . . But the voice they've never heard, because many unknown and new things will occur before she's able to sing: the voice of sighs, of malice, of the sorrows of all the women they've kept walled in. . . . The voice that's searching in the opened tombs."

Sarah thought of those generations of women. She imagined having known them all, having accompanied them: her only and trembling certainty.

"Oh, my God!" she added and she thought of Leila. Leila who was laying bare her shards. What a new, offensive harem! (she cried out), precisely without *haram*, without taboo. In the name of whom? In the name of what? . . .

She knew it was always like this under every heaven: the declarations of unavoidable war, whatever the charitable organizations may say about it, feed themselves only on some subterranean river of desperate and lucid love. . . . She shrank, destroyed by anger.

"This is the moment," she concluded later in a calmer voice, while Anne was packing her suitcase for her approaching departure, "this is the moment," she began again, "that Ishmael will really wail in the desert: the walls torn down by us will continue to surround him alone!"

It was her hope, or her challenge; it didn't matter much that she didn't know whether it concerned the coming day or the following year or the generation that isn't always the generation of "other people."

The plane Anne was supposed to take at dawn the next day was delayed for over an hour.

The two women waited among a group of migrant workers who had just spent their one month's paid vacation in their mountain village. Two or three of them, their faces tanned and more serene, were accompanied by their wives in long peasant dresses, a few with babies in their arms and their foreheads tattooed in minute detail.

The loveliest one—Anne heard this from Sarah who exchanged a few basic words with her—had only that morning abandoned her veil. Young, her eyes blackened with kohl but her whole face sharp with hope, she maintained a stiff posture of expectation until the moment of boarding.

"I'm not leaving!" Anne suddenly cried out. She stared intensely at the young woman traveler, smiled at her (that way the unknown woman would carry with her this sign of gratitude, as the others would take along their baskets and their pottery, all the way to the shantytown north of Paris that was waiting for them).

"I'm not going anymore!" Anne repeated, and as quickly as she could she rejoined Sarah, who was leaving the air terminal. They embraced.

In the old jalopy, on the road that led to the flat part of town, open as a courtesan seemingly easy to get, before it turned into the arcade-lined avenue that carries high its tight, white heart, the women—first one, then the other too—were humming.

"One day we'll take the boat together," the first one said.

"Not to go away, no, to gaze at the city when all the doors are opening. . . . What a picture! It will make even the light tremble!"

And the other one added that they would finally resuscitate the proud joy of the raiders of earlier days, the only ones in the city who had ever been called "kings," undoubtedly because they had been renegades.

Algiers, July–October 1978

The Woman Who Weeps

This uninterrupted dance of broken lines . . .
A. Adamov on Picasso's painting "The Woman Who Weeps"

"They all said I was wrong!" she said under her breath, then imperceptibly raised her voice. "They all told me: 'Your husband is not a French husband! You don't tell everything to a husband! . . . I . . .'" The sea with the low-pitched crashing of its swell diffused the sound of the voice.

"As for me . . . sleeping with someone every night was . . . (her speech was becoming feverish) it might just as well have been my skeleton that lay beside him. . . . He could see through me right to my bones."

A harsh laugh, a gasp. And she thought back upon all those years: "tombstone statuary" she used to say to herself at those grave moments at bedtime of before.

The sea breeze: grey and green. A blue trail disappearing in the west.

"So he beat up on me . . . (a look toward the horizon). He literally 'busted my face.'"

Then her voice broke. . . . She was going to add: "In those days, I would walk and walk the streets of Algiers as if my face were going to fall into my hands, as if I'd pick up the pieces, as if the pain were trickling down from my features, as if . . ."

And she thought: it was a city for just those kind of walks, a teetering space, streets half off-balance and willing accomplices when you're overcome by the desire to throw yourself off. . . . Blue everywhere.

She stood up, the past at her feet. Her two-piece bathing suit made her body, especially her thighs and abdomen, seem whiter.

"I'm going!"

One moment, her arms raised to the sky, she slipped a narrow dress of pale cotton over her unmoistened body. From the red canvas bag next to her, she took—slowly bending over to do this—a broad piece of white fabric with alternating stripes, some less shiny and more silky looking. She unfolded the sheet as if it were going to get away from her, and one could imagine her running across the immense beach after the immaculate cloth.

She wrapped herself up completely in the stiff material that, as it was crumpled, made a barely noticeable crunching sound: the man, still silent, heard it rustle despite the diffuse rumbling of the sea (his hearing had become much more acute after all those years in prison).

Now the feminine silhouette formed a rather billowing parallelogram; she remained there facing him, her neck and head completely free, but with the wind burrowing down under her armpits, she became a strange parachute, hesitating between earth and space. She smiled at him for the first time, in spite of all the whiteness.

From the bag she also took a kind of handkerchief, half covered with white lace, which she folded into a triangle. She placed it over the bridge of her nose, tied it into a knot at her neck, pulled the upper part of the silky sheet over her hair, which was cut very short. Above the mask of lace, her light-brown eyes, still smiling, seemed more almond shaped.

"Goodbye!"

The words hung suspended. The white silhouette, bending forward, walked away.

The man turned his head, following her with his eyes for a moment, then went back to staring at the sea. Grey and green: no trace of blue any longer in this sunless sunset.

The next day the weather remained the same. The sultry heat subsided toward the end of the afternoon: an overripe fruit that would slowly fall off. Miles away, the cities were buzzing in the dust.

The man went back to the same spot. He wasn't waiting exactly. You wait when your time isn't all your own. Since the time he had made the move, when it was barely dawning—

two rusted metal bars he had to bend with great care—since the moment his side had been covered with blood as he slid—a long and huge caterpillar—through the narrow little window, since that moment his time had truly been his own. The salt water had closed his wound into a scar; a brownish line crossed the right side of his back.

She focused her eyes on this unexpected feature when she spoke: "Little by little, other people fill you up . . . in a barely noticeable stream. For me, they began by filling me through my eyes. . . . All these past months in that house full of old aunts and cousins, I said to myself: "All I have to do is listen to other people. That's enough for me.""

She was thinking. Two or three sea gulls were flying low. A cry in the distance, but it was probably not a bird crying.

"Listen to the other. Simply listen to him and look at him. (A pause, as between two stanzas). Loving the other," she began again in a softer voice, just a little bit softer—"loving him while observing him; your own fever disappears, your own violence, the cries you've never let out! . . ." (the two sea gulls flew away, the sea invading the silence.) "The voice of the other reaches you, the voice of the one who's suffering or who has suffered . . . and who's unburdening himself, and there you are, weeping for him, for her, all you can do is weep for him, for her."

Her hand, much later, began to dig into the sand, to look for some pebble. This time, the veil in which she had been wrapped when she arrived, in which she would wrap herself when she'd be leaving in an hour or two, was lying on the ground like a dead skin.

"Sometimes I say to myself: I don't know where the edges of my body are, what my shape looks like. . . . What good are mirrors?"

At that very moment came the first caress. The man remembered the time it took, later on when he was once again huddling in his dark hole: she then raised her arm, looked at her fingers with great care, opened them wide, letting go of them in space, looking like a child because of her very concentration. . . . It was a good bit later that she reached for the man's leg; she touched his knee, examined its joints as if to test them, then her fingers brushed over his calf from top to bottom, down to his foot and back up again. She was caressing him with great delicacy.

"Your muscles are hard," she concluded, then: "I don't know how old you are. . . . Don't tell me, it makes no difference."

He, in turn, had put his hand on her slim fingers when they came back to his knee, then his thigh. So they stayed, hands entwined, and took their time looking at each other. Then he touched her right breast without baring it. She interrupted his beginning excitement.

"I'm going!"

Stood up. Rustling of fabric, despite the sea. The parallelogram all in white swaying with the same hesitation.

The woman disappeared, the man remained seated until the night, clear as it was, enveloped the whole stretch of sea, beginning at the farther corners in various parts on the horizon.

On the third day, while she was talking, but in a whisper now (those years of bourgeois marriage, the violent breakup, the long impulse toward the second man that tore her apart and that took her months to master, the second man, a pale and fragile adolescent . . .), was he listening, nothing was that sure, did he understand? Only then did she say to herself that, after all, he might speak a foreign language. . . . But at long last she was confessing, mumbling, letting it all flow out, as the sea continued its chant of a woman in confinement, the sea gulls no longer came, the bird cry had disappeared. In the distance, miles away, the cities in the dust had become dream cities, disappeared in the destructive strides of earlier centuries no doubt, and she was talking, finally opening herself up, her hand on the man's right knee.

She said: "Soon, when everything is out, all this dirt, all this garbage . . . soon I will put my dry mouth on this scar on your back, I will take my time, I will follow the trace of your wound with my tongue. . . . My face has been 'busted open' but I have not been disfigured, I have a mouth once more, I have lips again, a tongue . . . soon." And the past, in stonelike words, reached its bleak unfolding at last, little by little. That moment of concentration between the two vibrated with a subdued music (the sea barely rumbling in the distance).

Precisely at that moment, a first soldier, in a light-brown uniform and armed, appeared behind them.

The blowing of a whistle. . . . The woman stopped whispering, did not turn around.

Two other uniforms with rifles joined the first one. They didn't move either.

That day, the air was not as it had been before, sly and hazy. The diffuse circle of a sun, ready to disappear, was painting the horizon pink. At last the hope for a beautiful summer.

"We could get up and take a walk," the woman began. She was going to add "like lovers."

She didn't have the time to say it. The enormous animal, a German shepherd, came running, loping toward them; he seemed to be gamboling with happiness.

The man got up, turned toward the woman. He put his two hands out side by side, as when his wrists were chained together. His fingers lifted the white veil off the ground, then let it go. He started as if to say something: about the veil, about the woman who was waiting.

He went over to the animal, who, trembling with joy, began to make circles around them, perhaps ferocious, perhaps loving.

Some time later, the military silhouettes were walking away, surrounding the man, his torso bare. The German shepherd was no longer visible: no doubt he'd run ahead of them. At this spot the hill resembled a crumbling dune.

Facing the sea, without moving, her hands dug into the white veil she was twisting convulsively, the woman wept, the woman wept.

20 July 1978, Algiers

Yesterday

There Is No Exile

That particular morning, I'd finished the housework a little earlier, by nine o'clock. Mother had put on her veil, taken her basket; in the opening of the door, she repeated as she had been repeating every day for three years: "Not until we had been chased out of our own country did I find myself forced to go out to market like a man."

"Our men have other things to do," I answered, as I'd been answering every day for three years.

"May God protect us!"

I saw Mother to the staircase, then watched her go down heavily because of her legs: "May God protect us," I said again to myself as I went back in.

The cries began around ten o'clock, more or less. They were coming from the apartment next door and soon changed into shrieks. All three of us, my two sisters—Aïcha, Anissa, and I—recognized it by the way in which the women received it: it was death.

Aïcha, the eldest, ran to the door, opened it in order to hear more clearly: "May misfortune stay away from us," she mumbled. "Death has paid the Smain family a visit."

At that moment, Mother came in. She put the basket on the floor, stopped where she stood, her face distraught, and began to beat her chest spasmodically with her hands. She was uttering little stifled cries, as when she was about to get sick.

Anissa, although she was the youngest of us, never lost her calm. She ran to close the door, lifted Mother's veil, took her by the shoulders and made her sit down on a mattress.

"Now don't get yourself in that state on account of someone else's misfortune," she said. "Don't forget you have a bad heart. May God shelter and keep us always."

While she repeated the phrase several more times, she went to get some water and sprinkled it on Mother, who now, stretched out full length on the mattress, was moaning. Then Anissa washed her entire face, took a bottle of cologne from the wardrobe, opened it, and put it under her nostrils.

"No!" Mother said. "Bring me some lemon."

And she started to moan again.

Anissa continued to bustle about. I was just watching her. I've always been slow to react. I'd begun to listen to the sobs outside that hadn't ceased, would surely not cease before nightfall. There were five or six women in the Smaïn family, and they were all lamenting in chorus, each one settling, forever it seemed, into the muddled outbreak of their grief. Later, of course, they'd have to prepare the meal, busy themselves with the poor, wash the body. . . . There are so many things to do, the day of a burial.

For now, the voices of the hired mourners, all alike without any one of them distinguishable from the other if only by a more anguished tone, were making one long, gasping chant, and I knew that it would hang over the entire day like a fog in winter.

"Who actually died over there?" I asked Mother, who had almost quieted down.

"Their young son," she said, inhaling the lemon deeply. "A car drove over him in front of the door. I was coming home when my eyes saw him twisting one last time, like a worm. The ambulance took him to the hospital, but he was already dead."

Then she began to sigh again.

"Those poor people," she was saying, "they saw him go out jumping with life and now they're going to bring him back in a bloodstained sheet."

She raised herself halfway, repeated: "jumping with life." Then she fell back down on the mattress and said nothing other than the ritual formulas to keep misfortune away. But the low voice she always used to address God had a touch of hardness, vehemence.

"This day has an evil smell," I said, still standing in front of Mother, motionlessly. "I've sensed it since this morning, but I didn't know then that it was the smell of death."

There Is No Exile

"You have to add: May God protect us!" Mother said sharply. Then she raised her eyes to me. We were alone in the room, Anissa and Aïcha had gone back to the kitchen.

"What's the matter with you?" she said. "You look pale. Are you feeling sick, too?"

"May God protect us!" I said and left the room.

*

*   *

At noon, Omar was the first one home. The weeping continued. I'd attended to the meal while listening to the threnody and its modulations. I was growing used to them. I thought Omar would start asking questions. But no. He must have heard about it in the street.

He pulled Aïcha into a room. Then I heard them whispering. When some important event occurred, Omar spoke first to Aïcha in this way, because she was the eldest and the most serious one. Previously, Father used to do the same thing, but outside, with Omar, for he was the only son.

So there was something new; and it had nothing to do with death visiting the Smaïn family. I wasn't curious at all. Today is the day of death, all the rest becomes immaterial.

"Isn't that so?" I said to Anissa, who jumped.

"What's the matter now?"

"Nothing," I said without belaboring the point, for I was familiar with her always disconcerted answers whenever I'd start thinking out loud. Even this morning . . .

But why this sudden, blatant desire to stare at myself in a mirror, to confront my own image at some length, and to say, while letting my hair fall down my back so that Anissa would gaze upon it: "Look. At twenty-five, after having been married, after having lost my two children one after the other, having been divorced, after this exile and after this war, here I am busy admiring myself, smiling at myself like a young girl, like you . . ."

"Like me!" Anissa said, and she shrugged her shoulders.

*

*   *

Father came home a little late because it was Friday and he'd gone to say the prayer of *dhor* at the mosque. He immediately asked why they were in mourning.

"Death has visited the Smaïns," I said, running toward him to kiss his hand. "It has taken their young son away."

"Those poor people," he said after a silence.

I helped him get settled in his usual place, on the same mattress. Then, as I put his meal in front of him and made sure he didn't have to wait for anything, I forgot about the neighbors for a while. I liked to serve Father; it was, I think, the only household task I enjoyed. Especially now. Since our departure, Father had aged a great deal. He gave too much thought to those who weren't with us, even though he never spoke of them, unless a letter arrived from Algeria and he asked Omar to read it.

In the middle of the meal I heard Mother murmur: "They can't possibly feel like eating today."

"The body is still at the hospital," someone said.

Father said nothing. He rarely spoke during meals.

"I'm not really hungry," I said, getting up, to excuse myself.

The sobs outside seemed more muffled, but I could still distinguish their singsong. Their gentle singsong. This is the moment, I said to myself, when grief becomes familiar, and pleasurable, and nostalgic. This is the moment when you weep almost voluptuously, for this gift of tears is a gift without end. This was the moment when the bodies of my children would turn cold fast, so fast, and when I knew it. . . .

At the end of the meal, Aïcha came into the kitchen, where I was by myself. First she went to close the windows that looked out over the neighboring terraces, through which the weeping reached me. But I could still hear it. And, oddly, it was that which made me so tranquil today, a little gloomy.

"There are some women coming this afternoon to see you and to propose marriage," she began. "Father says the candidate is suitable in every way."

Without answering, I turned my back to her and went to the window.

"Now what's your problem?" she said a little sharply.

"I need some air," I said and opened the window all the way, so that the song could come in. It had already been a while since the breathing of death had become, for me, "the song."

Aïcha remained a moment without answering. "When Father goes out, you'll attend to yourself a little," she said at last. "These women know very well that we're refugees like so many others, and that they're not going to find you dressed like a queen. But you should look your best, nevertheless."

"They've stopped weeping," I remarked, "or perhaps they're already tired," I said, thinking of that strange fatigue that grasps us at the depth of our sorrow.

"Why don't you keep your mind on the women who're coming?" Aïcha replied in a slightly louder voice.

*

* *

Father had left. Omar too, when Hafsa arrived. Like us, she was Algerian and we'd known her there, a young girl of twenty with an education. She was a teacher but had been working only since her mother and she had been exiled, as had so many others. "An honorable woman doesn't work outside her home," her mother used to say. She still said it, but with a sigh of helplessness. One had to live, and there was no man in their household now.

Hafsa found Mother and Anissa in the process of preparing pastries, as if these were a must for refugees like us. But her sense of protocol was instinctive in Mother; an inheritance from her past life that she could not readily abandon.

"These women you're waiting for," I asked, "who are they?"

"Refugees like us," Aïcha exclaimed. "You don't really think we'd give you away in marriage to strangers?" Then with heart and soul: "Remember," she said, "the day we return to our own country, we shall all go back home, all of us, without exception."

"The day that we return," Hafsa, standing in the middle of the room, suddenly cried out, her eyes wide with dreams. "The day that we return to our country!" she repeated. "How I'd like to go back there on foot, the better to feel the Algerian soil under my feet, the better to see all our women, one after the other, all the widows, and all the orphans, and finally all the men, exhausted, sad perhaps, but free—free! And then I'll take a bit of soil in my hands, oh, just a tiny handful of soil, and I'll say to them: 'See, my brothers, see these drops of blood in these grains of soil in this hand, that's how much Algeria has bled throughout her body, all over her vast body, that's how much Algeria has paid for our freedom and for this, our return, with her own soil. But her martyrdom now speaks in terms of grace. So you see, my brothers . . .'"

"The day that we return," Mother repeated softly in the silence that followed . . . "if God wills it."

It was then that the cries began again through the open window. Like an orchestra that brusquely starts a piece of music. Then, in a different tone, Hafsa reminded us: "I'm here for the lesson."

Aïcha pulled her into the next room.

During their meeting, I didn't know what to do. The windows of the kitchen and of the other two rooms looked out over the terraces. I went from one to the other, opening them, closing them, opening them again. All of this without hurrying, as if I weren't listening to the song.

Anissa caught me in my rounds.

"You can tell they're not Algerian," she said. "They're not even accustomed to being in mourning."

"At home, in the mountains," Mother answered, "the dead have nobody to weep over them before they grow cold."

"Weeping serves no purpose," Anissa was stoic, "whether you die in your bed or on the bare ground for your country."

"What do you know about it?" I suddenly said to her. "You're too young to know."

"Soon they're going to bury him," Mother whispered.

Then she raised her head and looked at me. I had once again closed the window behind me. I couldn't hear anything anymore.

"They're going to bury him this very day," Mother said again a little louder, "that's our custom."

"They shouldn't," I said. "It's a hateful custom to deliver a body to the earth when beauty still shines on it. Really quite hateful. . . . It seems to me they're burying him while he's still shivering, still . . ." (but I couldn't control my voice any longer).

"Stop thinking about your children!" Mother said. "The earth that was thrown on them is a blanket of gold. My poor daughter, stop thinking about your children!" Mother said again.

"I'm not thinking about anything," I said. "No, really. I don't want to think about anything. About anything at all."

*

*   *

It was already four o'clock in the afternoon when they came in. From the kitchen where I was hiding, I heard them exclaim, once the normal phrases of courtesy had been uttered: "What is that weeping?"

"May misfortune stay far away from us! May God protect us!"

"It gives me goose bumps," the third one was saying. "I've almost forgotten death and tears, these days. I've forgotten them, even though our hearts are always heavy."

"That is the will of God," the second one would respond.

In a placid voice, Mother explained the reason for the mourning next door as she invited them into the only room we had been able to furnish decently. Anissa, close by me, was already making the first comments on the way the women looked. She was questioning Aïcha, who had been with Mother to welcome them. I had opened the window again and watched them exchange their first impressions.

"What are you thinking?" Anissa said, her eye still on me.

"Nothing," I said feebly; then, after a pause: "I was thinking of the different faces of fate. I was thinking of God's will. Behind that wall, there is a dead person and women going mad with grief. Here, in our house, other women are talking of marriage . . . I was thinking of that difference."

"Just stop 'thinking,'" Aïcha cut in sharply. Then to Hafsa, who was coming in: "You ought to be teaching *her*, not me. She spends all her time thinking. You'd almost believe she's read as many books as you have."

"And why not?" Hafsa asked.

"I don't need to learn French," I answered. "What purpose would it serve? Father has taught us all our language. 'That's all you need,' he always says."

"It's useful to know languages other than your own," Hafsa said slowly. "It's like knowing other people, other countries."

I didn't answer. Perhaps she was right. Perhaps you ought to learn and not waste your time letting your mind wander, like mine, through the deserted corridors of the past. Perhaps I should take lessons and study French, or anything else. But I, I never felt the need to jostle my body or my mind. . . . Aïcha was different. Like a man: hard and hardworking. She was thirty. She hadn't seen her husband in three years, who was still incarcerated in Barberousse prison, where he had been since the first days of the war. Yet, she was getting an education and didn't settle for household work. Now, after just a few months of Hafsa's lessons, Omar no longer read her husband's infrequent letters, the few that might reach her. She managed to decipher them by herself. Sometimes I caught myself being envious of her.

"Hafsa," she said, "it's time for my sister to go in and greet these ladies. Please go with her."

But Hafsa didn't want to. Aïcha insisted, and I was watching them play their little game of politeness.

"Does anyone know if they've come for the body yet?" I asked.

"What? Didn't you hear the chanters just now?" Anissa said.

"So that's why the weeping stopped for a moment," I said. "It's strange, as soon as some parts of the Koranic verses are chanted, the women immediately stop weeping. And yet, that's the most painful moment, I know it all too well myself. As long as the body is there in front of you, it seems the child isn't quite dead yet, can't be dead, you see? . . . Then comes the moment when the men get up, and that is to take him, wrapped in a sheet, on their shoulders. That's how he leaves, quickly, as on the day that he came. . . . For me, may God forgive me, they can chant Koranic verses all they want, the house is still empty after they've gone, completely empty. . . ."

Hafsa was listening, her head leaning toward the window.

With a shiver, she turned toward me. She seemed younger even than Anissa, then.

"My God," she said, emotion in her voice, "I've just turned twenty and yet I've never encountered death. Never in my whole life!"

"Haven't you lost anyone in your family in this war?" Anissa asked.

"Oh yes," she said, "but the news always comes by mail. And death by mail, you see, I can't believe it. A first cousin of mine died under the guillotine as one of the first in Barberousse. Well, I've never shed a tear over him because I cannot believe that he's dead. And yet he was like a brother to me, I swear. But I just can't believe he's dead, you understand?" she said in a voice already wrapped in tears.

"Those who've died for the Cause aren't really dead," Anissa answered with a touch of pride.

"So, let's think of the present. Let's think about today," Aïcha said in a dry voice. "The rest is in God's hand."

*

*   *

There were three of them: an old woman who had to be the suitor's mother and who hastily put on her glasses as soon as I arrived; two other women, seated side by side, resembled each other. Hafsa, who'd come in behind me, sat down next to me. I lowered my eyes.

I knew my part, it was one I'd played before; stay mute like this, eyes lowered, and patiently let myself be examined until the very end: it was simple. Everything is simple, beforehand, for a girl who's being married off.

Mother was talking. I was barely listening. I knew the themes to be developed all too well: Mother was talking about our sad state as refugees; then they'd be exchanging opinions on when the end might be announced: ". . . another Ramadan to be spent away from home . . . perhaps this was the last one . . . perhaps, if God wills it! Of course, we were saying the same thing last year, and the year before that. . . . Let's not complain too much. . . . In any event, victory is certain, all our men say the same thing.

And we, we know the day of our return will come. . . . We should be thinking of those who stayed behind. . . . We should be thinking of those who are suffering. . . . The Algerian people are a people whom God loves. . . . And our fighters are made of steel. . . ." Then they'd come back to the tale of the flight, to the different means by which each one had left her soil where the fires were burning. . . . Then they'd evoke the sadness of exile, the heart yearning for its country. . . . And the fear of dying far from the land of one's birth. . . . Then. . . . But may God be praised and may he grant our prayers!"

This time it lasted a bit longer; an hour perhaps, or more. Until the time came to serve coffee. By then, I was hardly listening at all. I too was thinking in my own way of this exile, of these somber days.

I was thinking how everything had changed, how on the day of my first engagement we had been in the long, bright living room of our house in the hills of Algiers; how we'd been prosperous then, we had prosperity and peace; how Father used to laugh, how he used to give thanks to God for the abundance of his home . . . And I, I wasn't as I was today, my soul grey, gloomy and with this idea of death beating faintly inside me since the morning. . . . Yes, I was thinking how everything had changed and that, still, in some way everything remained the same. They were still concerned with marrying me off. And why exactly? I suddenly wondered. And why exactly? I repeated to myself, feeling something like fury inside me, or its echo. Just so I could have worries that never change whether it's peace or wartime, so I could wake up in the middle of the night and question myself on what it is that sleeps in the depths of the heart of the man sharing my bed. . . . Just so I could give birth and weep, for life never comes unaccompanied to a woman, death is always right behind, furtive, quick, and smiling at the mothers. . . . Yes, why indeed? I said to myself.

Coffee had now been served. Mother was inviting them to drink.

"We won't take even one sip," the old woman began, "before you've given us your word about your daughter."

"Yes," the other one said, "my brother impressed upon us

that we weren't to come back without your promising to give her to him as his wife."

I was listening to Mother avoid answering, have herself be begged hypocritically, and then again invite them to drink. Aïcha joined in with her. The women were repeating their request. . . . It was all as it should be.

The game went on a few minutes longer. Mother invoked the father's authority: "I, of course, would give her to you. . . . I know you are people of means. . . . But there is her father."

"Her father has already said yes to my brother," one of the two women who resembled each other replied. "The question remains only to be discussed between us."

"Yes," said the second one, "it's up to us now. Let's settle the question."

I raised my head; it was then, I think, that I met Hafsa's gaze. There was, deep in her eyes, a strange light, surely of interest or of irony, I don't know, but you could feel Hafsa as an outsider, attentive and curious at the same time, but an outsider. I met that look.

"I don't want to marry," I said. "I don't want to marry," I repeated, barely shouting.

There was much commotion in the room: Mother got up with a deep sigh; Aïcha was blushing, I saw. And the two women who turned to me, with the same slow movement of shock: "And why not?" one of them asked.

"My son," the old woman exclaimed with some arrogance, "my son is a man of science. In a few days he is leaving for the Orient."

"Of course," Mother said with touching haste. "We know he's a scholar. We know him to have a righteous heart. . . . Of course. . . ."

"It's not because of your son," I said. "But I don't want to get married. I see the future before my eyes, it's totally black. I don't know how to explain it, surely it must come from God. . . . But I see the future totally black before my eyes!" I said again, sobbing, as Aïcha led me out of the room in silence.

*
* *

Later, but why even tell the rest, except that I was consumed with shame and I didn't understand. Only Hafsa stayed close to me after the women had left.

"You're engaged," she said sadly. "Your mother said she'd give you away. Will you accept?" and she stared at me with imploring eyes.

"What difference does it make?" I said and really thought inside myself: What difference does it make? "I don't know what came over me before. But they were all talking about the present and its changes and its misfortunes. And I was saying to myself: of what possible use is it to be suffering like this, far away from home, if I have to continue here as before in Algiers, to stay home and sit and pretend. . . . Perhaps when life changes, everything should change with it, absolutely everything. I was thinking of all that," I said, "but I don't even know if that's bad or good. . . . You, you're smart, and you know these things, perhaps you'll understand. . . ."

"I do understand," she said, hesitating as if she were going to start talking and then preferred to remain silent.

"Open the window," I said. "It's almost dark."

She went to open it and then came back to my bed where I'd been lying down to cry, without reason, crying for shame and fatigue all at the same time. In the silence that followed, I was feeling distant, pondering the night that little by little engulfed the room. The sounds from the kitchen, where my sisters were, seemed to be coming from somewhere else.

Then Hafsa began to speak: "Your father," she said, "once spoke of exile, of our present exile, and he said—oh, I remember it well, for nobody speaks like your father—he said: 'There is no exile for any man loved by God. There is no exile for the one who is on God's path. There are only trials.' "

She went on a while, but I've forgotten the rest, except that she repeated *we* very often with a note of passion. She said that word with a peculiar vehemence, so much so that I began to wonder toward the end whether that word really meant the two of us alone, or rather other women, all the women of our country.

To tell the truth, even if I'd known, what could I have answered? Hafsa was too knowledgeable for me. And that's what I would have liked to have told her when she stopped talking, perhaps in the expectation that I would speak.

But it was another voice that answered, a woman's voice that rose, through the open window, rose straight as an arrow toward the sky, that rounded itself out, spread out in its flight, a flight ample as a bird's after the storm, then came falling back down in sudden torrents.

"The other women have grown silent," I said. "The only one left to weep now is the mother. . . . Such is life," I added a moment later. "There are those who forget or who simply sleep. And then there are those who keep bumping into the walls of the past. May God take pity on them!"

"Those are the true exiles," said Hafsa.

Tunis, March 1959

The Dead Speak

to Lla Fatma Sahraoui,
my maternal grandmother,
in posthumous homage

I

At the grandmother's funeral, conversations are going on at a steady pace. Aïcha watches. Absent. They think she's not there. Because of her ashen face, those dull eyes they consider plain. Sagging shoulders, a body that's already withered, swimming in a light-colored tunic. The same one for years now, an undefined color. The visitors, women—a tense and curious crowd, white veils sliding over long black hair, breaking at the neck—the visiting women invade the dwelling that is too large. Seated, Aïcha watches.

Aïcha, the first name of an open flower, has been broken and wilted since time immemorial. During that war, no one counted the days or the months. And the time before the war seems a time swallowed up, of which even the memory has been erased.

The stronger swell of these last years, even if the virgins continued to blossom (poor, sad smiles and eyelids often reddened, their cheeks the radiance of a dawn despite themselves, their woman's bodies fully rounded . . .). As for the boys, as puberty approached, how the worry about them would claw at their mothers' hearts

    . . . —violation, who is going to violate them, the
    mountains, or some commando of the night, a
    musket shot at them . . . —

The swell has weighted everything down with bitterness, for certain women irremediably so.

At the grandmother's funeral, conversations are going on at a steady pace.

Aïcha, huddled on the floor. Two steps away, the dead woman stretched out underneath the immaculate sheet. Whiteness of woolens and silks everywhere, a few let black and shiny hair show through, faces marbled with redness. A woman sniffles gently. Barely droning, the heat of the place. Turned in on itself.

Aïcha watches. Her almost lashless eyes worn out from night-time tears. She doesn't weep. She wipes her face from time to time. The curiosity of white veils fussing over her. A wound made deeper once again, with every ceremony when the house must be opened to other people, for a wake or for a marriage within the tribe. . . .

Aïcha raises her head. The tribe? That was before. During that war, the grandmother stood straight as an oak tree in the storm. The past five years, they, mute shadows, would both move about aimlessly in these bourgeois spaces. On the second floor, all along the glassed-in terraces, Aïcha's son would trot behind old Hadda, dead today. Then he would come and curl up in the hollows of the mattresses in this very room. Two women alone, one child. Silence.

> "These five years of silence, I must say . . ."
> "Quiet, she's listening!"
> "As if she didn't know, poor thing, it's these five years of waiting that have killed the old woman."
> "Quiet, I tell you . . . Aïcha . . ."
> "And he?"
> "He?"
> "When did he arrive?"
> "The woman across the street, the one who sits at her window and spies . . ."
> "Well?"
> "She saw him come in the first time! Yemma Hadda hadn't died yet . . ."
> "Fortunate one!"

Aïcha daydreams. The visitors chatter. Successive places where her memory moors, where the same city women are, still there, present at these ceremonies of time. Fixed images, as if stopped behind her gaze that doesn't move.

> . . . the bed of a new mother, drained of her blood, muscles slack, next to whom whimpers the new-

The Dead Speak

born, lavished with blessings—the corpse of a
man shot the previous night, brought here, around
whom the hired weepers stand, suddenly rigid,
their lips half open for a cry that doesn't come
forth—same low table for coffee or mint tea, with
the same semolina cakes . . .

and these same women, present, chanting, whispering, bending
their head now to one then to another, rearranging their veil
with crisp little motions, causing the folds of its cloth to rustle
underneath their heavy thighs.

But everywhere, from all these years that founder, years mur-
dered under the jolts of war, behind the gagged mouths, surge
the suffocated cries, fading as at dusk or in a vast, last lingering chord—which terror has suspended above the buzzing and
slightly agitated background of these visitors. . . . Aïcha, shaking her head, tries to dismiss the buzzing within these spaces,
to retain only some of its mute visions.

Over there, the one in the semidarkness in the back, moonfaced under a white veil. Her two daughters-in-law seated on
either side of her, looking modest, with a black stare. Widows
as well. The oldest one saw her husband of fifty years and her
two sons fall in the small courtyard of her own house, near the
jasmine, in the light of the flares. The husband with the force of
a lion in repose. The sons, now men, supports on whom she'd
thought she could count for her old age. The preceding winter,
she had seen them both married the same night, in the midst of
choirs . . .

> . . . three men slaughtered in the same night. A
> raging horde, led by the son of the Maltese con-
> tractor,
>> Gate clanging against the patio wall,
>> Heavy ringing noises of the weapons and the
> cavalcade,
>> Broken lights of the kerosene lamps,
>> The horde upon the city. Spread out . . .
>> . . . The women's room. Shadows on the walls

of bare arms raised, clawing at their flesh. Shrieking, endlessly drawn out . . .

Over there, the one in the back, moonfaced, almost serene
today. Mute for two years now. Shows up only on occasions
of forced seriousness, other mourning to be shared, moments
of anguish of other families. Two years. There she is again
today. She is speaking. Aïcha watches her speak. Naturally, she
doesn't smile. The unchanging silk of sorrow stretched across
her features, lightly brushing the corners of her eyelids. But
she stretches her neck forward to listen. But she answers in
fragments.

The two daughters-in-law, behind her, gently touch their
pinkish cheeks underneath the veil. Tighten the fabric over their
moist forehead or under their chin. Soften their look.

Other women around. Aïcha knows them. They are the ones
who chronicle the flow of days and of destinies. The official
speakers. Without any need for slander. Out of simple concern
for giving an account.

Perhaps, too, for amplifying what happens through words,
through inflections, frayed sighs, and out of these making bal-
loons of hope or chasms of alarm.

All these dimmed palpitations within the surrounding noises
and the helplessness of suspended tears. Sounds too of the
repeated formulas. Words used to find a way out.

> —. . . obscure reason for women's murmuring,
> who—oh merciful God—, who will shed light
> upon you? . . . —

Aïcha tunes out the hubbub. But her slow, circular gaze seizes
on each face. Notices the humming emotion in each group.

> *And I, I who accompany the dead, whoever they*
> *may be, whether newly buried or already burrow-*
> *ing into the sand and mud underneath the stone,*
> *I the true shroud of the corpses, whether the most*
> *cleanly washed or those who stink underneath*
> *the ointments and perfumes, I who am the inter-*
> *rogative soul, let us say, who escapes, or searches,*

The Dead Speak

or waits, I who claim to be the paralyzing shell,
the last all-too-real mask, because I must reestab-
lish the original incommunicability as new and
unequivocal, I in all the places where multiple wit-
nesses congregate around a cold body, because
of the usual customary mores, witnesses already
forgetful, already denying but feeling the weight
of their common forgetfulness, I their inaudible
voice, I meticulously reestablish the distances, I
reevaluate the relationships.

*

* *

A sudden unreal tableau for Aïcha, motionless. Several city women flutter their prewar fans. They get settled. They get comfortable.

Right in the center of the room, the corpse. The shroud almost brushes against Aïcha's crossed knees. It outlines the shape of the head, continues along the body into a slight cone at the level of the stomach (the grandmother, tall and emaciated, suffered nonetheless from aerophagia). At the end, the feet form two horns.

Yemma Hadda, reduced to just a contour.

> "How many times, alas . . ."
> "Standing right before me, the last time. . . . I
> see her still, unfortunate woman! I . . ."
> "Don't tremble! Spell, spell out the name of
> God . . ."

How many times, at every wake, Aïcha would arrange another sheet around the hips and the feet. . . . Not here! Not in the middle. . . . Aïcha recoils, without getting up.

> —Get rid of the visitors, squelch the wave of mur-
> muring, stand up straight!—

Stand up straight, oh yes, despite the apparent uncertainty. Shoulders bare, body vibrant. Step over these huddled bodies. These submissive bodies. . . . Go and arrange the fabric in the same way over the sleeping grandmother.

"The last time,"
"My son woke me up at dawn: 'Yemma is
gone!' His voice broke. Poor thing, you would
have thought he was losing his own grandmother! . . ."
"Blessings be upon him . . ."

Yemma is sleeping, isn't she? Aïcha persists. If she were to
stretch out her arm, her hand would touch the shrouded face.
The same dialogue, then, used to end the days.

"Tell me," Hadda used to ask, "is the little one resting?"
Her features crumpled with fatigue, she would give thanks
with her blessings.
"He's sleeping, Yemma."
"That boy, he's going to be your rising sun! Don't forget that
I told you so!"
"May God hear you, Yemma Hadda."
That daily dialogue would end each dusk.
Yes, remove herself from the chatter. Forget the visitors.
A few gestures: raise the sheet, rearrange it as she had done
yesterday.

—Yesterday is coming back and I hear it. Yemma
Hadda is still worrying about the little one, planning his future. She promised it to me as a blanket
of destiny. . . . May God hear her! oh, if all of you
only knew!—

Aïcha sits. Yemma will speak no more. The little one . . .
Aïcha's boy, "Aïcha-the-outcast," she imagines the city's gos-
sip-mongers ululating:

—"An orphan, might as well call him a bastard,
neither known nor wanted by his father!"—

Aïcha, a brand-new mother, had found only this, Hadda's
virile confidence. Hadda, a distant aunt. One winter morning,
Aïcha on the doorstep, a suitcase in her hand, her five-month-
old child in her arms:

"You are the only one left of my mother's face
and blood . . ."

"Come on in, my daughter, yes indeed, it was I
who called for you."

Five years for Aïcha-the-outcast since that arrival.

Right in the center of the room, the corpse. The belly an am-
phora, accentuated by the sheet. In the back of the deep room,
a second sheet masks the mirror of the cherry wardrobe. A few
mattresses covered in gray. Everywhere, women's bodies piled
together like blurs of swallows caught in birdlime. In mottled
patches, an Aurès carpet shows through. In front of the door-
sill, right on the red stones, a jumble of pairs of black slippers.
For the old women take off their shoes before coming in. Take
off their veils. Then, after having found a space between two
rumps, they moan.

A final arrival has trouble making her way through. Some
fluttering of veils, a few greetings in a tone of resignation follow
her. She advances. Near the horizontal bulk, she stoops down.
Aïcha, suddenly attentive.

A second of silence. All the heads are bowed. The looks
concentrated. The hubbub drifts away, limp and slow, like an
ephemeral ship. In the center, with a ring-covered hand, the
lady lifts the sheet.

A glimpse of Hadda's face: eyelids deep inside each orbit,
the long line of her sharp nose, the color of wax that whitens
everything. One instant.

—To scream, to flee into a tearing of the widened
arms, to rip everything off—veil and the body's
skin—in this dread, turn the apparent serenity
upside down.—

Aïcha, motionless, watches. Nobody knows. And what is
there to know, the child . . .

"Hassan. . . . His name is Hassan," whispers
the woman who helps to guide the little boy to his
mother.

"Hassan, was it Yemma Hadda who named him?"

"His real name is Amine; the old woman called him Hassan from the moment he came into her house."

"So then she thought her grandson was dead?"

"No. . . . Five years without any news, yet she didn't give up."

"Look! . . . Aïcha. . . . Her son at her feet, but she doesn't move."

The child—"beautiful and strong" an unknown woman nearby, who seems gentle, compliments Aïcha, who does not smile—a quiet little boy, too quiet. Attentive eyes, with an embarrassing sort of heaviness, an almost absentminded resentment. The bulging and obstinate forehead of the father, that "hothead" who disappeared from the city, who has died they now say, a hero of the mountains or a traitor, who will ever know . . .

The child is silent. Reassured. Roused out of his deep sleep without crying. He never cries. Never! The silence of Hadda's dwelling has penetrated his being, a house that is too large, with its Syrian furniture, its modern kitchen, its second-floor trappings, spaces haunted by the waiting for the absent heir.

The child . . .

"Amine!" Aïcha calls.

He raises his eyes.

"Aren't you hungry?"

He doesn't answer. Studies the bulging sheet.

—Yemma is sleeping, my darling, my heart.—

Amine turns to his silent mother. Yesterday a man came into this same place. Hassan. The name living in the house all these years.

Without the uniform of heroes. Disappointing the child. Someone rather ordinary, barely a little taller than the milkman in the morning, barely less stiff than the sharecropper who comes every Friday. . . . He entered the room. Right here.

The Dead Speak

In a corner on her two mattresses, Yemma. She'd been helped up against the corner. Her ears flattened on either side on the large pillow, a down blanket across her. The waxen face near the whitewashed wall. The eyes immense but unfocused. The nose huge, and some paralysis of the face.

The man lowered his shoulders as he raised the curtain of the door. A few steps, then he stopped. Aïcha made a mute gesture with her arm in the direction of the grandmother. She whispered, the child didn't understand what. She took the boy by the shoulders tightening her fingers in a spasmodic way. Together, they left the room.

The man without a uniform and Yemma. The image is fixed. Amine scrutinizes the sheet.

Does he understand? Aïcha questioning herself, clutches him against her side.

> "That's all she has left!" mumbles a neighbor near the door, who from that spot has caught her movement.
>
> "The son returned from the mountains, hale and hearty! . . . He's her cousin, in short, a brother."
>
> "Does family count today?"
>
> "What is the fighting for, then? For the blood that perpetuates us? . . . Didn't you hear the speech yesterday on the square? 'We are all brothers!' "
>
> "Right you are, my sister, those are the right words. . . . May the men understand them the same way."
>
> "All I have to say is," another one sighs, "lucky is the man who, this past week of independence, has been able to see victory dawning."
>
> "Hadda, through the will of God, did see these days one last time!"
>
> "The neighbor who watches from her window . . ." the previous one began again.

"Let them talk, let them whisper . . . Aïcha said to herself, her hand on the frail shoulder of the little boy.

—Who'll tell me what tomorrow will bring?—

Then the refrain began inside her, there facing
all the women of the city, those who for all these
years under the burned mountain, rigid with hope,
had formed the foundering or trembling choir,
those who, all their veils swollen, scurried through
the alleys while the soldiers were searching for
who-knows-what terrorist, those who closed
doors of obscure hallways and who, breathless,
their ear against wood, recognized the rhythmic
step of the army rabble.

Those whose destiny it had always been to be
the ears and the rumors of the city, whose voca-
tion it had been to crouch down at the feet of
the husband coming home in the evening and to
undo his shoes and who, for the most part, no
longer had anything to undo but their anguish;
finally, those whose future it had been to recognize themselves as the unconscious leaven for the
adolescents of sudden resolve (—"my son . . . my
battered heart . . . my tortured flesh!")

All of them, sitting in groups today, believed
they were nobly keeping the dead woman company with the same posture and the same confabu-
lations, evoking her with expressions of regret, of
nostalgia—in short, burying her. As if we bury the
dead, as if they weren't continuing to live somewhere . . . but where? Then the refrain began inside Aïcha. An unexpected phrase. Whose words
moved her with a vengeance. They frightened her.
—"I have neither law nor master . . . the little phrase
began.—

"I have neither law nor master," she began again. She took
the words apart. Waited. Fear and confusion in order to understand . . .

The Dead Speak

Then she muttered the beginning of a prayer:—"There is only one God and Muhammad . . ."

*

* *

"There is only one God and Muhammad is his prophet!" an old blind woman stood up and interjected in a deep voice.

The same age as Hadda, she was the singer of the city. Her voice, hoarse at times, had kept a copper-toned sound to which the ears of the young and the old had always been sensitive. Reared up like an Arabic *Pythia* with many veils that made her taller. As soon as she intoned her chant, she became like the obscure mother of them all,

> . . . voice that anchors itself to all the separations
> of umbilical cords,
>   that resonates at all the seventh days after
> births,
>   that ululates at the fortieth days after deaths,
> which at the secret of every wedding night would
> introduce the sudden, the strange note of lament
> covered with virginal blood, the troubled terror
> before the solace of resignation, calm at last . . .

Voice of all mothers mute with powerlessness, contemplating the misfortune of their descendants. . . . Here is the blind woman of the city, once a courtesan. Since then, its pathetic priestess, tender contralto who recalls what for the dead, who . . .

"Hadda, my wound, the effigy of all mothers!"

"There is only one God . . . ," several old women in the group began again in chorus, providing the blind woman with time to improvise some more.

"Hadda, eyes open on the smile that comes after the massacre!"

The collective chant grew stronger a second time. The blind woman, thus supported, raised her emaciated arms theatrically to the sky.

". . . and Muhammad is His prophet!" finished the choir, from which a youthful voice pierced through.

"Hadda, whose young fawn returns to the source!"

Around Aïcha they were now all chanting. Her lips tightly closed, she suddenly heard the frail voice of her child utter a few fragments: ". . . is only one God!"

The copper-toned voice, taking the beginning notes higher and higher and holding them the length of two full breaths. Still tense, her eyes on the other faces in the darkness, Aïcha began to wait for what would follow. The moment when, having reached the peak, the blind woman's voice would burst forth into a long, piercing cry. And that would be the point where all the accumulated emotions of the chant would rupture sharply. Already, during the improvisation, a few experienced women were beginning to express their various opinions about the blind woman's being "in top form" as she mourned her contemporary.

The singer's recitative unfolded. She alone didn't refer to the dead woman as *Yemma*. Throughout the song's slow arabesques, Aïcha's silence grew more and more dense.

"Hadda, the conqueror of your blood, like your ancestor at the head of the horsemen in earlier days."

The collective litany grew weaker. Not that those present were feeling tired. But the blind woman was rushing the rhythm along. Motionless. Her arms behind her in a pose of lyrical meditation. The headdress on her reddened hair half fallen off, her swarthy face and sunken eyes, her powerful jaw. Suddenly shaken by nervous trembling.

She cut the alternating chorus short. No longer waited for the response. As if inspiration had become a mare for her that she was barely able to ride.

"Hadda," a shrill note becoming a piercing rattle. . . .

"Sobbing, are we already at the point of sobbing?" Aïcha asked herself plaintively.

Overcome by the aesthetic emotion, she finally began to weep.

"Hadda," the singer began again, a little softer, "open the royal road of deliverance to us! Hadda, now silent, speak to us!"

And the cry burst forth. Spasmodic. Long but powerless. Like a gurgling that the group's more vigorous chant drowned

The Dead Speak

out completely: traditional invocations, the Prophet's name, the hearts' frenzy . . .

"What did she say at the end?" one of the two young widows next to the moonfaced lady asked.

Rigid and silent, still standing up in her role as orator, the blind woman trembled, almost reeling. Then she sat down at the feet of the dead one, her hands on each sheeted cone, funerary statue, her flaming red hair completely undone.

Soundless tears flowing, Aïcha turned toward the woman asking the question. Her arms were still around her motionless child. She smiled, despite her face soaked with tears, less graceful than ever but its features softer.

"She said," with her boy in her arms, she raised herself halfway up, "she said, 'oh Yemma, speak to me!' "

"What's happening to her?" exclaimed an unknown woman in a corner.

"Aïcha . . . poor thing, she's weeping at last."

Compassion everywhere.

> "Blessed sorrow . . ."
> "The orphan is more unfortunate than the
> widow! Don't they say: 'You, my mother's
> orphan, you moan and your tears don't dry!' "

From her spot, her thin torso propped up, Amine's weight in her arms, Aïcha began her lament again under her breath. A childish, desperate moaning.

She rocked her head back and forth: "Yemma Hadda who has left us, speak to us, speak to me!"

"There is only one God," in the back of the overheated room, the consoling antiphon continued.

Tears were flowing down Aïcha's emaciated face. Aïcha, the first name of an open flower that will become nothing other than a faded fragment. . . .

> The little phrase—mother and child in sacral pos-
> ture—spiraled up a second time, a complete fall of
> grief. Aïcha thought it was a violent headache. . . .

But these words had nothing to do with those
the blind woman had spoken, almost indecent
ones, clashing with the words of the prayer that
were audible, now here, now there, in the room
once again buzzing with sound—noisy lamenta-
tion of July mornings, heat that makes the dead
grow putrid.

Surprising words Aïcha listens to inside herself:
already she was no longer watching the others.
She had yielded, she had melted away among their
sickly sweet moaning, she and the orphan boy in
her arms.

How to avoid the hardened phrase: "I have
neither law nor master!" . . . Hadda, her old aunt,
had she been her master? . . . Barely the hull of a
ship in distress and that since a long time ago.

"Only you, with my mother's face, with her
blood . . ."

These had been the first words of the outcast
when welcomed in the doorway. She had pronounced them mechanically, more out of humility.

"I have neither law nor master!" What law?
Except misfortune's law, more tenacious despite
these early days of independence . . .

*
* *

"Hassan, returned yesterday!" the busybody whispered for
the third time.

She was leaning against the dead woman's side, right in front
of Aïcha. She turned her head at a slight angle to the left, to the
right, the better to project the hissing of her words above her
fat chin.

Outside, a murmur filled the little courtyard.

"The Koranic readers," a child's voice announced from the
hallway. Inside, the confused noise of voices became weaker.

"The Friday prayer for Yemma Hadda, the fortunate one!"

exclaimed a woman almost joyfully. "Blessings be upon Yemma Hadda!"

Other squealing flared up here and there. The youngest ones were getting up. Others swished their veils. Several crumpled handkerchiefs were falling on the thick Aurès carpet.

Every woman was busy trying to figure out when the Koranic readers would begin, when the men would enter to lift the corpse, when . . .

"Out of the room, the room must be vacated!"
"Except for the old women. They just have to
cover their heads and shoulders again!"

During this agitated waiting and despite the new scattering, not one movement from the bulk underneath the sheet. Not a twitch or any sign of impatience from the long horizontal shape. The face, suffocated by the shroud, doesn't provide a single one of the starts one might have expected. Hadda, truly made of stone.

Well cleansed. Dressed in white underneath the white. New linen without a single stitch of sewing, as tradition requires.

Hadda with her large nose, with her look turned inward, waits.

Four men, one of whom is Hassan. He has just come through five years of battle, of mysterious activity, only to find his way to this pious moment. Uncover the body. He will hesitate at first, bending halfway down. He will lift the head of the grandmother with his two hands. His look dry, without showing any emotion.

"Amine!" Aïcha calls, the last one to move from her spot.

The younger women have disappeared into other rooms. The curiosity revived in their inquisitive glances from behind the shutters that overlook the little courtyard.

Aïcha is smothered under a blanket. She recoils a few steps. Finds herself squeezed between the old women. Right near her, the blind woman modestly puts the green silk scarf back on her tawny head.

—Four men! Hassan will carry the grandmother's head alone, for himself, for me. . . . —

The dead woman, all alone, right in the room's deserted center. Aïcha's prying eyes. Amine begins to whine plaintively, by fits and starts.

*

* *

The men came in, self-righteous silhouettes, ready to mete out justice. One of the four in wide, Turkish-style pants; the oldest with a sunburned face and an authoritative fez; finally, Hassan, the last one, narrow shoulders, no expression on his face.

Aïcha feverishly caresses Amine's head, who is now silent and clings to her. Suddenly,

—"I have neither law nor master," her lips mumble under her breath. Amine, thinking she's speaking to him, turns his frail little oval face to her.

—"But why? . . . why? Am I rebelling? . . ."

Upheaval that is verbal, so to speak, that does not become any clearer inside her aching head.

The four men go out. The center of the room is completely gutted, almost blood-let.

Aïcha gets up, suddenly the mistress of the house and yet absentminded. The visitors, about to leave, sit back down as if for a performance.

"Aïcha, absentminded? No! . . ." they remember bluntly: "repudiated!"

. . . some sly virgin will have come as a spy. Retaining her veil even among the other women, thus keeping her anonymity. Only a scrutinizing eye, the hole a hostile triangle in the completely masked face. She turns around from time to time in order not to miss a single detail. . . . The young inquisitor, often contemptuous, is slow and serious. . . . A world of women beleaguered, holding in its midst a spy, thus giving itself the illusion of mysteriousness. . . .

"There's always some impoverished cousin!"
"In every mourning period there is always one outcast!"

Commonplaces, hollow formulas that slip from one neighbor to the next. They offer their condolences. They go out.

"Am I rebelling, then?" Aïcha straightens up, her body drowning inside her ample tunic. She entrusts her son to the nearest of the matrons. Receives the expressions of compassion as she must, but she is leaning on the casing of the door. . . . Then heads toward the kitchens.

"The meal . . ."
"Will there be a meal for the guests?"
"For the men, surely not! See, they're staying outside. . . ."
"Hassan said. . . . I heard him say it," one woman, about to leave, intervened.
"What, what did he say?" several others asked.
" 'There's no point in serving a meal to the city people.' Those were his words. But he insists that everything should be given to the poor!"
"I just saw two slaughtered sheep."
"Yemma's couscous was famous! . . . She rolled her own! You thought the angels had prepared it, but with her fingers. . . . Wedding couscous, or couscous for the dead!"
"So that's what he said. . . . Ah, the men these days!"
"For the poor," another protested, "isn't that what matters most?"

Aïcha left the spasms of talk behind. . . . A few more hours, perhaps even till dusk, groups of women would hover around: those who had neither children nor husbands of supercilious authority, old and pale widows, so great in number now.

Cakes decorated with anise seed were handed out to them, piled up in majestic cones on trays of reed. Aïcha had prepared them herself the night before, helped by two young girls who lived in the house next door. Only three hours after Yemma's last sigh. Hours of continuous but gentle tears. Silent house; Aïcha alone with those young girls. At the critical moment, the younger one had ululated like a confused and upset puppy when it smells death for the first time.

Aïcha leaves the grandmother's room. Calls Hassan from below. But her throat stays dry, her hands are trembling.

"Oh son of my maternal aunt!"

The normal Arabic form of address. It could attenuate the despair of the cry.

Aïcha was going to begin this way had there not been the young girl's clamoring—Hasna, fourteen years old, her body in bloom, her breasts pomegranates.

> —Who could have muzzled her, who would
> have admonished her to "pray, pray to God and
> His Prophet," in foreseeing her uncontrollable
> fright?—

Hasna shrieked. Like a prolonged, self-complacent crying. Aïcha, haggard, in the middle of the patio, didn't need to call.

From the second floor, Hassan appeared, his face with the serious look above the balustrade. Aïcha made a convulsive gesture with her arms.

"Oh God," she sobbed, her neck bent, then, shaking and frenzied, dashed back into the room of the dead woman.

She sat down at the foot of the mattress, her eyes vacant, tears flowing down her still-pale face. Suddenly overcome by gentle nostalgia, an odd passivity. That is how Hassan found her as he drew the curtain aside, even before looking at Hadda.

He approached. The gaping stare of the dead grandmother. Close the worn eyelids with a sure hand, cover up that wide-open look, as if it had no voice. The brief elegance of the gesture, a belated sweetness after the flesh had been touched.

The Dead Speak

I who at the first moment of death, wrap the
marbled skin of new corpses in the winding-sheet,
I who fill the interior of the body grown cold
with the gently extinguished dream, all orifices
open, I who inexorably establish a more and more
oceanic distance between the most vibrant of the
witness-bearing sorrows and the staggering sealed
absence, I who . . . I?

Let us say, the befogged and barely distorted
voice, the tiny voice that desperately attempts to
cross over into the new darkness. . . . I?

I, eyes turned up noticing every call, I, the light
that goes out while the cracked voice hangs sus-
pended, in the helplessness of being heard neither
by a questioning ear nor even by some watch-
ful eye. . . .

I, old Hadda's invisible shroud, infiltrating
all the former, fallen anxieties, all the successive
bites of senile hope, I in the place of Yemma com-
forted, I, witness without memory, take cogni-
zance of Hassan's approach, the prodigal grand-
son, awaited for five years.

In front of her cousin, younger than she by several years, Aïcha realized she was weeping. Methodically, she took out a handkerchief, dried her hollow cheeks, wiped her nose soundlessly, got up. Left the room walking backward as if the old woman was still watching her.

One hour later, Hassan and Aïcha began to talk. The first words in so very many years; the young girls next door right nearby behind the curtain of the neighboring door. Hassan was giving orders. Was making decisions for the next day in a slow voice. A new accent in his speech, a gruffer accent than the city one, as if he were borrowing it from the waves of tattered nomads.
An accent that evoked pursuit. Aïcha thought it had a bitter tenderness.

And again, after exactly ten years, the old, the
wretched uneasiness. That which had dried her
up little by little. Had made her sour, then hateful, rebellious. Then had gone out, had left her
empty. Which had pushed her into marriage. The
last and most mediocre offer, from a suitor whom
she would earlier have haughtily refused.

"Twenty-eight and still unmarried!" She had
accepted. Knowing, even before the wedding,
that she would be repudiated. It was destined to
be. There was always one in every family. All the
more in the most venerable tribe of the maritime
city—pirates in days gone by, small craftsmen,
grocers, or the unemployed thereafter—

Wedding of bitterness. Her body already vanquished, she
who'd been the one in love when still a virgin—handsome as
a prince, the adolescent cousin when he'd taken refuge in their
home, with his narrow eyes, barely smiling, secretive, tender
perhaps. . . . The husband ran into the obstacle. Forcing the
surrendered body more and more ardently.

"Twenty-eight and still unmarried!" the merciless
husband exclaimed, his eyes full of hate, but in
reality filled with helplessness.

Barely the eighth day since their wedding. He
snickered, then spat on her.

Aïcha, lying down, gets up, wipes off her face.
Gets dressed again with precise movements. Imagines, as in an early morning dream, that she will
soon wake up. . . .

From that day on she refused to sleep with him. From then
on, he no longer held back; he had bottles of beer, with the sin-
ful smell, brought into his own house. The prohibition against
drunkenness, decreed by the partisans, subsequently made him,
the bully with the frizzy hair, as mad with helplessness as he
was before Aïcha's closed body.

The Dead Speak

Two months later, he repudiated her. She lived with her mother-in-law, a pathetic woman in her sixties who always complained about her misfortunes. Who helped her in child-birth.

At last Hadda's call; she had sent a messenger: "a broken home is no more serious than loneliness far away from one's own blood."

"What? . . . All that . . . ," Aïcha was remembering in front of Hassan who, in his slow voice and his new accent, was talking to her. And so this whole unfortunate history, through small decisions and imperceptible movements, through persistent re-fusal readjusting itself and flowing onward, a thin streamlet under laterite. This story had an origin,

"You!"
she thought the word was open, a veritable gift.
"You!" again the word like a cry of loneliness,
in a blank memory,
. . . "You!"

. . . the first time, Aïcha, barely twenty years old.
If not beautiful, at least serene and with a certain
gracefulness.
Aïcha, trembling and yet hardened, standing
before Hassan, only sixteen but a man. He'd been
wounded in the arm in a demonstration. He had
sought refuge in their house (Aïcha lived with a
humble mother, reduced by poverty. . . .) He was
hiding from the police. Lived with them for three
months.
Aïcha, troubled by his adolescent beauty, hope
whirling but immobilized—the young man
stretched out for hours on end in the peasant
room, his eyes open in the semidarkness. Aïcha,
wringing her hands, repeating:
—"You!"
Ten years later, the word comes back, hope
rekindled but . . .

That night, Aïcha at the feet of the dead woman, her eyes vacant, tears flowing. A woman immersed in yearning . . .

"As you wish, son of my maternal aunt!"

Her voice respectful (according to convention, and perhaps her unhappiness, too). She addresses him, now received in the city as the leader of the new heroes.

"Two sheep will be enough, I think. . . . The beggars no longer come to the door. The homes of the humble are known too well! In the evening, it will be better. . . ."

"Tomorrow evening, then. The lifting of the body at noon, before the Friday prayer."

"As you wish," she had repeated and she relived the impossible past. . . .

> That season then, the adolescent hiding in their
> home, the cherry trees had been abundant, the
> mint more velvety than ever, the evenings, ah! the
> evenings. . . .
>   Hassan would go out. A brown cape wrapped
> around him, disguising his outline and hiding his
> face; Aïcha would wait.
>   At midnight he would come in, conspiratorially.
> Behind the partition, Aïcha noticed the squeaking
> of the old box spring, the knocking of the pitcher
> he'd lift up to quench his nighttime thirst, that
> he'd put back down on the edge of the windowsill
> between the pots of basil and the square of scarlet
> geraniums. . . .
>   "You!"
>   The word swollen with the voice of youth.
> Sleep, within its boggy depths, held the stubborn
> call of the virgin. . . .

"You!" she repeats thereafter, two steps away from the dead grandmother. She, the outcast from now on, the dull and impoverished cousin . . . ah! there was enough to weep over for days and not only during a funeral.

"How sad his voice sounds," one of the young girls re-marked dreamily, listening behind the curtain, when Hassan left the room.

"You think so?" Aïcha responded, suddenly restive. She con-trolled her black sarcasm: "Here he is, the hero of the moun-tains and all the new girls lying in wait. . . ."

Then they prepared the cakes. The woman who would cleanse the body and her assistant arrived. The Koranic readers settled down in the courtyard one hour later for the wake. Aïcha didn't sleep. At dawn, she readied the rooms for the arrival of the visiting women, who came in growing waves.

*
* *

At the grandmother's funeral, conversations had been going on at a steady pace. One after the other, the ladies were leaving. Aïcha, assisted by the cook, a woman who specialized in funeral meals, now remained in the servants' quarters.

In a corner that served as pantry, two pinkish, scalped ewes were hanging suspended by their feet.

Her temples hurting, her mind empty, Aïcha rolled up her sleeves over her surprisingly strong arms. She helped the cook cut up the meat, a painstaking task. From the heavy pots and caldrons, the pungent odor began to rise little by little, the smell that itself sticks to the ribs, smell of spices roasting on the fire—paprika, which Hadda herself had left to dry the previous autumn, jumping around in the mutton fat.

"Mma!"

Coming out of a sleep heavy with clamminess and bad dreams, Amine appeared. His forehead moist, his arms reached for his mother, who, cleaver in hand, was methodically get-ting started on the second animal slaughtered. She raised her head, her face flushed with the effort and the heat. As a more and more redolent steam rose from the pots, Aïcha suddenly seemed young, an attentive nurturer. Which for a brief moment made her beautiful.

"Amine," she mumbled . . . "You!"

In the evening, platters of couscous and spicy meat came out of the house of old Hadda, now buried, carried in baskets by bunches of little boys and prepubescent girls, veiling their heads.

These groups dispersed toward the poorest of the neighboring houses, near the Roman amphitheater right before reaching the first hills.

II

Midday soon. July heat. In the avenue, that goes across the city right to the harbor area, the slow procession of men moves forward. The street still shakes from the preceding days of celebration. In a turn that comes out on an esplanade, the mosque waits, gleaming under an excess of flags.

Elderly men at the entrance. Faces impassive. With a keener look, the curiosity of other people more recognizable since this week of independence. These are the faithful who come to every Friday prayer, but this time, too, for Hadda.

"The old woman" they say. The most august of the devout women to have come to this religious service for so long. Everyone knows her virile authority, the priority her opinion held among the women, including her somber silence throughout the time of war.

With Hassan returned ("what *willaya* did he represent at this evening's political meeting? . . . Or was he trying to be nothing but a simple fighter from the mountains?" . . .), the old woman was leaving. And among the old people, she was the first one to do so, keeping herself outside the excitement that had inflated the city to the point of delirium.

A square of the faithful. Among them, the downtown grocer, the retired mailman, a few farmers who had retired to the city, employees of the court system and of the "indigenous" administration. About twenty men with graying mustaches, bald heads covered with a fez or a gray-blue skullcap. They gossip while they wait.

In the distance, a descending caterpillar, the procession appeared. The four pallbearers in front; the board carrying the dead woman seemed to be floating.

"How many times did she come down this street herself?" Saïd, the sharecropper, wonders.

He was supporting the funerary board, right behind the grandson. Among those accompanying the corpse, Saïd was obviously the only real mountain person. A bony face with a huge, drooping mustache, the same suit as the city people but a different head covering—a rounded dome wrapped in white muslin, ending in a slight tail just above the neck.

Saïd was being forgotten, neglected. The only man, however, to have spoken with Hadda throughout those arid years. . . .

Every Friday evening, he would come down from his hamlet. He'd leave his van there where in the past he used to unsaddle his horses and leave his cart. For twenty years, he'd go to sleep in his usual corner in the public Turkish baths. From five o'clock in the morning on, he'd be at the animal market as it opened. Once business was concluded, various merchandise wrapped up, he would go for the lunch that old Hadda had ordered and had served to him in a room off the vestibule.

She would make her appearance with the coffee. Would thank him for the sacks and the produce he had dropped off the night before. Then she'd listen to him talk about the harvest, the news from the mountain village—weddings, funerals, different disagreements—then . . . For the past few years, what was there to talk about but the fears insurmountable, the terror of massacres, sometimes the noises of nearby battles. . . . For months on end, the sharecropper hadn't been able to come, it wasn't until the spring of last year, when his entire herd (twenty-five sheep, two emaciated cows, and one little calf) had been burned in the main shed. The French army had occupied the town. When Saïd came back to the city, he scarcely had enough to buy some sugar, soap, and one or two rolls of cloth for the women. For the past year he couldn't have seen old Hadda more than four or five times.

Yet it was enough to foresee her approaching end. Besides, she herself: "You'll tell the little one . . ."

"If, God willing, the day ever comes, you won't forget to show the little one . . ."

"As for that branch of cousins who have the field next door, you'll remind the little one that the lawsuit is still in appeal! . . ."

She implied "after my death" with a stubbornness that Saïd's pious protestations could not shake ("Yemma Hadda, you'll be there yourself to . . ."). She'd continue her recommendations, including her many lawsuits, which she began in order to demarcate the boundaries of fields, property possessed jointly with the line of cousins and nephews that formed almost the entire population of the village where, in earlier days, Hadda used to be irrefutably enthroned.

Saïd had become the friend in whom she confided regarding her obsessive suits and her personal litigations. The last few years, he hadn't even dared to tell her that these lawsuits would cost her more than the value of the disputed pieces of land— a few dozen acres here, some olive groves there, some rocky hillsides . . . a cactus hedge . . . a more distant piece of land where the only things that grew were lentils and chick-peas.

With praiseworthy effort that she did not suspect, Saïd continued to give her supplies of oats and wheat for the winter's couscous, lambs to be slaughtered and offered to the poor at religious holidays, and finally in autumn, bushels of dried vegetables, sweet peppers already dried, wreaths of garlic and onions ready to be hung in the pantry. All this not only for the survival of the two women, but for feast days or funerals, occasions for gestures of charity and gifts of prestige.

"I'm going to get some things out to the neighbors," Hadda would declare.

"Look!" the young servant would say, "Yemma is sending you the first fruits of her harvest!"

From neighboring terraces, the women would thank her. The supposed wealth of Yemma Hadda remained a certainty.

Saïd thought of Yemma at one and the same time as a mother —to be venerated—as an employer—though sometimes a meddlesome one—and as . . . ? As "a symbol," he thought, "of the city's nobility," because of her knowledge of religious matters, her wisdom regarding ancestral mores, and her bitterness concerning temporal goods. He had a sense of how much the old woman cared about this appearance of wealth, despite misfortunes and public anxieties. As if this vanity would keep her going in the anticipation of her grandson's return.

"You'll tell the little one . . ."

"Yes, Yemma, I'm listening."

"Yes, Yemma, I promise!"

And he would promise. Under her veils, her prayer beads in

her hands, she was hardly shrinking—although her face was more shriveled and longer, making her nose seem more prominent. Her confidence in the grandson's return remained intact as if, in the mountains, everything would burn except the awaited heir. She only feared that her own death might occur before she'd be reunited with Hassan.

The mosque appeared. The cluster of the faithful parked on the esplanade went in; a few, in the courtyard, took off their shoes and began their ablutions.

In the prayer hall under the pillars, the feet of which were wrapped in a covering of light-colored reeds, the back of the room was already occupied by the pious in prayer. . . . Saïd, with the same movement of the shoulders and the torso as Hassan in front of him, slowly lowered himself in the columns' shadows to put the board on the ground. The murmurs of the congregation around him swayed with peculiar softness.

He took his place among the faithful crouched down in the first row. With a joy that surprised even him, he heard again the pure, almost wistful voice of the imam leading the prayer.

"It's been more than a year," Saïd thought as he stammered a Koranic verse, "ah yes, more than a year since I prayed here. . . . The previous time, too, it was for a funeral: a young boy, slaughtered through carelessness, a cousin of my second wife."

Saïd's ordinary piety needed no stimulation whatsoever, nor even daily observance. It would happen to him, sporadically, that he would pray every day with sudden fervor—generally during the month of fasting: then his activities would slow down, he would feel unburdened, and he would begin to frequent the village *cheikh,* a scholar from the East who had settled in the village to teach the boys the rudiments of Koranic knowledge. . . . In the evenings during the fast, the *taleb* would gather the mature villagers together, those of high moral standing, and would hazard an exegesis of the sacred texts.

Saïd had broken for good with the card and domino players. This wise change in his social life had undoubtedly gained him Yemma's respect. Certainly, before, he had opposed the administrator from France. (The latter had expected to brutally lay down the law, without even making use of the puppet administrators.)

Saïd had been forced to leave. In town, Yemma Hadda had protected him. The following year, when the administrator had been replaced, Saïd went back to his mountains with arrogant serenity.

> It is true, he brought back with him from this
> exile a second wife with whom the first wife, not
> displaying any of her bitterness, had to make
> her peace. . . .

Since then, Saïd had kept a close eye on the interests of old Hadda, already widowed at the time, and who, earlier during the events that had bloodied the country on 8 May 1945, had lost her only son, slaughtered with three of his comrades in the demonstration.

Under the columns, the collective prayer comes to an end. A movement disturbs the congregation. The *hazab* reads the Koran. Saïd, his eyes on the wooden board, recognizes fragments of the long recitative.

Once more pulled down into the past: "Who thinks of you now, Yemma Hadda?" he says to himself, seeing the lady again very clearly.

He thinks the word *lady*. In fact, it would happen to him at times on Saturdays, with the coffee, to call her "Lalla"—oh, my lady! As he was leaving her, he would just barely bow to her. Taking her aged hands in his, he would kiss them devoutly.

Hadda, sitting very straight, dressed in white, would bless him in the same words, her voice absent and calm. Saïd would get back behind the steering wheel of his loaded van. All the way along the new highway, built by the French army, he would feel protected by the grandmother's blessings, even when he'd have to stop at a military roadblock and some officer would have his stocks and jars checked.

Ah, yesterday's times! Times gone by . . .

Those trips home . . . In the village, his two wives would be waiting, each in a wing of the vast dwelling: the older one, his cousin whom he'd married when he was less than twenty, she barely fifteen, now a woman in her forties but still radiant. She was raising the five children she'd given him (unfortunately, only one boy, the last child).

The second wife, a mulatto whom he'd married in the city, lived in a room built for her on the other side of the orchard, with a terrace surrounded by vineyards and a thin jasmine tree. After seven years, he loved her as he had on the first day, though they'd tried to tarnish her reputation, a "dancer" they'd claimed. In fact, she was an orphan, employed until her adolescence as a servant in town in a café owned by Italians. Saïd had met her accidentally, was overwhelmed by her perfect body; she, such a young teenager, had calmly appreciated the honorable status that the sharecropper, even underneath his peasant manners, guaranteed her.

Saïd remembered the day he made his decision: his heart in turmoil, he'd come to consult Yemma. It was on her words that a second marriage would depend for him.

"An honest young girl and from a poor family," he'd specified in describing the mulatto girl.

Yemma Hadda, without his knowing how, seemed well informed. At first she said nothing. She let him drink his coffee. She finished her prayer beads as she pondered. She asked briefly what the first wife's reaction would be.

"I spoke to her," Saïd said after a moment's hesitation. Then in a softer voice: "All she answered was 'God has filled my home with five children to raise.'"

"May he protect you and have you return to her doorstep!" Hadda retorted, content to remind him of the Koranic rule of equity, in this case.

Saïd left, his peace of mind restored: true, the old woman had not said one word in favor of the young intruder, but then, she hadn't condemned her either.

The following Saturday, the sharecropper went back up to the village, the mulatto girl beside him, all wrapped up in a very stiff bridal veil. Since then, Saïd had had other children over and above the first five.

"Whatever happens within my home or doesn't, life goes

on!" Saïd sighed as he got up a few seconds later than his companions.

In that short space of time, an unknown man beside him had moved ahead of him and presented himself in his stead to lift the mortuary board with the other pallbearers.

At the exit, Saïd stepped into the front row of the procession that formed again on the esplanade.

Some of the members of the earlier procession dispersed at that moment—already it was one o'clock, the sun leaden, time to get home to the family table for the meal, then the mattress for a clammy afternoon rest.

Saïd found himself at the head of a smaller procession setting itself in motion to climb back up a more animated little street. At the end of it would be the cemetery.

Saïd took out a handkerchief of immense proportions. Wiped his forehead, then the edge of his heavy headdress. Passed his hand underneath the fabric that covered his neck. He started walking, as did the others; beside him, an old man was murmuring an incomprehensible soliloquy in a shaking voice.

Now that he was no longer helping to carry the funereal burden, he was watching the slow progress of the corpse, wrapped right to the level of his eyes, the board at a slight incline because the street ascended a few of the hill's buttresses. It was then that he felt the presence of the old woman even more.

She had always been an imposing presence to him. A somber kind of lady; an intimidating gaze: she never smiled. She scrutinized people all at once, a look that went right through, then lost interest.

Her voice, when she did converse, would address you, anonymous . . . Dressed in white most of the time . . .

> When still a child, Saïd would go to welcome her together with all the village children. . . . Yemma Hadda had arrived on horseback, forcing respect from these mountain people who knew her to be of their race.

The following days, she would receive every member of the family: cousins and other relatives, including the ones who were fighting her in court.

To him she seemed like a kind of mountain hawk because of her bony, prominent nose, her eyes set slightly apart, outlined in kohl, bird's eyes indeed.

When the august lady on horseback used to arrive from the city, once every spring and for important religious feast days, everyone would bow down and kiss her hand. After all, didn't she, through her two successive husbands, represent all the authority, destroyed—it was true—(confiscated, then divided many times over), of a once feudal family, still proud today, embracing within that pride the whole flock as it confronted the foreign administration.

"Two husbands," Saïd remembers. There he repeats what he has always known, having been too young himself to recall the husbands.

Two first cousins: she had been widowed very quickly from the first one because he'd been assassinated.

> . . . he had received an unknown man, passing through, as a guest in his house, had served him food himself, according to the village's traditions of hospitality, in the courtyard under the fig trees, far away from the women's quarters. . . .
> The other, restored, had put a bullet in his back, then had been able to flee across the orchards. A killer whose name had always remained unknown, though not his motive: to prevent his testimony, important to some legal case in town.

One year later, a cousin of the first husband had married the young widow, who already had a son. . . . Then, a few years after, Hadda suddenly surprised, even scandalized the village: the second husband, a handsome man it was true, was some-

The Dead Speak

what too fond of the dancers in the neighboring villages and, for the most part, spent his nights out. She, the abandoned wife, decided to leave and went off to the city. Yes indeed, a woman alone and not yet forty years old! . . . The division of property was advantageous to her, it was true. She even obtained separation from bed and board. The husband, after advances and entreaties that brought him discredit in the village, led a dissolute life, only to end up dying of juvenile tuberculosis, which his late nights of music and carousing had aggravated.

Saïd looks around. All of them: city people for the most part in their fifties; like himself, the generation of the humiliated. . . . "A herd to be exploited, sold, and shorn by France (he says "Francia," as if referring to a woman's first name). Today, the mountains throb, the wind swamps the streets and the walls with flags, a victorious vegetation, and all of us, they, I, we badly conceal our . . ."

He is looking for words, discovers his discomfort, comes back to the horizontal wooden board, which, at the level of his eyes, cuts off the horizon.

"We're not used to it," Saïd mumbles as he enters the cemetery that looks like a field in springtime, with the others. "Independence" . . . independence, a word, is it only the word that brings rapture?

Widowed a second time, Yemma came back to the village, took possession of her property again: a decayed house near the hills, with orchards all along the river. After a few months, she managed to avoid frittering away the inheritance.

Widow's veils, costume of immaculate silk, and always that hawk's face, that insistent dark gaze. From then on, Yemma Hadda focused the attention of the village on her severity, her sullen sadness.

Even faith itself, insofar as it was practiced, underwent Hadda's influence. She had suppressed the privileges and sales of various blessings from which, until then, her family had profited. By way of compensation, each year on the anniversary of Abraham's sacrifice, at her orders and in her presence, about twenty of the herd's fattest sheep had their throats slit. The gifts, in quarter pieces of meat, went to the poorest huts. . . . On the days that followed, all the sheepskins were washed at the spring, near the reeds. Then Saïd remembers the joy of his childhood—splashing naked to the waist in the rivers white with soapy foam. . . . Here too, as if the most ordinary tasks had become noble ones, Yemma Hadda would appear. Her scrutinizing look would wander across the peasant women who, their heads covered and their arms bare, were singing in the hills. . . . Times of unexpected happiness, of hesitant joy that Hadda, the somber lady, would observe.

Then she'd return to the city. Her village home would become silent, the door shut. Only the orchard, the sheds, and the animals remained under the supervision of a caretaker. . . . Saïd, a young man, would prowl around; on the other side of the slope, not far, the licentious nights could begin again. A few dancers from the South would reappear, the drum would once again be played after sundown, at the very place where the washerwomen had come at dawn. The moon smiled at the men of all ages, about thirty of them; once or twice, Saïd joined them.

A trance of dreams, music, and courtesans: for Saïd, the sharecropper, youthful madness could be summed up by these few evenings in which he, stealthily, associated with the dissolute group. Some of them, although their wives knew they attended these get-togethers, were numbered among the devout of the village. . . . Most often, five or six dancers, mostly young ones, sometimes faded but passionate, drove them mad. In order to deserve their favors, the males entered into a crazy competition. . . .

Saïd comes back to Yemma Hadda, rigid, closed to the cheerfulness of others. Didn't it used to be said that her second husband (she never referred to him) would roll bank notes into cigars and thus, like a king, smoke away his fortune in order to obtain the most beautiful of the courtesans traveling through, would end the night in some orchard, reappear the next morning and many nights thereafter in his abandoned home before going down to the city in order to entreat the lady, the only

and true mistress who refused him. He had died of his ex-
cesses as much as of tuberculosis. Since then, everyone called
the widow *Yemma*, this widowhood or loneliness having hardened her overnight. A little later, Saïd entered into her service.
He felt honored and wished to marry Yemma's daughter, the
supreme honor. Never dared to declare himself: she was given
in marriage to a man in the city, died in childbirth, and the boy,
Hassan, was raised by the grandmother. Even then, Saïd never
noticed a yielding in Hadda. Not even one due to the aging
process. An immovable statue, that is how he saw her.

"We are all humble, submissive, . . ."

He excluded Hadda. Today it was as if, on the wooden board,
the authentic past of the city was being transported through the
streets. . . . For the first time, as he spoke the word *city,* Saïd
didn't think of a foreign place.

> The evening before, he had expressed his desire to
> Hassan to carry the remains to the mountains. "To
> our village," he had mumbled. Hassan had scru-
> tinized the sharecropper's face, surprised at this
> request, at the loyalty it betrayed.
>
> "Burying her here or there . . ." he answered, "it
> is all our land, no matter where. . . ."
>
> What did the young man know? This bit of
> past, from now on scattered in the fog. Knowing
> that an old woman, dead at seventy, one week
> after independence, would inalienably remain part
> of that village, half destroyed besides. . . .
>
> "Did she wish it so? Were you told something?"
> Hassan questioned him.
>
> The grandmother's voice came between. The
> sharecropper heard it clearly: "You shall tell
> him . . . you will tell him. . . ."

"The dead speak, I tell you, . . ." Saïd thought, "but if she
doesn't say it to you. . . . Did you know her, do you know that
her untamed heart underneath that gnarled body lived there. . . .
O you, hero of the mountains!"

Saïd thought these last words with peculiar mockery. He immediately felt guilty about it afterward. Stuttering, he answered Hassan's questions. . . . The dialogue between the two men remained hanging in the air. "The dead speak," Saïd repeated accusingly; the years paraded past him, slid away behind his back as if for good—only the corpse, once again placed on the ground.

A man in the procession moved to the front to push open the cemetery door. The bearers raised their burden again, the followers spread out, not in any order, directly to the hole down there, a small hillock of fresh earth on either side.

Saïd stopped, leaned his back against the stunted fig tree. Then he knew that at last the past was over, not just yesterday's war and its repercussions, but an acrid taste of life, a way in which to bend beyond, to sit down in front of an intimidating lady, to breathe inside a hut. Everything was beginning; who was being buried, an old woman? They were burying sadness, nobility too, and its pitiless austerity.

The sharecropper was the first one to leave the cemetery, certain small-minded city people noticed. The following days they also noticed that Hassan, the heir, considered himself heir to nothing, not to any wealth, not to land, only to the word of those who had died, his companions whom he had been forced to bury in numbers too large to count in the course of his recent tumultuous past.

III

The cemetery was asleep. All those who'd come along in the procession were leaving, some by themselves, others in little groups. Hassan, standing, was waiting for the gravedigger to finish his work.

A noble work, he thought; he could have made the suggestion: "—brother, give me the shovel, I too know how to. . . . I know!"

The repeated gestures of tradition: for the one who slides the breads into the oven with a wide motion of the elbow, for the half-blind old woman who, arms raised, cuts the cord above the belly of the new mother, for the man who hunches his shoulders as he falls when hit by a murderous bullet, finally for the one who's going to drop bits of soil on a face that's ready to rot, on the vulnerable shape of the corpse. . . .

"At that moment, and only then, with the tomb still open, the rebellion suddenly broadens, grows deeper. . . . But the human being, whoever it may be that's lying there, is seized, worn-out or hardened—depending on the case—by a certain serenity when the living brother begins the cruel gesture—cruel but gentle (". . . earth, cover up this body; earth, make it dissolve; earth, push your worms of death up, earth . . . my mother!").

Hassan lets the gravedigger leave. Some money slipped into the laborer's hand. A few blessings to be received. Alone facing the grandmother. Alone after five years of silence.

"She is dead," Hassan repeats to himself with a touch of resentment. Should he feel sadness? It was lucky to have found her alive the night before, but he knew her will to wait would be the stronger one. . . . Still, five years!

Recently, Hassan has been measuring time. Others are already summing it up: "seven years," as they say in the classical and conformist histories: "the Seven Years' War," "the Hundred Years' War." Here the formula is set: "The War of Liberation." Liberation of the physical setting and of other people, but . . .

Finally alone, Hassan notices to what extent the ceremony has weighed heavily upon him since the morning; so many people, so much coming and going, so many words, so much strolling around. . . . Why? . . . Because the grandmother had gone to sleep?

"Before, it was before," he said to himself with a shrug of irritability, "it was before that death required so much display!"

Welcome it with infinite precautions, answer it when suddenly its blackish mug has darkened a home, has dug a hole into the family network, answer it with precise words, with collective prayers, with the sighing of women.

"Before! . . ." he said again with a shudder. He turned his back on the tomb, grey and humid.

The young man—thirty years old, somber bearing, ordinary face, slightly curly and already greying hair, his shape a bit stocky—took a few steps in this garden of the dead: rare flowers, the grass burned by the scorching heat, a few knotty olive trees still standing in a corner; especially from there, near an old weathered wall, there was an extraordinary panoramic view over the city and its harbor. In the distance, the Mediterranean.

Hassan recognizes the place, between the wall and a cupola that once had seemed an impressive monument to him, of which now only some remnants are left: the corner where he used to take refuge as a child when accompanying Yemma Hadda every Friday. She used to come and kneel on her daughter's tomb—the little boy would wander off, away from the tombs, didn't much like to hear the monotonous recital of prayers and conversations that every woman holds, kneeling down that way before death.

"Come and pray on your mother's tomb!" some neighbor, accompanying the grandmother, would reproach him.

The little boy would turn away, find the familiar spot near the wall, against the structure with the cupola—the mausoleum of a saint of the previous century, so they claimed.

As then, Hassan leans against this wall, observes the small city: a narrowed landscape, holding on to its former almost-rustic beauty, the Roman circus in the middle like an immense and punctured eye, of reddish stone, seeming like the ruins of recent despair. The white village hadn't changed, but it seemed as if a new atmosphere had enveloped it. The harbor now appeared reduced to such modest proportions with its ten or so boats and its motionless fishing piers, its aging lighthouse at one end; its torpor seemed definitive.

These past few years, all the inhabitants had turned in the other direction toward the arid mountains, from which in earlier days mountain people had come down barefoot, with baskets of Barbary figs or dried fava beans, from which something like a new scent comes forth that might chase away the rancid past of the city, huddled under its own decay for so long.

> —From the mountains a laughing death de-
> scended, light-footed as this spot, a death on the
> wings of victory! . . . —

Hassan left the cemetery, closing its gate as if it belonged to a house of which he'd been the host. Without looking behind him, he went down the rocky slope that led him back to the adjacent districts, the most underprivileged of the town. Only then did he begin to question himself about the grandmother: "That sharecropper, yesterday. . . . What did he want to tell me, that man; I couldn't make him talk? . . . He really was more upset than I! . . . He loved Yemma Hadda."

Hassan concluded this without any emotion. He felt his spirit had dried up. "A cash register," that's how he would gladly have defined himself. In the capital city during the preceding days, he had attended the unfolding of the convulsive celebration almost imperturbably.

He crossed the town. He nodded his head rapidly two or three times to answer the greetings of a few shopkeepers. "Go home. . . ." He had made this a strict rule, yet it was as if that law weighed him down. Anxiety grasped him as he thought about the decisions he would have to make: Aïcha and her son, what was to be done with them, surely she couldn't stay in the house by herself. . . . Did he really know where he himself would go? For some time now, he no longer felt at home anywhere, yet he was resigned to having to establish himself somewhere, no matter where, provided that he could continue to see the mountain when he looked up, its somber crests, its watershed. Like a convalescent's need.

He pushed the door open, coughed briefly and entered, went

straight up to the second floor without calling anyone at all. As he arrived, a rustling of dresses, whispering: the neighbors who were still there were hiding from him. His head lowered, he climbed up the stairs that led to the rooms that Old Hadda had kept for him.

The previous evening, in one of these rooms, he'd found the desk, crammed with old letters, from his high-school days. He hadn't looked for anything specifically; one or two lines in his old handwriting had barely moved him—notes taken from readings in a notebook of fifteen years ago. He was not in the mood to delve into his own past. Later, when the time came to make adjustments, to settle accounts . . .

He entered the same room, ran his hand over one or two of the books he'd taken off the shelf the night before, while the old woman was dying below. He stretched out on a sofa. The room seemed cool: curtains drawn since morning, in the back an enormous wardrobe that smelled of mothballs. On the wall facing him, a simple engraving such as one finds in all humble homes, with Abraham, his son, and the serene face of Gabriel, an engraving he himself had hung there in earlier days: undoubtedly during the period when he cultivated folklore in order to conceal his anguish. He contemplated the picture with a sober heart, even a hardened one.

Then he turned over on his side, his body tired, and tried with difficulty to fall asleep.

> *I, the anonymous voice who accompanies the dead, the invisible fog that belongs to all separations, the jumble of unreality that borrows the convulsion of a moment of death, the satisfaction of a last sigh, and thus of Hadda's last gaze— waxen mask, eyes wide open from the moment Hassan made his entrance—hope halted, I sometimes draw the conclusion that at a burial one often doesn't bury whom one thinks.*
>
> *Of course, the dead lies waiting with a sharp desire (sorely tested by some whose time is spent in formalities and ceremonies), desire for the*

The Dead Speak

earth, its sand that little by little will swallow up each pore, its subjacent waters that will wet the back and scalp of the human finally become plant again, as soon as the last shovelful of earth has been cast. The silence of the cemeteries barely closed off—blissful solitude—the dead one breathes one last time, a consolation even the worms of the woman-earth do not notice. Finally, the fall toward the abyss begins—a voluptuous drift, a gradual drowning . . .

Do I need to say that I speak only of the dead of this earth of sun, of those who by chance were not enclosed in coffins of lead. No need at all to wait for the wood to rot first, for the lead to liquify in order that the dead may finally receive their veritable deliverance, the one in which they will again assume their original form, featureless and without character, in which plant life and human memory are mysteriously interwoven. . . .

I, then, am the collective voice, who comes and goes from one to the other of these subterranean presences, of these inhabitants of the deep, in the hollow of the immense sound holes of the planet, lightly touching one here, encircling another one there. Who will say why the dead speak? I surge to the surface, I prowl, I pursue one who lives, I bewitch an innocent, I make an old man hum with childhood, I especially pierce a healthy adult, a forgetful one, a renegade, or one who wants to be. . . .

Old Hadda . . . Her burial: a minor fact, the undertow of a half-consumed world, after the war and even more with the swell of the beginnings of peace. Old Hadda: when she was born, in an earlier century, in that village where the share-cropper Saïd still lives, a generation of defeat had populated that corner of earth . . . Algeria. . . . One place on earth where at times (five years, or

*ten, or fifty . . .) the somber arrow of time digs
in, sharpening hearts and flesh. . . . Are the people
humble, is the wretchedness deep? . . .*

The young girl Hadda grew up with that yearning, her woman's share was commonplace, a bravado unexpected at that halfway point, but the
entire outline of her life was altered by it. . . . The
life of a peasant woman, then the sudden refusal—
oh, in all a minor refusal—but because of it a face
was drawn: a somber lady of true nobility recovered, the mask's pride that no longer reveals itself
as mask, but true awaiting, but harsh hope. . . .

*I, attendant of the dead, for old Hadda I do my
best to summarize a sketch of life.*

A burial of no importance, surely, but there is
the gloom of an impoverished cousin, there are
the daydreams of a sharecropper in a procession,
while the witnessing glances are focused on the
grandson alone. In his heart reigns an arid expanse. Worse than oblivion.

*Still the dead speak. The old woman's voice
murmurs to Aïcha, touches the sharecropper's
memory with loyalty. What does the man, toward
whom Hadda's last hopes were directed, notice of
all this? Nothing.*

Hassan, "the hero of the mountains" as a bitter
Saïd named him, Hassan has stretched out on a
sofa in the room. His body tired, he turns on his
side. He'd like to fall asleep.

*I, the voice that goes spinning, that flows from
one to the other, that suddenly brings the rustling of memories to a heart in turmoil, memories,
old whisperings, music, I who for hours, sometimes days, after a burial have trouble leaving and
stay to prowl around like a drunkard looking for
his way home, I across from the sleeping man
on the sofa, I am measuring the insuperable distance between him and Hadda, a lady lying down,*

The Dead Speak

straight, her head already that of a boneless monster. . . . The dead speak, certainly, who would measure their ambiguity?

*

* *

In the days that followed, in the city where Yemma Hadda had held court, various leaders were giving ringing speeches about the new order to be established, about the society bruised but free at last to begin its reconstruction. Hassan was one of those who spoke: two or three thousand people were listening in the square; among them were many women, placed in the back, a moving expanse of white veils.

For a long time he spoke about the dead, all those dead buried beneath the underbrush, dead in battle, massacred, "all the dead who would have lived," he said. His speech was received with such prolonged enthusiasm that the ululations of the women ascended in langorous spirals from the esplanade above the harbor where the meeting was being held to the cemetery, where Aïcha had come by herself to pay her respects. It was the seventh day after Yemma's death. By her side, her little boy—already five years old—was contemplating the panorama of the city over the wall, a view made iridescent by the shifting and colored dots of the meeting.

1970 and 1978

Day of Ramadan

The days of the fast, time grows longer, houses become deep, shadows translucent, and the body languid.

"They're flying, the seasons," Lla Fatouma would begin.

"Jack be nimble, Jack be quick," Nadjia intoned, "the fast is flying by."

"You'll see, when it comes in winter! Sweet and gentle like wool, winter Ramadan is," and Lla Fatouma, heavy and imposing, would go to her housework.

"I remember it," Houria, the oldest of the daughters, mumbled, "yes, it was wintertime when I started fasting . . . . I was ten!"

"No, it was fall," the second one corrected her. "The oranges were still green, I'm sure of it. I was eight and I was fasting one day on, one day off."

Nfissa was watching her sisters without saying a word. The father had gone out, Lla Fatouma was now saying her prayers in a corner of the large living room, while Nfissa piled up the sheepskins they had used during the afternoon siesta. The others were bustling about, but in anarchy due to the change in the household routines during these first days of Ramadan.

"Time grows longer, houses become deep, shadows translucent, and the body languid": again, Nfissa's mind is analyzing, then wanders haphazardly through memories—before, during the same season, she and Nadjia couldn't wait to start fasting (when would they finally get permission? The family refused to wake them up in the middle of the night for the meal that would help them through). Before, it was only yesterday . . .

Yesterday, Nfissa had been in prison . . . Ramadan among the truly sequestered, that prison in France where they had been grouped together, six "rebels"—they said—who would be judged.

They had begun the fast with the cheerfulness of the ascetic: exile and chains had become immaterial, a deliverance from the body that turns around in circles inside the cell but suddenly no longer runs up against the walls; two French women who'd been arrested in the same network had joined the Islamic observance and, despite the blandness of the evening soup, how peace of mind superseded the gray hours, how the evening song, despite the guards, seemed to clear the distance across the sea, to reunite them with their country's mountains!

"The first Ramadan away from suffering," Lla Fatouma murmured, going back to her kitchen.

"It's still all wrapped up in it, though," Houria groaned softly.

Only Nfissa, pretending to read, heard her. She raised her eyes to their elder sister: twenty-eight and already a widow.

"If only he'd left me a child, a son who'd bring his image back to me," she'd complained for months on end.

"Raising a child without a man, you've no idea what a bed of thorns that is!" the mother retorted. "You're young, God will bring you a new husband, God will fill your house with a whole crop of little angels yet!"

"May God will it so!" the others responded in chorus. From the kitchen the smell of grilled paprika was beginning to emerge.

"Four o'clock already! . . . Just two more hours of patience."

"I've felt neither hungry nor thirsty!" Nadjia exclaimed as she twirled around. Unexpectedly, she believed herself to be at some party, turned on the radio, did a quick dance step.

"Fasting with laughter and joy," she declared with false cheer, "My fast will count doubly!"

Houria had left the room, trailing longing in her wake. Nfissa stared at her younger sister for a long time: nineteen, her eyes lit with pride, thin to the point of being worrisome.

"You ought to be less noisy," she advised with an indulgent half-smile. "Houria remembers!"

"I remember too! You may have been imprisoned, but I too was in prison, right here, in this very house you think is so wonderful."

Nadjia's voice became harsh; she jumped up, gave a short, sharp laugh, and stood stock-still, confronting Nfissa, ready for a new quarrel.

"You're not going to start that again!" Nfissa grumbled, picking up her reading.

"If you're going to get angry, well then, your fast will count for nothing!" Lla Fatouma, in her bright voice, interjected from the kitchen door.

Her arms were bare, she had taken off her organza top without any further ado, was wearing nothing but an undershirt scalloped in the old-fashioned style. She'd just been kneading the dough for the small cakes and, rosy from the effort, was coming out to wash her hands in the basin in the courtyard. The household was becoming a women's kingdom, with the father not returning until sunset, a few minutes before the muezzin's chant would be heard through the vineyards and the languid jasmine vines. The village mosque was close by.

At her mother's words, Nadjia shrugged her shoulders in helpless sadness. Lla Fatouma, without having heard the conversation, had understood: during the last two years of the war, the father had made Nadjia stop her studies. Since the independence, she wanted to pick them up again, wanted to go to the city and work, be a teacher or a student, no matter, but be working: a family drama was brewing.

"Ramadan is the truce of all grudges. A black heart will never obtain remission . . ." Lla Fatouma murmured as she came back in.

She crossed the room, put her blouse back on with slow and regal motions, then went back to her pots. When the fast was broken, Nfissa and Nadjia, in front of the low table stacked high with dishes, were waiting for the others, the father included, to end the evening prayer. The meal would take place in almost total silence because of the father, who, as soon as he'd had his coffee, went out to participate in a religious watch.

Then the neighboring women would come to visit, chattering in the courtyard, folding their veils back themselves. With heavy sighs they would sit down on the sofas.

"For the seven years of the war, everyone has been staying at home," one of them began.

"With our daughter in the hands of the enemy, how could we possibly bring ourselves to drink coffee!" another exclaimed, referring to Nfissa and showering her with blessings.

Nadjia greeted the arrivals, exchanged the interminable formulas of politeness with them, then vanished. To Nfissa, who came in vain to bring her back: "No!" she snorted, "All that babbling, eating cakes, gorging oneself before morning, is that why we've suffered bloodshed and mourning? No, I won't have it . . . I . . . ," and her voice was filled with tears, "I thought, you see, that all this would change, that something else would happen, that . . ." Nadjia burst out crying, pushed her face into her pillow, on the same bed she'd slept in as a child.

Nfissa left the room without answering.

"If only you could smother the memory!" an old woman, who had lost her two sons in the war, was saying in the middle of the general conversation, "then you might be able to rediscover the Ramadans of before, the serenity of before."

A silence fell, uncertain, imbued with regret.

"Happy are the martyrs of the faith!" Lla Fatouma said gravely, coming back in, a teapot in her hand.

The smell of the mint spilled out into the night-enveloped courtyard, and Houria went out to wipe her tears.

1966

Nostalgia of the Horde

"Little mother," Nfissa begged, snuggled up against the great-grandmother in the bed, "tell us about your husband. . . . Nobody but you knew him . . . not even father!"

The great-grandmother remained lucid. It had been Ramadan then; in the next town, everyone was visiting the house of a friend during the indolent evening watches, and the children were trotting down the shadowy streets, their arms loaded with pastries to be taken to the oven.

At the house, the father had come home with nuts, almonds, dates, and raisins, he had scattered them in small piles in front of his four daughters, they had pulled the grandmother out of her religious meditation in order to pluck the petals off the hearts of palm in front of her.

"Tell us about your husband, little mother," Nadjia begged in turn.

"I was married at the age of twelve. . . . As only daughter, I'd been spoiled by my father. So there I was in my new home, not knowing how to do anything at all: I couldn't knead bread, I didn't know how to turn the sifter for the couscous . . . and I hadn't a clue on how to work the wool! And what good is a woman who doesn't know how to work wool? One day, my father-in-law brought his wife a ton of wool, which she divided among her four daughters-in-law, myself included. Each of us had to do everything alone: wash the wool, beat it, clean it, then card it and spin it, and finally weave either a robe for the husband or . . ."

"And you learned all that?" Houria exclaimed.

"At twelve?"

"What I found the hardest of all, you see, my little girls, was getting up early! . . . How I used to sleep when I was your age! . . . One day, I don't know why, I didn't wake up until eight o'clock. . . . Eight o'clock, you realize what that means?"

The old woman shook her head, smiled maliciously while feeling her dentures with her index finger.

"My mother-in-law, shocked by my laziness, had said to my husband: 'Go get her father! We didn't invite a princess into our house!' Of course, she was right. So I wake up, I yawn, I stretch, when all of a sudden I hear my father coughing behind the door to my room. I get up, really terrified. Shaking all over, I ask him to come in.

"Calmly, my father begins to question me: 'What's going on? Why did they call for me?'

" 'It's nothing, really,' I answered, in embarrassment. 'I didn't wake up this morning.'

"So then he looks at me, very severely, and threatens me: 'The next time if I come and find you in bed at such an hour, you'll be weeping tears of blood!' and then he went away."

By now all the girls were together in the big bed around the great-grandmother.

"And then . . . go on!"

"Years later, I heard the rest. . . . After having left my room, he had met up with my father-in-law, who was his best friend, in the street. He got very, very angry, and this time it was for real it seems: 'What is this, you make me come here just because she gets up at eight o'clock and that during Ramadan? Look here, you; she's still a child: you, I warned you!'

"It seems that the other one had to apologize to him. . . . I, of course, knew nothing about this, and from that day on I was so afraid that my father would have to come back like that, coughing behind my door as I woke up, that I was up at four in the morning every dawn, at the time my husband used to get up to leave for his father's fields. I would already have kneaded and baked the bread in the oven, sometimes put the meal on the *kanoun,* by the time my mother-in-law and my sisters-in-law would get up. . . . Then I'd have the whole morning indoors at my loom to work on my weaving and continue the blanket or the woolen veil I'd be making."

"Is it that loom standing over there?" one little girl asked.

"The very same one," the grandmother answered. "Not to brag, but after some years in my husband's house, there was nobody who could spin and weave better than I. . . . My mother-in-law used to say about me: 'Look at Fatima, she spins wool as fine as a serpent's tongue!' "

The little girls were completely settled in the enclosed bed, a lamp was lighted, Nfissa would ask again: "Your husband, little mother, you still haven't talked about him!"

"My husband, alas, may God forgive him and grant him salvation, after the death of the 'old one,' who was a righteous and good man, my husband became violent and brutal. . . . Sometimes he would beat me. . . . Once for almost nothing at all: I had forgotten to put away a plate of cakes after breakfast. He came in at the end of the morning, noticed my mistake, grabbed the *taimoum* stone that he used for his ablutions. Next thing I knew, he threw it at my face! . . . The stone cut open my forehead just above my eye (the Prophet, may he be praised, protected me!) and then my husband went back to praying imperturbably."

"And then?"

"Then . . . My sisters-in-law are going crazy because that very same day my father is coming to visit. What am I going to tell him? Knowing that my husband beat me, he would have made me leave on the spot. My sisters-in-law are begging me: 'Make up a lie! We don't want you to leave!' Even the old lady chimed in and advised me: 'Tell your father that it was the heifer'—'It was the heifer you gave me,' I told him when he started worrying about my wound. 'When I wanted to milk her, she kicked me!' 'Curses upon that heifer that almost blinded my daughter!' my father cried out, immediately swearing upon the Koran that he'd take back the heifer that very day, directly to the slaughterhouse. . . . And there I was, crying all night, for I loved that heifer so much . . . but I cried softly so that my husband could sleep!"

Is it because of all these memories that the grandmother started going back to the mosque in the village?

"You shouldn't!" her son said to her before getting into his carriage with Nfissa and Nadjia, whom he was taking to the city. "Very few women go there, now that this is France."

"France?" the grandmother grumbled, "So what?"

During that time, she once spent a whole day crying, a grief as profound no doubt as that for her heifer in earlier days: the imam of the village had died.

"For twenty years I'd prayed right behind him. He was so good at saying the *tarawih:* he recited the longest suras to start with, then the shortest verses, then twenty kneelings."

The seventh day after his death coincided precisely with the beginning of Ramadan, and although the cheikh was painfully missed, the blessed month was greeted with joy: the children were lighting candles and ran through the little streets singing hymns, the men were praying all night long . . .

The twenty-seventh day of fasting, Lla Toumia dared to evoke the dead, Omar and Rachid were playing in a corner, throwing apricot pits for marbles.

"In his youth, my father would spend this "night of Destiny" reciting as many suras as possible. One year, on the same occasion, he broke his fast with an apple and he ran to the mosque. He read sixty suras straight through, without stopping. . . . In the end, his master interrupted him: 'Kneel down, oh Mahmoud!' my father kneeled down and his master left."

"The night of the twenty-seventh day," the old aunt who was visiting remembered, "the *tolbas* take turns reciting the Koran and each one of them stands on one leg only. . . . Emulation takes hold of them: who will hold out the longest, who, in religious fervor, will not feel his body any more?"

"That was then! These days, new times, only the heathens reign supreme. . . . Our own sons (the woman who was speaking stood up and got ready to leave), yes, our own sons sometimes fall into faithlessness!" she moaned and wrapped herself in her veil of rigid silk.

"The best ones have disappeared!" the old woman sighed.

The children, girls and boys alike, would hold each other tight on these evenings when the nostalgia of the horde would inexplicably infiltrate the hearts (any pretext would do: a wedding, a death).

"Your great-great-grandfather," the great-grandmother began again, "may God have mercy upon him! had five sons, one of whom was your grandfather. . . . The first one, Baba Taieb, had a mania: at regular intervals he'd moan: "oh Allah!" Sometimes his brothers, embarrassed, would reprimand him: 'Say God's name to yourself, or under your breath, but why this cry?' 'It's not my fault! It happens without my being aware of it, it is soothing to me!' . . . One day I came back from the cemetery with a group of women; from afar we saw a man walking, wrapped in a huge green coat, a bright green perhaps, but the green of Islam nevertheless. Suddenly, a cry: 'Oh Allah!'—'Poor man,' said one woman, 'he must be a dervish.' I had to admit, with some bitterness that's for sure: 'He's no simpleton, he pretends to be a dervish. . . . That is my husband's brother!' . . . Even at funerals he'd place himself in the middle of the *tolbas* as they were reciting. As soon as they'd stop just to catch their breath, he'd bellow: "Oh Allah!" and we, his relations, his wife, his daughters, we'd be groaning in a corner: 'Baba Taieb doesn't know how to control himself!' "

The storyteller stopped, reeled off her prayers as she unwound her beads between her fingers, then began again: "The second son was nicknamed 'the pilgrim who left for Mecca and returned naked' "

"Naked?" they laughed uproariously.

"They'd robbed him over there, and all he was wearing was his gandoura. His brothers all had to pitch in to buy him some clothes. When he'd put together all his savings from his work as cobbler for his journey to Mecca, they had tried to hold him back: 'Keep your money for your old age, you don't even have any sons!' 'No!' he answered, 'This time, my heart is unmoored with the desire to see the House of God' and that is how he departed."

"And the third one?" a little voice asked.

The storyteller took her time: her moist eyes were shimmering with the light of the past.

"The third one, a coachman, was a man of means: Hadj Bachir, died at forty on the road that goes down to the plain. The coach was pitching dangerously, he took the lead, jumped off, and fell in the ditch, but the coach fell on top of him. The other travelers, who hadn't budged, were all fine. . . . They brought him to the next town, they helped him into the vestibule of the Turkish baths and left him there to die: death took half a day to fetch him, they said. Some of the merchants who came through and who knew him, gathered their thoughts before him, daydreaming, then left full of sorrow: 'What a man lies dying there!' they sighed. . . . They say that a sweltering heat came down over the city that same day."

"And nobody went to get a doctor for him?" one of the young listeners asked.

"In those days," the great-grandmother answered in an irritated voice, "if you said 'doctor and hospital,' it meant a doctor from France and a French hospital."

"The fourth one," she began again after a silence, "they called the Sudanese, because he went to live in the Sudan for seven years. When he came back, his nieces and nephews asked, 'What's it like there, uncle?'—He said: 'All day long they sleep on their belly. . . . As soon as the sun sets, they get up and then what nights! dancing, singing, poetry competitions, circles of storytellers. . . . In that country, they live by the moon!' Sometimes he'd also say: 'When I would tell them about the water at home that runs through drainpipes, they'd laugh, they wouldn't believe it or they'd say only: Paradise, is that where you live?' "

"And the fifth one, little mother?" one child said.

"The fifth one was your great-grandfather, may God protect him and keep him. . . . I married him at twelve, he was twenty-eight . . ." she stopped.

Later on, she began her story again, but not in the same tone: seeing those sweet little faces all around her probably reminded her of similar scenes, herself married at twelve or thirteen, and finding the one they then called the "old woman" in the new house, the woman who at eighty still couldn't make up her mind to die. . . .

"She was my father-in-law's mother, everyone's grandmother, yet unwanted by them all, to such a degree that in the end she stayed in my room. For eight years she didn't leave her corner. Her daughters-in-law (including my mother-in-law) didn't like her. Unfortunately, those things happened even in the old days. When she began to grow weaker, I warned them in the courtyard, and all they answered was: 'the old woman won't die; she's the one who'll bury us all!' One week later, I closed her eyes and went out again to tell them: 'Mma Rkia is dead!' and they started sobbing, wretches that they were, and pulling down at their hair!"

For a moment, the storyteller was silent, blinked her eyelids: "For those eight years, she had been talking to me from her corner, oh how she would talk! And I listened to her. . . . She was a young bride the year that the French came into our town. The entire family had gathered in the largest room, as big as a barn, and nobody would leave it, neither man nor woman. Only the *cheikh*, your ancestor, son of a Turkish janissary and a Berber woman, stood watch in the doorway, day and night. . . . During those days of constant fear, Mma Rkia gave birth to a daughter. Outside they could hear the noise of the carnage and the bullets, but by her side her sister-in-law had begun to curse the new mother's fate: 'A daughter! you've given us a daughter! . . . only good enough for a race of slaves!'—Feeling deeply ashamed, Rkia thought: 'Is that my fault?' Later on, she said to herself: 'Girl or boy, weren't we all there, crammed together as if in a chicken coop at the coming of the jackal?' 'Ah, my darling,' the old woman would say to me, 'I can still hear that woman cursing, cursing! . . . Suddenly, my newborn daughter uttered a first moan interrupting the silence, then a second one that was longer and more distinct, then she died. . . . I've always thought that God took her away from me because of my sister-in-law's curses; she belonged to the race of hired mourners, that evil one! Later, I had five boys, five boys but not a single daughter, alas. . . . That was the year the French occupied our town!' Mma Rkia sighed."

1965

Postface

Forbidden Gaze, Severed Sound

I

On 25 June 1832, Delacroix disembarks in Algiers for a short stopover. He has just spent a month in Morocco, immersed in a universe of extreme, visual richness (the splendor of the costumes, reckless frenzy of *fantasias,* the pomp of a royal court, the rapture of Jewish weddings or of street musicians, the nobility of royal felines: lions, tigers, and so forth).

This Orient, so near and of his own time, offers itself to him as a total and excessive novelty. An Orient as he had dreamed it for *The Death of Sardanapalus*—but here washed clean of any association with sin. An Orient that, in addition, and only in Morocco, escapes from the authority of the Turks, loathed ever since *The Massacre at Chios.*

Thus, Morocco is revealed as the place where dream and its incarnation of an aesthetic ideal meet, the place of a visual revolution. In fact, Delacroix can write a little later: "Ever since my journey, men and things appear to me in a new light."

Delacroix spends only three days in Algiers. This brief stay in an only recently conquered capital city directs him, thanks to a felicitous combination of circumstances, toward a world that had remained foreign to him during his Moroccan trip. For the first time, he penetrates into a world that is off-limits: that of the Algerian women.

The world he had discovered in Morocco and that he freezes in his sketches is essentially a masculine and warrior world, in a word, a virile one. What his eyes saw was the permanent spectacle of an exteriority made up entirely of pomp, noise, cavalcades, and rapid motion. But, as he passes from Morocco to Algeria, Delacroix crosses, at the same time, a subtle frontier that is going to invert every sign and will be at the root of what posterity shall retain as this singular "journey to the Orient."

*

*   *

The adventure is well-known: the chief engineer of the harbor of Algiers, Monsieur Poirel, a lover of painting, has in his employ a *chaouch,* the former owner of a privateer—the sort who used to be called a rais before the 1830 conquest—who, after long discussions, agrees to allow Delacroix entry into his own home.

A friend of the friend, Cournault, reports the details of this intrusion to us. The house was situated in what used to be the rue Duquesne. Delacroix, in the company of the husband and undoubtedly of Poirel as well, crosses "a dark hallway" at the end of which, unexpectedly and bathed in an almost unreal light, the actual harem opens up. There, women and children are waiting for him "surrounded by mounds of silk and gold." The wife of the former rais, young and pretty, is sitting in front of a hookah. Delacroix, Poirel reports to Cournault, who writes it down for us, "was as if intoxicated by the spectacle he had before his eyes."

With the husband as intermediary and impromptu translator, he begins a conversation and wants to know everything about "this new and to him mysterious life." On the many sketches that he draws—women seated in various positions—he writes what seems to him to be the most important and not to be forgotten: specification of colors ("black with lines of gold, lacquered violet, dark India red," etc.) with details of costumes, multiple and strange references that baffle his eyes.

In these brief and graphic or written annotations, there is an almost feverish hand at work, an intoxicated gaze: a fugitive moment of evanescent revelation standing on that borderline in motion where dream and reality converge. Cournault notes: "that fever that the sherbets and fruits could barely appease."

The completely new vision was perceived as pure image. And as if this all-too-new splendor might blur the image's reality,

Forbidden Gaze, Severed Sound

Delacroix forces himself to note down, on his sketches, the name of every woman. Like a coat of arms, watercolors bear names like Bayah, Mouni and Zora ben Soltane, Zora and Kadoudja Tarboridji. Penciled bodies coming out of the anonymity of exoticism.

This abundance of rare colors, these new-sounding names, is that what arouses and thrills the painter? Is that what causes him to write: "It is beautiful! It is straight out of Homer!"

There, during that visit of a few hours with women in seclusion, by what shock, or at least by what vague stirrings was the painter seized? This heart of the half-open harem, is it really the way he sees it?

From this place through which he had passed, Delacroix brings back some objects: some slippers, a shawl, a shirt, a pair of trousers. Not just trivial tourist trophies but tangible proof of a unique, ephemeral experience. Traces of a dream.

He feels the need to touch his dream, to prolong its life beyond the memory, to complete what is enclosed as sketches and drawings in his notebooks. It's the equivalent of a fetishist compulsion augmented by the certainty that this moment lived is irrevocable in its uniqueness and will never be repeated.

Upon his return to Paris, the painter will work for two years on the image of a memory that teeters with a muted and unformulated uncertainty, although well-documented and supported by authentic objects. What he comes out with is a masterpiece that still stirs questions deep within us.

Women of Algiers in Their Apartment: three women, two of whom are seated in front of a hookah. The third one, in the foreground, leans her elbow on some cushions. A female servant, seen three quarters from the back, raises her arm as if to move the heavy tapestry aside that masks this closed universe; she is an almost minor character, all she does is move along the edge of the iridescence of colors that bathes the other three women. The whole meaning of the painting is played out in the relationship these three have with their bodies, as well as with the place of their enclosure. Resigned prisoners in a closed place that is lit by a kind of dreamlike light coming from no-where—a hothouse light or that of an aquarium—Delacroix's genius makes them both near and distant to us at the same time, enigmatic to the highest degree.

Fifteen years after these few days in Algiers, Delacroix remembers again, reworks it, and gives the 1849 Salon a second version of *Women of Algiers*.

The composition is almost identical, but the recurrence of several changes has rendered more obvious the latent meaning of the painting.

In this second canvas—in which the features of the characters are less precise, the elements of the setting less elaborate—the vision's angle has been widened. This centering effect has a triple result: to make the three women, who now penetrate more deeply into their retreat, more distant from us; to uncover and entirely bare one of the room's walls, having it weigh down more heavily on the solitude of these women; and finally to accentuate the unreal quality of the light. The latter brings out more clearly what the shadow conceals as an invisible, omni-present threat, through the intermediary of the woman servant whom we hardly see any longer, but who is there, and attentive.

Women always waiting. Suddenly less sultanas than prisoners. They have no relationship with us, the spectators. They neither abandon nor refuse themselves to our gaze. Foreign but terribly present in this rarified atmosphere of confinement.

Elie Faure tells us that the aging Renoir, when he used to refer to this light in *Women of Algiers,* could not prevent large tears from streaming down his cheeks.

Should we be weeping like the aged Renoir, but then for reasons other than artistic ones? Evoke, one and a half centuries later, these Bayas, Zoras, Mounis, and Khadoudjas. Since then, these women, whom Delacroix—perhaps in spite of himself[1]—knew how to observe as no one had done before him, have not stopped telling us something that is unbearably painful and still very much with us today.

Delacroix's painting has been perceived as one approach to a feminine version of the Orient—undoubtedly the first one in European painting, which usually treated the theme of the odalisk as literature or evoked only the cruelty and the nudity of the seraglio.

The distant and familiar dream in the faraway eyes of the three Algerian women, if we make an attempt to grasp its nature, makes us in turn dream of sensuality: a nostalgia or vague softness, triggered by their so obvious absence. As if behind those bodies, and before the servant lets the curtain fall once more, a universe is displayed in which they might still live continuously, before they take their pose in front of us, who look on.

For that is exactly it, we look on. In reality, that look is forbidden to us. If Delacroix's painting unconsciously fascinates us, it is not actually because it suggests that superficial Orient within a luxurious and silent semidarkness, but because, by placing us in the position of onlookers in front of these women, it reminds us that ordinarily we have no right to be there. This painting is itself a stolen glance.

And I tell myself that, more than fifteen years later, Delacroix remembered especially that "dark hallway" at the end of which, in a space without exit, the hieratic prisoners of the secret keep to themselves. Those women whose distant drama cannot be guessed at except for this unexpected backstage scene that the painting becomes.

Is it because these women are dreaming that they do not look at us, or is it that they can no longer even glimpse us because they are enclosed without recourse? Nothing can be guessed about the soul of these doleful figures, seated as if drowning in all that surrounds them. They remain absent to themselves, to their body, to their sensuality, to their happiness.

Between them and us, the spectators, there has been the instant of unveiling, the step that crossed the vestibule of intimacy, the unexpected slight touch of the thief, the spy, the voyeur. Only two years earlier, the French painter would have been there at the risk of his life. . . .

What floats between these Algerian women and ourselves, then, is the forbidden. Neutral, anonymous, omnipresent.

*

*   *

That particular gaze had long been believed to be a stolen one because it was the stranger's, the one from outside the harem and outside the city.

For a few decades—as each nationalism triumphs here and there—we have been able to realize that within this Orient that has been delivered unto itself, the image of woman is still perceived no differently, be it by the father, by the husband, and, more troublesome still, by the brother and the son.

In principle, they alone may look at the woman. To the other male members of the tribe (and any cousin who may have shared her childhood play becomes potentially a voyeur-thief) the woman shows—in the early days of an easing of the customary rigors—if not her entire body, at least her face and hands.

The second period of this easing turns out, paradoxically, to be dependent upon the veil.[2] Since the veil completely covers the body and its extremities, it allows the one who wears it and who circulates outside underneath its cover, to be in turn a potential thief within the masculine space. She appears there above all as a fugitive outline, half blinded when she can only look with one eye. The generosity of "liberalism" has restored to her, in some cases and certain places, her other eye and at the same time the integrity of her gaze: thanks to the veil, both her eyes are now wide open to the exterior.

Thus, there is another eye there, the female gaze. But that liberated eye, which could become the sign of a conquest toward the light shared by other people, outside of the enclosure, is now in turn perceived as a threat; and the vicious circle closes itself back up again.

Yesterday, the master made his authority felt in the closed, feminine spaces through the single presence of his gaze alone, annihilating those of other people. In turn, the feminine eye when it moves around is now, it seems, feared by the men immobilized in the Moorish cafés of today's medinas, while the white phantom, unreal but enigmatic, passes through.

Forbidden Gaze, Severed Sound

In these lawful glances (that is to say, those of the father, the brother, the son, or the husband) that are raised to the female eye and body—for the eye of the dominator first seeks out the other's eye, the eye of the dominated, before it takes possession of the body—one runs a risk that is all the more unforeseeable since its causes may be accidental.

It takes very little—a sudden effusiveness, an unexpected, unusual motion, a space torn open by a curtain raised over a secret corner[3]—for the other eyes of the body (breasts, sex, navel) to run the risk in turn of being fully exposed and stared at. It is all over for the men, vulnerable guardians: it is their night, their misfortune, their dishonor.

Forbidden gaze: for it is surely forbidden to look at the female body one keeps incarcerated, from the age of ten until forty or forty-five, within walls, or better within veils. But there's also the danger that the feminine glance, liberated to circulation outside, runs the risk at any moment of exposing the other glances of the moving body. As if all of a sudden the whole body were to begin to look around, to "defy," or so men translate it. . . . Is a woman—who moves around and therefore is "naked"—who looks, not also a new threat to their exclusive right to stare, to that male prerogative?

The most visible evolution of Arabic women, at least in the cities, has therefore been the casting off of the veil. Many a woman, often after an adolescence or her entire youth spent cloistered, has concretely lived the experience of the unveiling.

The body moves forward out of the house and is, for the first time, felt as being "exposed" to every look: the gait becomes stiff, the step hasty, the facial expression tightens.

Colloquial Arabic describes the experience in a significant way: "I no longer go out *protected* (that is to say, veiled, covered up)" the woman who casts off her sheet will say, "I go out *undressed,* or even *denuded.*" The veil that shielded her from the looks of strangers is in fact experienced as a "piece of clothing in itself," and to no longer have it means to be totally exposed.

As for the man who agrees to share in this, his sisters' or his wife's most timid of evolutions, the slowest possible one, he is thereby condemned to live ill at ease and sick with worry. He imagines that no sooner will the lacy face veil, then the long body veil, be lifted, than the woman will (she can't help it) move on to the stage of fatal risk, that of uncovering the other eye, the eye-that-is-sex. Halfway down this slippery path, he glimpses the only stopping point of the "belly dance," the one that makes the other eye, the navel-eye, grimace in the cabarets.

Thus the woman's body, as soon as she leaves her seated waiting in the cloistered interior, conceals dangers because of its very nature. Does it move around in an open space? All that is suddenly perceived is that straying multiplicity of eyes in and on that body.

Around this feminine drifting away, the dispossessed man's haunting feeling of paranoia crystallizes. (After all, the only man in Algiers who, in 1832, permits a foreign painter to penetrate into the harem, is precisely a former little pirate, now a conquered *chaouch* who is henceforth accountable to a French civil servant.)

In Algeria, it was precisely when the foreign intrusion began in 1830—an intrusion contained at all costs at the doorways of impoverished seraglios—that a gradual freezing up of indoor communication accompanied the parallel progressive French conquest of exterior space, an indoor communication becoming more and more deeply submerged: between the generations, and even more, between the sexes.

These women of Algiers—those who have remained motion-less in Delacroix's painting since 1832—if it was possible yesterday to see in their frozen stare the nostalgic expression of happiness or of the softness of submission, today their desperate bitterness is what must strike our most sensitive nerve.

At the time of the heroic battles, woman was watching, woman was crying out: the gaze-that-was-witness throughout the battle, which ululations would prolong in order to encour-age the warrior (a cry, extended, piercing the horizon like an infinite abdominal gurgling, a sexual call in full flight).

But, throughout the nineteenth century, the battles were lost one after the other, further and further to the south of the Algerian territories. The heroes have not yet stopped biting the dust. In that epic, women's looks and voices continue to be perceived from a distance, from the other side of the frontier that should separate us from death, if not from victory.

But for those born in the age of submission, feudals or proletarians, sons or lovers, the scene remains, the watching women haven't moved, and it is with a retrospective fear that the men began to dream of that look.

Thus, while outside an entire society partitions itself into the duality of the vanquished and the victorious, the autochthons and the invaders, in the harem, reduced to a shack or a cave, the dialogue has become almost definitively blocked. If only one could force that single spectator body that remains, encircle it more and more tightly in order to forget the defeat! . . . But every movement that might recall the fury of the ancestors is irremediably solidified, redoubling the immobility that makes of woman a prisoner.

*

* *

In the oral culture of Algeria, primarily in the thoroughly occupied small towns, there develops the almost unique theme of the wound, which comes to replace the lively unpredictability of the expression of ironic desire, in poetry, in song, and even in the patterns of the slow or frenzied dances.

The fact that the first encounter of the sexes is not possible except through the marriage ritual and its ceremonies sheds light on the nature of an obsession that profoundly puts its mark on our social and cultural being. An open wound is etched into the woman's body through the assumption of a virginity that is furiously deflowered and the martyrdom of which is consecrated by the marriage in a most trivial manner. The wedding night essentially becomes a night of blood. Not because the partners become better acquainted or, even less, because of pleasure, but a night of blood that is also a night of the gaze and of silence. Hence the razor-sharp chorus of long cries uttered by the other women (a sisterhood of spasms that tries to take flight in the blind night), hence also the din of the gunpowder in order to better envelop that same silence.[4]

Now, this look of the sex steeped in blood sends us back to the first look, that of the mother at term, ready to give birth. The image of her rises up, ambivalent and flooded with tears, completely veiled and at the same time delivered naked, her legs streaked with blood in spasms of pain.

The Koran says, and this has been often repeated: "Paradise is found at the feet of mothers." If Christianity is the adoration of the Virgin Mother, Islam, more harshly, understands the term *mother* to mean woman without pleasure, even before seeing her as the source of all tenderness. Thereby obscurely hoping that the eye-that-is-sex, the one who has given birth, is no longer a threat. Only the birthing mother has the right to look.

II

During the time of the Emir Abdelkader, nomadic tribes loyal to him, the Arbaa and the Harazeli, found themselves besieged in 1839 in Fort Ksar el Hayran by their traditional enemy, the Tedjini. On the fourth day of the siege, the assailants are already scaling the walls, when a young Harazeli girl, named Messaouda ("the happy one"), seeing that her men are ready to turn their backs, calls out:

> "Where are you running like that? The enemies
> are on this side! Must a young girl show you how
> men are supposed to behave? Well then, take
> a look!"

She climbs onto the ramparts, lets herself slide down the other side, facing the enemy. Thus exposing herself willingly, she speaks these words at the same time:

> "Where are the men of my tribe?
> Where are my brothers?
> Where are those who used to sing songs of love
> to me?"

Thereupon the Harazeli came running to her aid and tradition reports they did so while clamoring this war cry that was also a cry of love:

> "Be happy, here are your brothers, here are your
> lovers!"

Electrified by the young girl's call, they pushed back the enemy.

Messaouda was brought back in triumph, and ever since, the "Song of Messaouda" has been sung by the tribes in the Algerian south, recalling these facts and ending with this exact exaltation of the heroic wound:

> "Messaouda, you shall always be a wrench for
> pulling teeth!"

In the history of Algerian resistance struggles during the last century, numerous episodes, indeed, show women warriors who left the traditional role of spectator. Their formidable look would prod the men's courage, but suddenly also, right where the ultimate despair dawns, their very presence in the boiling movement of battle decides the outcome.

Other accounts of feminine heroism illustrate the tradition of the feudal queen-mother (intelligent, a tactician of "virile" courage), for example, the distant Berber woman Kahina.

The story of Messaouda, more modest, seems to me to present a newer aspect: surely a variant on heroism and tribal solidarity, but above all it is here connected with a body in danger (in completely spontaneous motion), with a voice that calls, challenges, and abrades. In short, it heals the temptation of cowardice and allows a victorious outcome.

"Be happy, here are your brothers, here are your lovers!" Are these brothers-lovers more upset to see the completely exposed body, or are they more "electrified" by the feminine voice that runs off? This sound at last comes forth from the entrails, brushing past the blood of death and of love. And this is the revelation: "Be happy!" The song of Messaouda is the only one that consecrates this happiness of women, completely inside a mobility that is improvised and dangerous at the same time: in short, that is creative.

Very few Messaoudas, alas, in our recent past of anti-colonial resistance. Before the war of liberation, the search for a national identity, if it did include a feminine participation, delighted in erasing the body and illuminating these women as "mothers," even for those exceptional figures who were recognized as women warriors. But when, in the course of the seven years of the national war, the theme of the heroine becomes exalted, it is exactly around the bodies of young girls, whom I call the "fire carriers" and whom the enemy incarcerates. Harems melted for a while into so many Barberousse prisons, the Messaoudas of the Battle of Algiers were called Djamila.

Since that call by Messaouda and the antiphonal response of the "brothers-lovers," since that race forward of woman's pride set free, what do we have as a "story" of our women, as feminine speech?

Delacroix's painting shows us two of the women as if surprised in their conversation, but their silence has not stopped reaching us. The halting words of those who have half-lowered their eyelids or who look away in the distance in order to communicate. As if it concerned some secret, the enlightenment of which the servant is watching for, and we cannot quite tell whether she is spying on them or is an accomplice to them.

From childhood on, the little girl is taught "the cult of silence, which is one of the greatest powers of Arabic society."[5] What a French general, "friend to the Arabs," calls "power," is something we feel as a second mutilation.

Even the yes that is supposed to follow the fatiha of the marriage ceremony and that the father must ask of his daughter—the Koran requires this of him—is ingeniously squelched almost everywhere (in Moslem regions). The fact that the young girl may not be seen uncovered in order to utter her acquiescence (or her nonacquiescence), obliges her to go through the intermediary of a male representative who speaks in "her place." A terrible substitution for the word of one by another, which, moreover, opens the way to the illegal practice of the forced marriage. Her word deflowered, violated, before the other deflowering, the other violation intervenes.

Besides, even without the *ouali,* it has been agreed that this yes, which they are waiting for directly from her, may be expressed, because of her "modesty" in front of her father and the man of the law, through her silence or through her tears. It is true that in ancient Persia, an even more characteristic practice has been noted[6]: to consecrate the marriage, the boy makes his agreement heard loudly and clearly; the fiancée, the girl, is put in the next room amid other women, near the door over which a curtain falls. In order to make the necessary yes audible, the women hit the young girl's head against the door, causing her to moan.

Thus, the only word the woman must pronounce, this yes to submission under the pretense of propriety, she breathes out with discomfort, either under the duress of physical pain or through the ambiguity of silent tears.

It is told that in 1911, during various Algerian campaigns, the women (mothers and sisters) would come and roam around the camps where the so-called indigenous conscripts were penned in, would come to weep and tear at their faces. The image of the tearful woman, lacerating her cheeks to the point of hysteria, becomes for the ethnologists of the time the only image "in motion": no more women warriors, no more women poets. If it doesn't concern invisible and mute women, if they're still an integral part of their tribe, they can only appear as powerless furies. Silence even of the dancer-prostitutes of the Ouled Naïls, their bodies covered down to their feet, their idol-like faces weighed down by jewels, their only sound the rhythmic one of their ankle bands.

Thus, from 1900 to 1954 in Algeria, there is a closing down of an indigenous society, more and more dispossessed of its vital space and its tribal structures. The orientalizing look— first with its military interpreters and then with its photographers and filmmakers—turns in circles around this closed society, stressing its "feminine mystery" even more in order thus to hide the hostility of an entire Algerian community in danger.

However, this has not prevented the spatial tightening from leading to a tightening of family relationships during the first half of the twentieth century: between cousins, brothers, etc. And in the relationships between brothers and sisters, the latter have been most often—always thanks to the "yes-silence of the tears"—disinherited to the advantage of the males in the family: here is another face of that immemorial abuse of trust, of that alienation of material goods and bed and board.

Thus, doubly imprisoned in that immense jail, the woman has the right to no more than a space that is doomed to become ever smaller. Only the mother-son relationship has grown stronger to the point of obstructing all other exchanges. As if the attachment to the roots, which grows more and more difficult for these new proletarians without any land and soon without a culture, should again pass through the umbilical cord.

But beyond this tightening within the families, by which only the males benefit, there is the attachment to the oral roots of history.

The sound of the mother who, woman without a body and

without an individual voice, finds once again the sound of the collective and obscure voice, which is necessarily asexual. For in the spinning around of the defeat that ended in tragic immobility, the models for finding a second wind and oxygen have been sought elsewhere,[7] in places other than this kind of immense nourishing womb in which the long chain of mothers and grandmothers, shaded by patios and shacks, nurtured the emotional memory. . . .

The echoes of the battles lost in the last century, details of color very much worthy of a Delacroix, reside among the illiterate storytellers: the whispered voices of those forgotten women have developed irreplaceable frescoes from these, and have thus woven our sense of history.

In this way, the enlarged presence of the mother (woman without body or, conversely, of multiple bodies) finds itself to be the most solid knot in the almost complete incommunicability between the sexes. But at the same time, in the realm of the word, the mother seems, in fact, to have monopolized the only authentic expression of a cultural identity—admittedly limited to the land, to the village, to the popular local saint, sometimes to the "clan," but in any case, concrete and passionate with affectivity.

As if the mother, recoiling on this side of procreation, were masking her body from us, in order to return as the voice of the unknown ancestress, timeless chorus in which history is retold. But a history from which the archetypal image of the feminine body has been expelled.

A hesitant sketch in stipples floats on the surface, all that's left of a culture of women, now slowly suffocating: songs once sung by young girls on their verandas,[8] quatrains of love from the women of Tlemcen,[9] magnificent funereal threnodies from the women of Laghouat, an entire literature that, unfortunately, is becoming further and further removed, only to end up by resembling those mouthless wadis that get lost in the sands. . . .

Ritual lament of the Jewish and Arabic women folksingers who sing at Algerian weddings, this outdated tenderness, this delicately loving nostalgia, barely allusive, is transmitted little by little from the women to the adolescent girls, future sacrificial victims, as if the song were closing in upon itself.

We, children in the patios where our mothers still seem young, serene, wearing jewelry that doesn't crush them—not yet—that often adorns them in inoffensive vanity, we, in the faint murmuring of those lost feminine voices, we still feel its old warmth . . . but rarely its withering. These islets of peace, this intermission to which our memory clings, are these not a small part of that plant life autonomy of the Algerian women in the painting, the totally separate world of women?

A world from which the growing boy removes himself, but from which today's young, self-emancipating girl distances herself as well. For her in particular, the distancing amounts to shifting the location of her muteness: she exchanges the women's quarters and the old community for an often deceptive one-on-one with the man.

Thus, this world of women, when it no longer hums with the whisperings of an ancillary tenderness, of lost ballads—in short, with a romanticism of vanished enchantments—that world suddenly, barrenly, becomes the world of autism.

And just as suddenly, the reality of the present shows itself without camouflage, without any addiction to the past: sound has truly been severed.

III

As the war of liberation in Algeria was just barely getting started, Picasso, from December 1954 to February 1955, goes to live every day in the world of Delacroix's "Women of Algiers." There he comes face-to-face with himself and erects around the three women, and with them, a completely transformed universe: fifteen canvases and two lithographs carrying the same title.

It moves me to think that the Spanish genius presides in this manner over a changing in the times.

As we entered our "colonial night," the French painter offered us his vision that, the admiring Baudelaire notes, "breathes I don't know what heady perfume of evil haunts that leads us rather quickly toward the unplumbed limbo of sadness." That perfume of evil haunts came from quite far off and will have become even more concentrated.

Picasso reverses the malediction, causes misfortune to burst loose, inscribes in audacious lines a totally new happiness. A foreknowledge that should guide us in our everyday life.

Pierre Daix remarks: "Picasso has always liked to set the beauties of the harem free." Glorious liberation of space, the bodies awakening in dance, in a flowing outward, the movement freely offered. But also the preservation of one of the women, who remains hermetic, Olympian, suddenly immense. Like a suggested moral, here, of a relationship to be found again between the old, adorned serenity (the lady, formerly fixed in her sullen sadness, is motionless from now on, but like a rock of inner power) and the improvised bursting out into an open space.

For there is no harem any more, its door is wide open and the light is streaming in; there isn't even a spying servant any longer, simply another woman, mischievous and dancing. Finally, the heroines—with the exception of the queen, whose breasts, however, are bursting out—are totally nude, as if Picasso was recovering the truth of the vernacular language that, in Arabic, designates the "unveiled" as "denuded" women. Also, as if he were making that denuding not only into a sign of an "emancipation," but rather of these women's rebirth to their own bodies.

Two years after this intuition of the artist, there appeared the descendants, the carriers of the bombs, in the Battle of Algiers. Are these women merely the sisters-companions of the nationalist heroes? Certainly not, for everything takes place as if the latter, in isolation, outside of the clan, had made a long trek back, from the 1920s to almost 1960, in order to find their "sisters-lovers" again, and that in the shadow of the prisons and the brutal treatment by the legionnaires.

As if the guillotine and those first sacrificed in the coldness of the dawn were needed for young girls to tremble for their blood brothers and to say so.[10] The ancestral accompaniment had, until then, been the ululation of triumph and of death.

It is a question of wondering whether the carriers of the bombs, as they left the harem, chose their most direct manner of expression purely by accident: their bodies exposed outside and they themselves attacking other bodies? In fact, they took those bombs out as if they were taking out their own breasts, and those grenades exploded against them, right against them.

Some of them came back later with their sex electrocuted, flayed through torture.

If rape, as a fact and a "tradition" of war, is in itself horribly banal ever since wars have existed, it became—when our heroines were its victims of expiation—the cause of painful upheaval, experienced as trauma by the whole of the Algerian collective. The public condemnation of it through newspapers and legal intervention certainly contributed to the spread of scandalous repercussions: the words that named it became, where rape was concerned, an explicit and unanimous condemnation. A barrier of words came down in transgression, a veil was shredded in front of a threatened reality, but one whose repression was too strong not to return. Such repression submerged a solidarity in misery that for a moment had been effective. What words had uncovered in time of war is now being concealed again underneath a thick covering of taboo subjects, and in that way, the meaning of a revelation is reversed. Then the heavy silence returns that puts an end to the momentary restoration of sound. Sound is severed once again. As if the fathers, brothers, or cousins were saying: "We have paid plenty for that unveiling of words!" Undoubtedly forgetting that the women have inscribed that statement into their martyred flesh, a statement that is, however, penalized by a silence that extends all around.

Sound severed once again, the gaze once again forbidden, these are what reconstruct the ancestral barriers. "A perfume of evil haunts," Baudelaire said. There is no seraglio any more. But the "structure of the seraglio"[11] attempts to impose its laws in the new wasteland: the law of invisibility, the law of silence.

Only in the fragments of ancient murmuring do I see how we must look for a restoration of the conversation between women, the very one that Delacroix froze in his painting. Only in the door open to the full sun, the one Picasso later imposed, do I hope for a concrete and daily liberation of women.

February 1979

NOTES

1. The innovative talent of the painter Delacroix contrasts with the traditionalism of Delacroix the man. Cf. his very conservative image of woman when, after his visit to Algiers, he notes in his journal, referring to the harem: "It is beautiful! It is straight out of Homer! The woman in her women's quarters busy with her children, spinning wool or embroidering splendid fabrics. That is woman as I think she should be!"

2. Veiled women are, in the first place, women who are free to circulate, therefore more advantaged than the women who are completely secluded, the latter usually being the wives of the most wealthy. According to Koranic tradition, the husband may not prevent his wife from going to the baths—the *hammam*—at least once a week. But what if he is wealthy enough to have his own *hammam* built inside his home?

In the town where I was born, in the thirties, the women used to go to the baths veiled, but they would go at night.

The veiled woman who circulates during the day in the city streets is, therefore, a woman in the first stage of so-called progressive behavior.

Since, furthermore, the veil signifies oppression of the body, I have known young women who, when they reached adolescence, refused the principle of having to be veiled when circulating. The result was that they had to remain cloistered behind windows and bars, and so see the exterior world only from afar. . . . A half measure among the men of the new middle class: as much as possible, they let their women circulate in individual cars (which the women themselves drive), thus to shelter the body (steel playing the role of the ancestral fabric) and to circulate in a way that "exposes" them as little as possible.

3. There is a traditional story told about the love between the prophet Muhammad and Zaineb, the most beautiful of his wives. A story born from a single look.

Zaineb was married to Zaid, the adopted son of the Prophet. One day, the latter needed to speak with Zaid. And so he approached his tent. Zaineb told him that Zaid was not there. She hid herself behind a tapestry, but "a gust of wind lifted the curtain" and the young woman, scantily dressed, became visible to Muhammad, who retired, distraught.

Zaid then sets Zaineb free again. But Muhammad will have to wait until a Koranic verse intervenes, making the union with a former wife of an adopted son legitimate. He will marry Zaineb, who will remain, together (and often in competition) with Aïcha, a favorite wife (cf. Gaudefroy-Demonbynes: Mahomet).

4. Cf. a wedding song of western Algeria:
   Oh, girls, I beg you
   Let me sleep with you!

Women of Algiers in Their Apartment

Every night, I'll make one [of you] "explode"
With my gun and rifle!

5. See *La Femme arabe* (The Arab woman) by General Daumas, written shortly before the author's death in 1871 and published in 1912.

6. See P. Raphaël du Mans, *Etat de la Perse en 1660* (*The state of Persia in 1660*) (Paris, 1890).

7. *Elsewhere* because the origin of political nationalism is as much due to the emigration of workers to Europe in the 1920s as to the movement of the new ideas from the Arabic East where large numbers of educated Arabic speakers and Moslems are trained (the Parti Progressiste Algérien—P.P.A.—and the ulema movements).

8. The "songs . . . from the verandas" are those of the *Bokala* game, in which the young girls respond to each other in rhyming couplets, as signs of portent.

9. These are the *hawfis,* a kind of popular, feminine poetry that is sung. Ibn Khaldoun already mentions this traditional genre, which he calls *mawaliya.* This same kind of feminine literature is found in places other than Tlemcen, but always in small towns of the Algerian north.

10. See, before 1962: Zora Drif, *La mort de mes frères* (The death of my brothers).

11. *La structure du sérail* by Alain Grosrichard (1979).

ACKNOWLEDGMENTS

"There Is No Exile" was published in *La Nouvelle Critique,* Paris, 1959, a special issue on Algerian literature.

"The Dead Speak" was published in part in *Algérie-Actualité,* 1969.

"Nostalgia of the Horde" is a text that, as do some others, enters as collective feminine murmuring into the composition, third part, of my novel *Les alouettes naives* (Julliard, 1967).

I chose that story as the end to this collection, for the memory of a chain of grandmothers comes back to the year 1830, in which Delacroix appears in Algiers as the only foreign witness among so many invaders.

A.D.

Glossary

Afterword

Glossary

Barberousse: famous Turkish privateer in the history of Algeria; also name of the most notorious prison in colonial Algeria, where torture and the guillotine were openly used.

chaouch: official at the gate of an important personality, in charge of announcing the arrival and departure of guests; a person who would fetch coffee and run errands; a "gofer."

cheikh: title given to an old notable, a scholar, or a master.

dhor: one of the five prayers Muslims are required to say daily.

fantasias: a fantasia is an equestrian competition in, and display of, riding skills organized on special occasions; also, the title of a painting by Delacroix.

Fatma: Proper name; also common pejorative noun by which the French colonizers designated Arab women and housemaids.

"gene": word coined by the translator for the French word *gégenne,* used in the original text to designate an instrument of torture.

Hadja: title given to a woman who has made the pilgrimage to Mecca.

hammam: the Turkish baths.

haoufi (hawfi): a kind of popular, feminine poetry.

hazab: reader of the Koran in the mosque.

kanoun: a small, three-legged portable clay pot filled with coals.

ouali: a holy man, a religious figure; also, a civil servant.

Pythia: attending, female oracle priestess at Delphi.

taimoum: a stone that, in the most arid regions, is used instead

Glossary

of water for the ritual ablutions required before the daily prayers.

taleb: student of the Koran.

tarawih: prayer during Ramadan preparatory to the fasting the next day.

tolba: plural form of *taleb* (q.v.).

willaya: there were six "fighting willayas" as command divisions in Algeria during the war, which fought not only the French but each other.

Yemma: the respectful title for older women, and the Arabic for "mother."

ulema: Muslim theologians, jurists, scholars; also, religious and political organizations of Algerian leaders during the colonial era.

Afterword

On a balmy spring day in 1957, a young Algerian girl not yet twenty-one years of age hailed a taxi in Paris. She was on her way to Julliards, the prominent publishing house that had just accepted her first novel. *La soif* was soon picked for publication by Simon and Schuster, translated as *The Mischief,* and praised by the *Sunday New York Times* of 12 October 1958. She was famous.

The contract she was about to sign was technically void, since she was not of age. But the young author had more pressing worries. Photo sessions had been scheduled with *Elle,* a successful, somewhat highbrow women's monthly whose editors had requested a bio sheet. Concerned about her family's reaction to a story that spoke of erotic self-indulgence and had been written at a time when she should have been studying for exams, she impulsively decided to cut her hair, change her birth date, and use a pen name.[1] It did not work. A few weeks later,

1. To this day, all studies, even scholarly ones, give the incorrect birth date, 4 August 1936. It was chosen, she says, because it was her parents' anniversary—maybe not such a good idea if she wished to elude detection. She later discovered that her idealistic father, a self-professed socialist who admired the French Revolution, had selected it as the date for his own wedding because he wanted, he said, "a true marriage between equals." In French history, 4 August 1789 marks the day when class privileges were abolished. Her real birth date is 30 June 1936. Djebar, who likes to ponder such coincidences, pointed out that 30 June was also the eve of Algerian independence, formally granted on 1 July 1962, and the day of her joyous homecoming after an exile of eight years.

These details, and other quoted words or phrases that follow, are from my interviews conducted with Assia Djebar, but they do not appear in the interview section of this essay. All such material will henceforth be identified in parenthesis as unpublished (unp.). Any quote attributed to Djebar that is not so marked is included in the interview below.

she was found out by her mother, who was browsing through the magazine rack at the hairdresser's.

While the taxi hurtled through the streets of Paris, the young writer asked her fiancé, an Algerian nationalist who would soon be on the run from the French police, to recite the ninety-nine ritual modes of address to Allah in the hope of finding herself a nom de plume. She selected *djebbar,* the phrase that praises "Allah the intransigeant," but in her haste spelled it "djébar," unwittingly transforming the classical Arabic into the vernacular term for "healer." The accent has since been dropped, but at least one French scholar versed in Arabic, Jacques Berque, called her "Djebbar" while reviewing her 1985 novel, *L'amour la fantasia* (Love and fantasia). As for Assia, she has said, "it was just a family first name that everybody liked" (unp.). But it has far-reaching symbolic resonances. In standard Arabic, it designates Asia and the mysterious Orient, thus "orientalizing" its bearer. It also happens to be the name of the Egyptian princess who rescued Moses and is so honored in Algerian lore as a holy woman and called "Pharaoh's sister." In the vernacular, it designates the flower variously known as the immortelle or the edelweiss. Twenty-some years later in this collection of short stories, first published in 1980 as *Femmes d'Alger dans leur appartement,* the "healer" signed her presence in the text as that of a *sourcière,* a magic dowser who taps into the subterranean reality of woman's silence to exorcize the death-in-life of the harem and to bring her forgotten sisters a kind of immortality.

Assia Djebar has been called the most gifted woman artist to come out of the Moslem world in our century. Openly feminist, a willing spokeswoman for her housebound sisters, fearless critic of her tradition-shackled brothers, bold experimenter in metahistorical fiction, confident in her role as a prominent Third-World writer and international lecturer, Djebar is a woman of contrasts whose negotiation of the troubled waters of post-colonialism is commendable.

By the early eighties, the former university lecturer, who had declined many an invitation from American universities "because they'd want me to play a role with which I am not comfortable" (unp.), had become comfortable on the lecture circuit of academe, equally at ease in the West as in her native Islam. The reason has to do with the circumstances surrounding the writing of this collection of short stories she calls "dear to my heart." In the wake of the extremely successful project that preceded it by a year, *La nouba des femmes du mont Chenoua* (Celebration of the women from Mount Chenoua), a film she wrote, directed, and produced, *Women of Algiers* put her back on the international map. Both film and book garnered the greatest praise in France, Germany, and Italy, where *Nouba* won first prize at the Venice Film Festival. Although the collection deals quite openly with the plight of ordinary Algerian women, it also raises far-reaching issues concerning such women and their society that go beyond the exotic, sentimental clichés Europe inherited from colonial paternalism. Born of the colonial war against France, *Women of Algiers* is about the cost of war to both men and women; the cost of a tradition that denies the human dignity and integrity of both; the sheer human waste of maintaining one group as subservient to the personal and political needs of another. It gives a voice and a body to "the inappropriate/d other" of Western patriarchies,[2] the native's mute mate who stands simultaneously as the other of the West and the other of man. It is the same woman who wails on the far shore of Conrad's *Heart of Darkness,* lips moving without a sound; the same native woman who, on this continent, hides in the wildest crags of Prospero's island: silenced, erased, invisible. Ever closer to us, she is Caliban's own Sycorax, who, says Shakespeare, was born in Algiers. Far from being limited to "the plight of the Algerian woman," this collection of short stories speak to all of us.

Not counting innumerable critical essays, newspaper articles, prefaces written to other people's works, and her co-translation of two novels from Arabic into French, Djebar has published a

---

2. The phrase is Trinh T. Minh-ha's title to the special issue she edited for *Discourse* 8 (Fall–Winter 1986–87), "She, the Inappropriate/d Other."

book of poetry, the present collection of stories, seven novels (the eighth is in press and she has finished the ninth), and one play—as well as having adapted and directed many others as she collaborated with her first husband in running an experimental theater on the outskirts of Paris in the 1970s. She has written and directed two long features. A film on her life, produced by French television, is in the works for summer or fall 1992. And, come 1993, she will be shooting her third film in Algeria. Still, she is more famous in Europe than in the United States, an imbalance the present translation should quickly remedy. There already exist two English versions of her densely theoretical Postface to *Women of Algiers*, "Forbidden Gaze, Severed Sound,"[3] an essay on the politics of female representation; but, they were done without consulting her. Thus, she was more than pleased when, a few years back, I solicited her collaboration in seeing through a complete translation of the present collection. This, then, is the first English translation of *Femmes d'Alger dans leur appartement* undertaken with her consent and cooperation.

Among specialists in Third-World studies, Djebar's work has been admired for years. But it was her first novel in almost two decades, *L'amour, la fantasia* (1985), that won her back the public's love. *Les alouettes naïves* (Innocent larks), had come out in 1967, and some were beginning to fear that she would never publish another line. A best-seller for many weeks in France and in North Africa, *L'amour* received the 1985 Franco-Arab Friendship Prize for literature. In the usually staid *Times Literary Supplement,* Ivan Hill was moved by not only "a passionate search for identity but also a cultural and historical exploitation of thought and literacy," and what he called "Djebar's linguistic spree." In France, where *L'amour* was originally published, the critics were unanimous. Speaking of her "latinity," Jacques Berque, an eminent scholar in compara-

3. Lee Hildreth, trans. "Forbidden Sight, Interrupted Sound," in the special issue of *Discourse* (see note 2), pp. 39–57; and J. M. McDougal, trans. "A Forbidden Glimpse, a Broken Sound" in *Women and the Family in the Middle East,* ed. Elizabeth Warnock Fernea (Austin: Texas University Press, 1984), pp. 337–51.

tive colonial history, gushed for the mildly left-of-center *Nouvel observateur:* "This fulgurant outburst of romanticism, this meditation on sociology, this semibiographical confession, . . . all merge into an intricately woven narrative that carries its reader far, far away from Camus's austere Mediterranean classicism."[4] Given Camus's status as the official representative of things Algerian for the past fifty years (*The Stranger* was published in 1942), the comparison was far from random. In the interview below, Djebar coolly distances herself from the famous Algerian-born Frenchman and, with a keen sense of her own territory, claims "all of it, including the hinterland, [whereas] Camus only hugged the shore."

As a Moslem woman, educated in the French system while her country was still under de-facto colonial rule and witness to eight years of a brutal war while still in her twenties, Djebar is the only writer of her sex and her generation who has managed an impressive output both before and after her country's accession to independence. Her entire corpus grapples with issues attending the passage from colonial to postcolonial culture: the definition of a national literature, the debate over cultural authenticity, the problematic question of language, and the textual inscription of a female subject within the patriarchal object.[5] Against this background, *Women of Algiers,* crucial signpost into new territory, illuminates the commitments of the early works and adumbrates the beginning of a meditation on history: the birthing of a strong feminist voice speaking terrible truths, but one that speaks with neither acrimony nor resentment—what she describes as, "my own kind of feminism."

Bruised by the controversy back home surrounding her first

4. Ivan Hill, "A Love-Hate Affair." *Times Literary Supplement,* 13–19 April 1990, p. 404; Jacques Berque, "La langue de l'envahisseur," *Le nouvel observateur* 1086 (30 August–5 September 1985): 54 (my translation).
5. Another writer to raise such issues, is, of course, Kateb Yacine, clearly one of Djebar's literary fathers—as he was for all of the North African writers— who died in 1989. CARAF has just brought out the translation of his masterpiece, *Nedjma,* with an incisive Introduction by Bernard Aresu on just such issues.

Afterword

film, and having been told that "short stories do not sell," she had given the manuscript to a small, independent French feminist publishing house,[6] rather than battle Algeria's state-controlled SNED, the house that had earlier published her play, *Rouge l'aube* (So red the dawn, 1969), and her poetry, *Poèmes pour l'Algérie heureuse* (Poems to a happy Algeria, 1969). Since *La nouba,*[7] a state-financed film, censors had looked askance at her work. When I met Assia Djebar for the first time in Algiers in 1976, she was preparing to shoot this film. In our first conversation, Djebar confided that she had presented the project solely as a documentary on the war, glorifying male heroism, in order to get past the censors. She promptly turned it into a semifictional record of women's participation in, and retrospective comments on, the war, with plenty of harsh criticism about the human and social cost of such heroism.

She had intended *Women of Algiers* primarily for an Algerian public. Unfortunately, Algeria was not ready to look at the cracks in its socialist mirror. The overwhelmingly favorable reaction in France, however, where people still stop her on the street to talk about it, took her by surprise. It has gone through at least one reprinting there (1983). In Italy *Women of Algiers,* now in its second reprinting, became hugely successful, undoubtedly helped along by her no-less-successful first film and, Djebar surmises, by the fact that "Italian feminists . . . come from all social classes," a discreet, wry reference to the rather haute-couture tone of French feminism. In firmly proletarian contrast, Antonella Boralevi, writing for *Il messaggero,* gave Djebar the whole front page of the literature section, saluting her as the *Pasionaria* of modern-day Algeria (23 March 1988). On this continent, American-based, Tunisian-born scholar Hédi Abdeljouad called the collection,

6. Editions des femmes; the use of the lowercase was meant to signify the editorial team's decision to break away from patriarchal, authoritarian modes of production.
7. First produced for Algerian TV, it was later viewed by packed houses and provoked intense debate at a time when the official campaign to refurbish woman's traditional image was losing speed. Obviously, the censors were not about to let themselves be embarrassed again.

Afterword

"a landmark in her career and in Maghrebine esthetics in general."[8]

In North Africa, Djebar is commended or censored depending on the ideological fluctuations of current regimes. In the Middle East, she is controversial for having sponsored the French translation of *Ferdaous,* a novel by Nawal Al Saadawy,[9] Egypt's former health minister, a sociologist, and a medical doctor, who eventually was fired then jailed for speaking about women's issues, including the terrifying experience of her own ritual excision as a child. With unflinching honesty, Djebar talks of a culture that glorifies woman's biology the better to subjugate her. Her latest published work to date, *Loin de Médine* (So far from Medina, 1991), a meditation on Islamic history prompted by the bloody fundamentalist street riots of 1988 in Algeria, could make her persona non grata in Saudi Arabia, where the holy city of Medina is located. *Médine* looks at the history of the Prophet's struggle against hostile warring tribes in the Saudian sands. The story brings back into prominence the dozen or so women in the Prophet's entourage, in order to remind us, if we had forgotten, that without these women's courage, Islam might not have survived. The subtitle calls them "daughters of Ishmael," highlighting their physical as well as spiritual wanderings within the religious patriarchy.[10]

Médine has already been the subject of a documentary film shown twice on French television and distributed throughout

8. Hédi Abdeljouad, review of *Femmes d'Alger dans leur appartement,* by Assia Djebar, *World Literature Today,* Spring 1981, p. 362.

9. *Ferdaous* was published by des femmes in 1981, and as *Woman at Point Zero* in 1983 (London, ZED). Fearless, Saadawy has continued to write. English readers may refer to *The Hidden Face of Eve: Women in the Arab World* (London: ZED, 1980). In 1991, Saadawy's women's association was declared illegal, all its documents were destroyed, and its assets were confiscated. Djebar's introduction to Saadawy's novel was intended to gain the Egyptian woman an international audience.

10. For an excellent survey of the issue, in particular the degree of social and economic autonomy tribal women maintained as a carryover from their own cultures, including nonmonogamous habits, see Leila Ahmed, "Women and the Advent of Islam," *Signs* 2 (1986): 665–90.

Europe. In Algeria and Morocco, people took to the streets when excerpts were published, "the bearded ones to burn me and the beardless ones to defend me" (unp.). The tense and bloody events of winter-spring 1992, following the overwhelming victory of the FIS (Front islamique de salut, or Islamic Salvation Front) in the national elections; the fundamentalists' refusal to share power despite being democratically elected; president Chedli's resignation and the army's subsequent takeover, against which Djebar spoke publicly from Paris—all have proved her worst fears correct. In every major Algerian city, women's groups banded together and thousands of women descended into the streets to refuse the contemplated return to religious law. As this is being written, the Arabic translation of *Médine* is under way but has yet to appear in the Islamic world; judging by these preliminary reactions elsewhere, however, it will not pass unnoticed.

The interview that follows flows out of several conversations over the years. The first one took place in 1976 on the flower-filled terrace of an opulent hotel, high in the hills of Algiers. Neither of us could afford to stay there, but the wide expanse of open gardens made privacy possible. It was better, she hinted, that I not look as if I was interviewing her. Islam had just been reinstated as the state religion in Algeria's brand new charter, sounding the death knell of public female participation in the new society, and in spite of President Boumédienne's official Campaign for the Emancipation of the Maghrebian Woman, the streets of Algiers were empty of women, veiled or not. Our next encounter occurred in 1987, during the annual conference of the African Literature Association at Cornell University, where the subject of translating this collection was broached. But Assia Djebar, in the wake of the huge success of her 1987 novel, *Ombre sultane* (Sultana's shadow), was busier than ever. It took until the summer of 1990 for the two of us to sit down in the little courtyard overhung with lilac that huddles at the back of her tiny house on the outskirts of Paris, which looks so much like an Algerian villa.

When I left after a three-hour talk, mindful of her fall from favor upon completion of her first film, I promised to send her

Afterword

the transcripts if she would, in turn, answer additional questions. At this writing, she is still an Algerian civil servant, a visiting lecturer on loan to the Algerian Cultural Center in Paris. Some of these additional questions were undoubtedly too bluntly phrased. As her first balking reply makes clear, she was in no mood to provide "frankly autobiographical" details. Eventually, we taped three more hours in the summer of 1991, and a last hour in December of the same year.

Culled from these successive sessions, the interview below spans the bulk of a long and varied professional life, expanding on the relationship between writing and film, and on her changing poetics and its relationship to the other arts as well as to French, the conquerors' language ("they came, they killed, they conquered"), on whose canonical masters the writer passes irreverently iconoclastic judgment: "It's the dead ones I worship!" Finally, Djebar leaves us with tantalizing glimpses of the work in progress, the final two books of a projected quartet (of which *L'amour* and *Ombre sultane* are the first two)—a quartet that should be read, she claims, as an "architectural metaphor." Wary as she was, she nonetheless delved progressively deeper into her writing, to that *coeur intime,* that inner "core" or inner "heart" (the French phrase signifies both) of which she was initially so protective. Eventually she gives us richly autobiographical material, even if she would probably insist it is not. I was careful not to ask.

WOMAN'S MEMORY
SPANS CENTURIES

An Interview with Assia Djebar

C Z   *Assia Djebar, can you tell us about your origins, your family, your school years? What possessed the dutiful daughter of good Moslem parents, in what you yourself have many times called a puritan environment, to become a French writer in a culture that did not encourage women to write?*

Afterword

A D   *I'm afraid I can't. I cannot face such frankly autobiographical questions and you can see by my other interviews that I've never been good at answering them.
Mother, father, brother, sister, they're of no interest
here. I've been asked too many times before.*

C Z   *I do not wish to pry, so let me rephrase.* Women of
Algiers in Their Apartment *was published in a country where short stories do not sell and yet it sold like
crazy. It was supposed to be a diary of things Moslem,
yet it was embraced by readers across borders. It was
intended for women of the Third World, and still
women of the First recognized themselves in it. How
are readers to approach it?*

A D   *When I am asked to introduce myself to an audience that may not have read all of my works, I use
this little skit: "I was born in Algeria. Between the
ages of twenty and thirty, I wrote four novels. I then
stopped publishing for about ten years. For two years,
I worked on a film among the women from my tribe,
deep into the familiar territory of my childhood. Afterwards, I came back to writing. I had just turned forty.
It's at that point that I finally felt myself fully a writer
of the French language, while remaining deeply Algerian."*

*I use it as a way to get this across: What interests me
is the relationship between writing and autobiography
because, unlike the usual schema of female writing in
the Western tradition, which is all subjective, I started
writing as a wager, almost a dare, to keep as far away
from my real self as possible. When it came to my fiction, I would open some sort of parenthesis from my
real life. And then came* Les alouettes naïves.

C Z   *If I understand you, in the early novels you remained
in hiding from yourself, so to speak. How did you
manage to get out from behind yourself?*

A D   *I remember it all too well. I can even pinpoint for
you today the exact spot where I became blocked. I*

was writing Les alouettes naïves, *sketching the life
of a newly married young couple. At first, I thought
that this private stuff did not belong in there; it was
going off in a different direction from the rest of the
book, depicting mutual erotic fulfillment right smack
in the middle of a war story. I think now that, at bottom, even though I thought I was writing as far away
from my own self as possible, my fiction had suddenly
caught up with me. I could not help it. My life as a
woman tripped me up.*

C Z *Critics have usually grouped together your two war
novels* Les enfants du nouveau monde *(Children of
the New World, 1962) and* Les alouettes naïves. *However,* Alouettes *signals a radical turning point in your
writing from which you never looked back. Woman's
erotic self-discovery stands at its very center, sym-
bolically and structurally. Female eroticism makes up
the novel's* coeur intime. *Woman's erotic awakening
takes up the center of the middle part in a tripartite
structure—structurally, the center of the center.*

A D *In* Alouettes, *when I finally realized that I could not
help it, when I understood that writing always brings
one back to oneself, to that inner core or heart, as
you so justly call it, I felt as if . . . as if I was exposing myself doubly. First, because as an Algerian, but
one living—or so it seemed—as a Westerner, I was
somewhat exposed already. Second, because writing
about my innermost self felt like exposing myself further: I more or less chose silence. As if I could not see
past that inner core, as if . . . to write was to commit
suicide.*

*Your questions now force me to ask myself: Why is
it that autobiographical questions are so abhorrent?
I believe that it is because, all through my first three
novels, my writing consisted in systematically turning my back on my own life—in short, in refusing the
autobiographical dimension of writing. This realization leads me today to reconsider my violent reaction*

*to your biographical questions, earlier. Now, I am
almost glad you posed them. Well . . . almost!*

c z   *This middle part, in* Alouettes, *is a problem as far as
plot development is concerned; it interrupts the linear
sequence, and fractures the temporal structure. Yet it
is crucial on the level of images and their symbolism,
since you use the same images in* Women of Algiers.
There are no accidental symbols in writing.

a d   *You are forcing me to look back, to move upward in
my memory. I was myself living in a blissful state of
happiness, a love story outside of time, a private happiness that was a bit static. There I was, among the
exiles. I decided to write a novel that would delineate
the various stages of political consciousness awakening
among them. These were young people for the most
part, and not all war veterans—a very mixed bag. My
relationship to autobiography, as it may have started
then, consisted above all in the fact that I was struck
by the realization that we were all marginal participants, actors on the sidelines, if I may use a phrase that
may not please everyone.*

c z   *Compared to your slim earlier novels,* Les alouettes
naïves *is a huge book of almost five hundred pages.
Some pieces that look like leftovers, or else are clearly
sequels to it, were included in* Women of Algiers, *a collection published thirteen years later. What triggered
your decision? Were they politically too sensitive to
use at the time of the publication?*

a d   Women of Algiers *is still dear to my heart. For instance, "The Dead Speak" represents the surge of
the autobiographical element, a surge triggered by
the death of my own grandmother, eight days after
Algeria's independence of 1 July 1962. For the last
story, "Nostalgia of the Horde," I got the idea from
my former mother-in-law, who was able to show me
that a woman's memory spans centuries—just one*

woman. She would talk of an obscure, forgotten old woman she used to know who used to talk of the old days. This is precisely how Algerian women "relay" the past: they tell the (his)story of colonization, but tell it otherwise.[11] Listening to her, I thought to myself, "I shall write a collection of short stories." I wanted to show the whole world that I was starting in a different key, catching my second breath as a writer. Once the decision was made, I suddenly felt reconciled with myself. For ten years, I had experienced not quite a full break, but a kind of suspension from myself. I made a discovery: to write about oneself is to put oneself in mortal danger.

C Z   *Were there other reasons? I am thinking of what was happening on the political plane in Algeria, a slow tightening of the screw, as far as women's civil liberties were concerned. On the aesthetic plane, was not the film, the change in medium, a new relationship to the eye, forcing you to reconsider your own vision? Or were you still plagued by the old language question?*

A D   *Ah! the language question. I know I've told many others before that my silence had to do with my problematic relationship to language. That's what I claimed largely to be left in peace.[12] But your questions force me to reconsider, and I am persuaded that there was something else at the bottom of it—at the bottom of me. I know, for instance, that I had to wait until* L'amour, la fantasia *to be able to take charge of my writing, to be able to inscribe my innermost self in my work. You are right here too. I could not have done it*

---

11. In French, *histoire* indiscriminately refers to both "story" and "history."

12. Djebar meticulously dissects her relationship to language in Marguerite Le Clézio's interview "Ecrire dans la langue adverse," *Contemporary French Civilization* 10 (December 1986): 230–44. Unfortunately, it has not been translated. Given Djebar's wariness, the piece is a tribute to the exquisite patience of the interviewer and remains the authoritative statement on this aspect of Djebar's poetics.

without the mediation of painting and the "interces-sion" of painters.

C Z   *You're not claiming that the language question played no part in it altogether, are you?*

A D   *It was not the language per se but what I call the gap between the two languages, French and Arabic, a gap that mirrors the yawning gap between two societies that still go on functioning side by side, but keep their backs stiffly to each other. I've said it many times. The upbringing that I received from my own mother and others around me had two absolute rules: one, never talk about yourself; and, two, if you must, always do it "anonymously."*

C Z   *Anonymously? I think you must specify further for non-Maghrebian readers. How strict was the taboo? Was it for mixed company only?*

A D   *The taboo still persists today, even when there are only women present. Take a look at* L'amour, la fantasia. *When women are alone together, only older women may talk; the young ones must keep silent. This gen-erational rule of order is just as binding among men. The older men always have the floor, ahead of, and often instead of, the younger ones.*

As for speaking anonymously, one must *never* use *the first person pronoun. Back home after the war, I found myself in a very traditional milieu in my mother-in-law's household. No sooner was I alone with a group of women than I would pose questions, ask for personal opinions or personal details. Whatever their age, the women were always reticent. To them, it felt like prying; it was indecent. I, on the other hand, also had a Western experience, a Western mode of behav-ior. When I throw myself into writing a novel, I must confront the opposite strategy: to write a Western nar-rative, I must speak subjectively, I must start with the first-person pronoun. That's when I realized that the problem goes far beyond the territorialization of this gap between the two languages. Within that gap there flowed eighteen years between* Alouettes *(1967) and* L'amour, la fantasia *(1985); a gap for which, as you yourself have said,* Women of Algiers *serves as the signpost into new territory.*

C Z   *I've always suspected that making the film is what got you through. Teaching yourself how to make a movie was teaching yourself how to arrive at a different kind of writing, would you say?*

A D   *Absolutely. The film was the decisive factor. I was just coming out of two years of film work during which I had used primarily the eye and the ear. I started the first short story, "Women of Algiers in Their Apartment," and wrote it extremely fast, even though I had spent ten years without publishing. As you know, the idea was that the story was going to be the seed for the next project, a film on the urban women of Algiers. It was intended to match its other half,* La nouba, *a film on the rural women of the hinterland.*

C Z   *And what happened to the film project?*

A D   *My private life took a different turn. I married my second husband, an Algerian poet living in Paris. Had I proceeded with the second film, I would have had to go back to Algeria and invest perhaps two years of my life. The logistics of filming are rather daunting. Instead, I went back to writing with a great sense of relief and joy: I was in charge again. This time, I positioned myself neither as an outside observer, nor as an Algerian woman, nor as a colonized being. I defined myself as a* gaze, *a way of looking upon my very own space. That's where my film on Algiers would have started.*

C Z   *A multitude of gazes—Delacroix's painting "Women of Algiers in Their Apartment" is all about this. Who*

Afterword

gazes at whom? You have given L'amour, la fantasia
the same beginning. I'd call it your matrix scene. In
L'amour, *all of the city of Algiers is on the ramparts,
men, women, children, gazing at the invaders' ships
coming in on the tide, while on deck, the invaders
themselves are intently gazing at the city they have
come to conquer. Who is subject and who is object:
do they themselves know?*

A D   *I had not thought of the parallel, but you're absolutely
right. What was it you said earlier about there being
no accidental symbols? I could not have pulled it off
without the prior film experience that brought to my
writing a moviemaker's gaze. Film gave my writing a
vision; French became my camera. In contrast, my film
work always starts with sound. The music researcher,
so passionate about ancient songs—I have been her, or
she has been me, for a very long time. I used to go to
the institute to listen to old folksongs from Laghouat
or Tlemcen. And when I taught history, I realize now
that I always included oral material, almost without
thinking.*

C Z   *How do you see the connection, then, between these
"new" stories, those that were written after* Alouettes,
*and what I have called the novel's missing piece, the
sequel from* Alouettes *that you inserted in the collection?*

A D   *They are connected through the theme of memory
and the question of our relationship to memory. I
had begun by writing "Day of Ramadan," but I only
started to understand this connection when, after
writing "The Woman Who Weeps" and "Women of
Algiers," I was seized by the urge to bring my grandmother into it, to bring the past into a dialogue with
the present. In my yearning to hear her immaterial
voice, I conceived of a story that became "The Dead
Speak." That done, I realized with a start that I had the*

makings for a collection of short stories. Delacroix's painting only came to me after that.

C Z *We could say, then, that Delacroix's painting triggered, not your writing, but your reading of yourself; a backward gaze, as it were, on what you had just done; a gaze that positioned you with regard to him, the Westerner, and with regards to your work, the world of women.*

A D *Absolutely. I wrote the Postface when I had just moved to the little house you know. As it happened, I then discovered that it had belonged to another Algerian writer, Elissa Rhais, a woman of Jewish descent who had exiled herself and spent her final years in it, writing. I felt under her sisterly protection, there, and decided to track down her heirs and buy it. And I did. I spent a couple of weeks on the Postface, weaving a kind of textual meditation that would serve as a reflective background to the stories I had just put together. At this point, I wondered—you probably won't agree—whether the Postface should not be the preface. "Forbidden Gaze" would have opened the collection, become the Overture. What do you think?*

C Z *I think your first instinct was right. Had you placed "Forbidden Gaze" first, the whole tenor of the collection would have been harsher, much less compassionate. As it is, it's pretty unbearable. Judging by the fact that it has been translated twice into English already, it is also read abroad as the most radical of your essays.*

A D *The Postface was intended to unify the stories. Only after I had written it, did I tackle the short preface, the Overture. It enabled me to raise the issue of a woman's language, the circulation of woman's voice, my relationship to Arabic, and it helped me define my own kind of feminism.*

C Z *Do the strong women ancestors to whom you pay homage explain your feminism?*

Afterword

A D   *For me, feminism has always been tied up with the question of language, but not just French.* Women of Algiers *is my first response to the official policy of Arabization, which I loathe. In my films, I have experimented with the different versions of the Arabic language in Algeria. I had an Arabic sound track and a French sound track for* Nouba. *I lived immersed in the language of the hinterland, an experience that ran quite contrary to the current efforts to impose a version of classical Arabic upon the land, an "Arabization from above" that has become, for me, the linguistic equivalent of war. Official Arabic is an authoritarian language that is simultaneously a language of men. As you yourself have told me, there are few good men in my fictional universe.* Women of Algiers *is a world without men.*

C Z   *At the very least we can say that you come down rather hard on the men. Take the grandson in your favorite story, "The Dead Speak."*

A D   *Well, I came back on my birthday, the real one, 30 June, literally on the eve of independence. As you can surmise, I knew quite a few of these guerrilla fighters who, upon their glorious homecoming, turned into apparatchiks.*

C Z   *Unsavory as some of them are, your treatment can also be generous and often compassionate. Again, look at "The Dead Speak."*

A D   *You're too generous yourself. What compassion I felt consisted in showing that neither men nor women had yet been able to cut the umbilical cord that bound them to an overly painful past. They still can't. Because of that, my women have no children.*

C Z   *As you know, you've been attacked for your demeaning portraits of women who, perpetually pregnant (or distraught at being childless), glorify the procreating body that keeps them subjugated.*

Afterword

A D   *When I think of the female body, I do not see it as a procreating body but as an erotic body. While writing* Women of Algiers, *I found other themes much more intriguing: problems of language, the status of the Berber language and the Berber culture, for one. What interested me in "Women of Algiers," was how to explore the relationship between the written word and the voice—particularly, woman's voice.*

C Z   *Is this how you discovered feminism?*

A D   *Yes. It was an extremely fertile period of my intellectual life. I would go back and forth between Paris and Algiers, thinking all the time about the possibility of a dialogue between a European woman and an Algerian one, its modalities. Look at what happens in "Women of Algiers." It is the Algerian woman who comes to the help of the French one, whereas this was a period when we'd hear, all day long, that "the feminists from the West," as they were reverently called, had something crucial to give us, Moslem women, a lesson to teach us, ready-made recipes that would save us.*

C Z   *Continuity or discontinuity: Do you then see a radical break brought about by your newly found feminism? Is there a before and after* Women of Algiers?

A D   *Continuity or discontinuity? For two solid years, making the film, I had stared in awe and wonder at my own region, the region described by Camus in* Noces *(Nuptials, 1937). But, whereas I claimed all of it, including the hinterland, Camus only hugged the shore. I had all of it, the many landscapes and the many faces. It was sheer happiness to find my own space again. The camera moved constantly back and forth from past to present. Likewise,* Alouettes *is structured by this pitching back and forth, between the time of childhood, the depth time of lost paradise, and the present. So there is visual continuity between my film and my fiction.*
    Next, leaving aside the cinematic influence, what

Afterword

*I also see is the double register of my writing, the
scriptive discontinuity. There is, for instance, Sarah's
Western voice as opposed to that of the water carrier,
in the divan you call lyrical. It was connected to an
increasing feeling of disenchantment toward my own
country that had never been in my work before, something akin to despair. Working a whole year (1977) in
the hinterland, I had discovered a new closure. Ma-
terially, the peasants were living better than they ever
had under the colonizer; but their bettered lot was
simultaneously accompanied by a general, harsh return
to the cloistering of the women. Writing "Women of
Algiers" I suddenly understood that I had arrived on
stable ground. A lot has been said: that I intended to
cancel out my early novels, for instance. Those who
claim that, don't know what they're talking about. My
early novels are well-constructed, taut stories. I have
said many times that they were written as parentheses
in my real life. Because of this, some think I should
cross out the first three and claim that my true career
started with* Alouettes. *I don't.*

C Z   *Do I dare, then, ask the Françoise Sagan question?*

A D   *Don't you dare! It's been a long time since anyone has
referred to me as another Sagan. Those who read me
do know that our writings could not be more dissimi-
lar, now. We had the same publisher, that's all. I prefer
to play down this particular coincidence. The criticism
that was showered upon me at the time touched me
little. What with a husband who was wanted by the
police and the attendant turmoil, I thought that the
revolution—correction, I never use that term; I call
it "the Algerian war"—that the war was so much a
part of my everyday life, that I could not possibly have
turned it into literature.*

    I wish to specify here: I have never *used the term*
revolution, *even at the time when it was flooding and
drowning every discourse, public or private. This long*

aside is to tell you that this *is what I understand by
the term* form, *a certain kind of rigor and precision
in one's thinking. That's what I intended for* La soif;
that's what I came back to with Ombre sultane. *You
might call it an ethic.*

C Z   *Going beyond your training as a historian, what else
determined your calling?*

A D   *The years of high school were crucial because I was a
boarder for seven years. I was only allowed home to
the little village where my father taught once a week.
Out of four or five hundred little girls, we may have
been three or four Algerians. I was usually the only
Algerian girl in my classes, because I had elected the
toughest (*elite *as we used to say) syllabus. I had asked
to study Arabic as a foreign language and was told it
was not allowed. So, I went for the hardest track to
show them: Greek and Latin. I never could pass up a
challenge.*

   *I lived through all this aspect of colonization with-
out making much of a fuss about it. But, in my third
year, two things happened: I made a friend, the daughter of an Italian settler, and together we discovered
literature. We stumbled upon the published letters
of Alain Fournier to Jacques Rivière,[13] impassioned
arguments as to what should constitute literature. It
was a sort of calling for them, certainly: they fought
about the early Claudel, all of Mallarmé, the early
Gide—in other words, what was considered the avant-*

---

13. Rivière, who died in 1925, was a novelist and the gifted editor of what
was to become the prominent review (and subsequently, a press as well) *La
nouvelle revue française*. Associated with Proust, Gide, Claudel, and Valéry,
and later, with Sartre, NRF single-handedly ruled the literary roost on the
side of neoclassicism between the two world wars. His sister Isabelle was to
marry Alain Fournier, who would write the single most influential symbolist
novel in French literature, *Le grand Meaulnes* (Big Meaulnes, 1913). Their
plea for a strong, austere, and classical style has obviously left its mark on
Djebar.

garde for their time, writers that our teachers had told us were too difficult for us. Their fervor profoundly influenced me.

C Z   *Has your own career measured up? Do you reread yourself?*

A D   *Back home, my first novel was called minor. My university colleagues never mentioned my novels or would say, semidismissively, that their wives read them. It took me a while to realize these were gut reactions against anything coming from a woman. I don't reread myself, but I remember with great precision what I set out to do. With* Women of Algiers, *I miscalculated in targeting an Algerian public that did not materialize. Let's not forget that it was not published in Algeria. I was even asked why I had bothered to give it to a feminist press. People had a pretty set idea about who I should or should not be.*

     Well, with L'amour, la fantasia *they had to change their tune. I was now the writer of a book that* Révolution africaine *had pronounced—allow me to quote, I can't resist—"the most important book of the decade." I was no longer someone they could patronize.*

C Z   *Are you read in different ways on each side of the Mediterranean? Is there a culture-specific reader response to the Djebar phenomenon?*

A D   *I did not understand the paradox at the time, but a neighbor in France recently told me that her friends still remember the publication of* Femmes d'Alger *as "a momentous event." In Algeria, my usual public consists of some 30,000 persons, who faithfully buy any book of mine within six weeks of publication. I had aimed no further.*

     Des femmes sold all of its first printing, 15,000 copies, and sold it fast. Short stories do not sell in France, some people had told me. There was astonishment at seeing mine so successful; all the more so that,

since Alouettes naïves, *French readers had forgotten
me. From this standpoint, the press behaved quite
handsomely with me, leaving it up to me how to pro-
mote my book. I refused quite a few token interviews
from journalists who wanted me on their shows "to
talk about the plight of the Algerian woman," when
they had not even read the book.*

Then came L'amour, la fantasia. *It was clear that,
although scholars' reactions were favorable, few had
expected such a book. What touched me most were the
reactions of ordinary readers, often exiled from Africa
or the Maghreb, who would write or come all the way
to meet me. In fact, it was the men who felt themselves involved by the question of language; I'm not
sure why. I am not talking about one or two but six
or seven men who, independently of each other, have
commented on this. A Syrian reader even said, "Only
Marguerite Duras can tackle the question of language
with as much power." As for me, I'm flattered, but I
don't see the connection.*

C Z   *I do, I do. Don't pay attention to her agent-provoca-
teur-of-feminism side. Think of her use of silence, all
these unconscious drives that bubble up to the surface,
a bit like a Proust who would have gone minimalist.*

A D   *The one I prefer is* Le ravissement de Lol Z. Stein *(The
ravishing of Lol Stein, 1964). The others I could teach,
because I could keep my critical distance from them;
not this one. It cuts too close. Have you noticed? Of
"the three great ladies of French literature"—Duras,
Sarraute, and Yourcenar—all were born outsiders; not
one of them has had a French childhood.*

C Z   *Do you feel any common bond with Duras, who is a
filmmaker as well, just like you. Something about the
influence of vision on written texts?*

A D   *I'd see Yourcenar, rather, as my first influence, because
she, too, poses the question of history. Her style is a*

*bit dense, in an old-fashioned sort of way, but I am
fond of it. As for Duras, I am touched by this disem-
bodied voice that is on the verge of self-decentering. In
short, I do read them, but I have no conscious desire to
emulate them—not that I know of.*

*For me—pardon the horrible phrase—French litera-
ture has nothing to do with living writers: It's the dead
ones I worship! I did settle my accounts with France,
once and for all, by writing* L'amour, la fantasia. *Of
course, I went through my Proust period. But I am
partial to poets, Henri Michaux, René Char, those I
discovered with my little Italian friend in boarding
school. I was put through the existentialist grid when
cramming for my first year at the university. I think
that's why I never got hooked. At the beginning of the
war, dutiful revolutionaries were supposed to admire
model couples, Sartre-Beauvoir or Aragon-Elsa. For
the Algerian brothers, Aragon was the Victor Hugo of
the revolution [she laughs]. But for me, there can be
no meeting ground between politics and art—even if I
admire* Le fou d'Elsa *(Elsa's fool, 1963) by Aragon.
I can't read this way because I can't write this way,
I suppose. So, when the brothers asked me who my
writers were, I would mention foreigners. The one who
counted most—and still counts—was Cesare Pavese.*

*The French translations of Pavese came out while
I was a student in France, 1956 or 1957, and they
were a revelation. There were my own landscapes,
my childhood, the same types of people and customs
I had known in my village. Since then, Italians have
remained the people of Europe among whom I feel
at ease; their writers are writers with whom I feel
at home.*

C Z *Perhaps they are better able to understand your work,
unencumbered by the Nordic baggage of French intellectuals who tend to put a cool Cartesian grid over
their Latin emotions, or at least pretend that they do.*

Afterword

A D   *I saw this when I went to Venice to present my film.
My first serious relationship with European women
started with filmmakers, the Italian and the German
women directors. Italian feminists, in particular, come
from all social classes. They would enter into my films
with a generosity and a warmth I received nowhere
in France. French people could grant me my stance of
woman dissecting women, but they could not tolerate
my dissecting colonial history: their colonial history.
The Italians and the Germans would stay to talk to
me about films for hours, and talk technique, too. The
sound-image connection I discovered in films gave me
the courage to begin the quartet.*

C Z   *How so?*

A D   *I know. You're going to ask me about triggers, aren't
you? I started my historical research on the nineteenth
century less than two weeks after finishing* Zerda, *my
second film.*[14] *The archival documents I incorporated
gave me the lead I needed to plunge into* L'amour, *by
providing me with a similar editing technique. Remember the sentence I use in the voice-over of* Zerda:
"*Painters and photographers always come after the
battle is over.*" *I meant to imply that pictorial archives
can lead one back in time, in memory, only so far. So
I decided to use the French language to move back up
the chain of violent images—including the violence
that happens off camera—as if looking at the conquest
simultaneously from both sides.*

   But the other trigger, as I have said before, was that

---

14. As a historian, Djebar had been asked by Pathé-Gaumont, a film company, to sift through some old reels stored in a warehouse. They turned out
to be discarded newsreels on the colonies. Out of the colonial discards, the
"gazing" that the colonizer refused to acknowledge, she wove *La zerda et
les chants de l'oubli* (Zerda, and the songs of forgetting, 1982). *Zerda*, is a
vernacular word to designate a popular festival, a merrymaking celebration.
The film *Zerda* celebrates retrieving those pieces of the collective past she had
thought were lost forever to the collective memory.

Afterword

*I suddenly realized that I had never used the French
language to speak of love. I looked up all of the words
of love I knew in an Arabic dictionary and I began
to wonder about myself: Who was I? A Berber? An
Arab? I was Francophone in my writing, but who or
what was I in my life? There was a zone of silence, in-
habited by words of love I pronounced only in Arabic
and kept safe in my memory. One morning I found
myself writing the famous first lines of* L'amour, la fantasia, *my formal entrance into French language: "A
little schoolgirl going to school for the first time on an
autumn morning, her hand in the father's hand."*

C Z   *Was it a lead-in to the rest of the quartet, as well?*

A D   *Exactly. With* L'amour, *I wanted to reintegrate my
own autobiography, so I had to settle my quarrel with
the language first. That's when I understood that the
French language, for me, had nothing to do with Sartre
or Camus. The French language, for me, is the language of those people coming onto my land with the
colonial conquest. Those first few official conquerors—
they came, they killed, they conquered. They write, and
kill as they write—in the act of writing. Hence, before
diving into my present life and sounding my own inner
self, I had to describe the childhood of this language
that structures me. So, in* L'amour, la fantasia, *I evoke
the language of the nineteenth-century conquest in
conjunction with that of the little girl learning to write
it for the first time.*

C Z   *This overriding concern for structure, for the inner
logic of symbolic patterning in your narratives, is this a
carryover from the well-constructed, taut stories with
which you started your writing career?*

A D   *It is my best and most consistent feature. I should have
been an architect [she laughs]. When presenting my
novels in Germany not too long ago, I found myself
thinking about the quartet in architectural metaphors.*

Afterword

L'amour, la fantasia, *the first volume, is the entryway
of a traditional Arab house; you know, the visitors'
vestibule, when you've barely come inside from the
street; not the "patio," the private inner courtyard re-
served to the women, but the minicourt that leads into
it. Whereas* Ombre sultane, *the second book, represents the private inner chambers, the space where the
women are free to be alone together. The third remains a book about women. In the traditional house,
as you must have done many times, women used to
go up on the terraced roofs in order to gaze far, far
away, toward the horizon. I think I shall call it "Un
silencieux désir" (So silent a desire). I go further up,
before the French conquest. Then I plunge back down
again into the autobiographical childhood material
of* L'amour, la fantasia, *but from a different vantage
point. The fourth volume is a coming back to the early
historical themes that govern* L'amour, la fantasia. *This
time, I shall push back prior to 1830, before the French
conquest. It is the history of palace coups, Turkish
deys, Machiavellian plots and counterplots—Mediterranean power plays from which the French are totally
absent. They no longer exist.*

C Z *You are going back to the time of "before," the pre-
history of French history, down to the "subterranean"
(your favorite word) foundations, then?*

A D *Exactly. I cannot let go of the question of who we were
before. Somewhere in me something must account
for the* métissage, *this wild mixture sown into me by
my own father. To me, it's quite obvious: I am the
schoolteacher's daughter.*

C Z *What would have happened if you had written under
your own name? Once you had been found out, did
you ever think of it?*

A D *I have been asked often why I did not keep my father's
name, "Imalayen," which is gloriously Berber. At the*

time, I was really obsessed with not being found out by my parents; also, for a book cover, I thought it might be too long. I toyed with using my mother's name, "Sarahoui." I would have claimed back my mother's name as others used to claim the clan's name in the old days. But, in her culture and tradition—what you can see in La nouba—*it would have been a way to show off. All of Cherchell would have easily made the connection. I wished to spare her. So I stayed with Djebar. Every time I finish something and have to sign my name, I am tempted to use the correct spelling, djebbar, and then I decide against it. I like the idea of this letter, silently hiding between two languages and two cultures. So, my last and not least motivation, the last "trigger" I shall give you for your collection, is that I remain, as well, the descendant of my mother's clan. I am Cherchell's daughter, the city that is, for me, Algeria's true capital—before the time of the Turkish deys, before Algiers, Juba's own Caesarea—which is why I think I'll call the fourth book, perhaps, "Les oiseaux de la mosaïque" (Birds of the mosaic).*

C Z   *You're referring to all the wonderful mosaics found in Cherchell and Tipasa?*

A D   *Roman mosaics and Libyan statuary that our conquerors took upon themselves to send to the Louvre museum. I have this image in me of all these statues of naked women from centuries ago recovered from the soil of my native land. As the French arrive, I see our men digging them up from the earth, but unable to look at them. To them, these are just naked, pagan statues; and yet, these are our grandmothers. Today, their granddaughters, wrapped up in opaque, white veils from head to toe, are only allowed out of the house at night for the weekly ritual visit to the Turkish baths.*

C Z   *These birds, caught in the silent mosaics of the past, are the reincarnation of the innocent larks, I'm sure. You've come back full circle.*

Afterword

A D   *Yes, I've come back to the question of woman. As you
said, there is no accidental symbol.*

This stubborn return to her signature symbol, woman's
body, is typical of a writer who has had to fight her way
through a colonial condition aggravated by cultural gender
expectations. The tendency to rebel against what is expected
of her has often triggered her choice of topic, and it accounts
in no small part for the transformation of her own poetics:
the gradual invasion of the autobiographical into writing
exercises that were initially conceived as "some sort of parenthesis from my real life." Consider the first novel that made
her famous, for which, on a self-imposed dare, she decided to
write "as far away from my own self as possible."
Stories about amoral characters by young girls of good
breeding, who were not supposed to know about such perver-
sities, were all the rage then. Barely out of her teens, Françoise
Sagan had just published *Bonjour tristesse* (1954). Djebar
sent her manuscript to the same publisher, a decision that,
in spite of what she now claims, cannot have been altogether
a "coincidence." It has all the bravado of a James Fenimore
Cooper, the bumpkin from the New World, taking up the pen
to prove that he could write as well as the darling of the Old
World, Sir Walter Scott. More to the point, the Sagan parallel
was used as a gauge of her talent. Even the favorable reactions
of the American press were interlaced with references to "a
Sagan soufflé."[15] For the French pundits, she was the proof
that *mission civilisatrice,* the imperial will to civilize that
consisted in turning "one of them" into "one of us," could
succeed. For the Algerians—who, in the midst of a nationalist war, espoused committed literature—she was a shameless
hussy. In the disparaging words of A. Nataf, *La soif* was a
piece of bourgeois trash, "devoid of the primary Algerian
reality of war, suffering, and courage."[16] With the immedi-

15. Jean Campbell Jones, review of *The Mischief,* by Assia Djebar, *New York
Times,* 12 October 1958, p. 52.
16. A. Nataf, review of *La soif,* by Assia Djebar, *Présence africaine,* no. 16
(Oct.-Nov. 1958): 120.

ate publication of a second, somewhat similar, novel, the typecasting on both sides of the Mediterranean was complete.

Some of the new pieces in *Women of Algiers* were written to combat such expectations, and they show clearly polemical intents. "The Woman Who Weeps," sketched in just one day, expresses outrage at a country where freedom from subjugation for all did not seem to include women. Leila's plaintive question in the opening short story, "Were there ever really any brothers . . . tell me, were there?" boldly implies that the brothers have betrayed the revolution by betraying their women. "Women of Algiers" is the first story, and it gives its title to the collection, an index of the paramount importance of its polemical stance.

The confusing state of an increasingly fragmented society is reflected in the collection's fragmented format. *Women of Algiers* presents a series of painful personal questions without ready answers. Mixing newly written pieces, such as "Women of Algiers," with older ones ("Ramadan" dates from the Tunisian exile of 1959, and "Nostalgia of the Horde" goes back to the early sixties), Djebar attempted to bridge two crucial periods, before and after the revolutionary homecoming, in an effort "to bring the past into a dialogue with the present." It led her to a formal experimentation that layered at least three styles: first, the new (for her), oneiric narrative born of her film experience, shifting through levels of perception and time, as in "Women of Algiers"; second, the older, more openly ideological type previously used in her war novels, as in "Horde" or "Ramadan"; and, third, the metafictional writing about writing, as in the meditation on the representation of woman's body that shapes the famous Postface, "Forbidden Gaze, Severed Sound." This experimentation positioned the Algerian self as subject, honing her third literary manner from bourgeois novels to war novels to the free-flowing, polyphonic quartet now in progress. *Women of Algiers* remains essential to a good understanding of the evolution of Djebar's corpus. It is an evolution increasingly anchored in an Algerian reality that is presented as highly personal and idiosyncratic, but that is, for this very reason, representative of a community brutalized by memories of a colonial war, uncertain as to its true history, and perhaps mired in self-doubts. This, I believe, accounts for its backward rather than forward stance, and goes a long way toward explaining why the collection has been mauled by some critics for its regressive rather than progressive glance at the woman's question. Reviewing the collection for the general public, and exasperated at the self-effacing suffering of its female protagonists, Marie-Blanche Tahon, for instance, calls *Women of Algiers* "an essentially male-centered epic," a clearheaded assessment but a singularly limited one.[17]

Djebar left for France in the fall of 1954. On 1 November 1954, war broke out in Algeria, only a few months after the French debacle at Dien Bien Phu on 7 May. This was the beginning of the end for the French empire. By 1958, Djebar had been expelled from Sèvres, the elite normal school with a highly restrictive admission quota where she had been the first colonial admitted on full scholarship; her younger brother was in jail; and her brand-new husband was wanted by the French police. Hoping to sneak back home, the newlyweds smuggled themselves to Tunisia but were refused permission to cross over into Algeria, she says, because "the word had been given to get the women out of there—not that there were very many" (unp.). Female combatants and female logistical participants were being pulled back. In 1956, a historic secret meeting on Algerian soil in the area of La Soummam in eastern Kabylia had produced a consensual platform between all contending revolutionary factions and, among other things, had reluctantly formalized the participation of women in the war, largely because the losses among male combatants were increasing. Two years later, La Soummmam was but a memory. Frantz Fanon's glowing picture of these heady days in *A Dying Colonialism* notwithstanding, problems soon developed between progressive, educated young

17. Marie-Blanche Tahon, review of *Femmes d'Alger dans leur appartement, Ecriture française dans le monde: La tribune des Francophones* 5 (1981): 114.

women eager to do their part and traditional, regressive, male guerrilla fighters eager to stop them. Even if, as Djebar herself grants, their number was never very large—a fact on which pro- and anti-feminist scholars agree—the symbolic impact of the women's presence can hardly be overestimated: they slept on the ground in the bush, they ran dangerous urban missions on equal terms with strange men in strange places, they were allowed everywhere unveiled and free of male control. Indeed, Pontecorvo's controversial film *The Battle of Algiers* uses the breaking of such Moslem taboos with maximum visual impact, showing those young girls (whom Djebar would call the fire carriers in *Women of Algiers*) discarding the veil, bleaching and cutting off their traditional plaited hair: young women who bantered and flirted away with the French soldiers in order to walk through the checkpoints and plant their bombs throughout the European district.

The disappointment of their being dispensed with was bitter. While the first successful flush of nationalistic pride would constitute the stuff of Djebar's third novel, with its upbeat title, *Les enfants du nouveau monde*, this particular period of disappointment in her life would become the subject of her fourth and much darker novel, *Les alouettes naïves*, with a less than upbeat ending: "the war that had just concluded between people was being reborn within the couple."[18] That novel would link, for the first time, the personal war between men and women to the larger war of national liberation. The undertow of uneasiness that often disrupts the lyrical surface of *Alouettes* would eventually erupt in *Women of Algiers*.

While in Tunis, working with refugees, Djebar wrote hard-hitting pieces for Fanon, then editor of the revolutionary *El-Moudjahid*. The newspaper—which did not become the official organ of the party until 1962, after the FLN (Front national de libération, or National Liberation Front) had triumphed as primus inter pares among the contending guerrilla factions in those *willaya* wars that "The Dead Speak" so

18. Djebar, *Les alouettes naïves*, p. 423. Hereafter page citations will be given in the text to the French editions of her works cited in the Bibliography below (my translations).

wrily allude to—functioned in those preindependence days, she says, as "the hopeful voice—and the paper—of Algerians at war" (unp.). In Tunis, Djebar also resumed her studies in history and completed the equivalent of an M.A. thesis with famous French historian Louis Massignon. Somewhat of a mystic himself, he was the ideal director for a research project dealing with one of Tunis's twelfth century holy women. The choice of topic was not random. It brought together the question of the precolonial past with that of women's role in shaping and transmitting it. Mythic tribal grandmothers presented as guardians who "relay" the collective memory abound in her corpus. In *Women of Algiers,* it is the strong great-grandmother who, in "Nostalgia of the Horde," opens the past up to her own great-granddaughters. In "The Dead Speak," it is another strong grandmother—so determined that, married twice, she secures her freedom and her property from her second husband to raise her children alone, "and she not yet forty"—who keeps the family, the village, and the clan together while the men are at the front. This homage to her own maternal grandmother is a typical feature of Djebar's imagination, always triggered by a specific personal detail. The recurring avatars of the ancestor-grandmother make up the collective group of women dancing in the cave of *La Nouba,* celebrating that wildest woman of them all, the Berber queen who held off the invaders and went by the name of Kahina, meaning, "inspired soothsayer," a title that hailed her ability to "relay" past and future.[19]

19. The real Kahina was Dihya, a woman of the Djarawa tribe in the Aurès mountains, an ethnic Berber and a Jew, who pushed back the Arab invaders all the way to the Libyan border at the end of the seventh century and held them off for five years before being killed in battle. The wild woman of origins, whom Kateb Yacine calls *la femme sauvage,* is a constant of his corpus; he sees her as a metaphor for the nation itself, Ur-mother of the tribe. Her memory is a revered part of Algerian folk beliefs: a deep ravine, on the hilly outskirts of Algiers, is named after her (Ravin de la femme sauvage). The difference between Kateb and Djebar is that she uses real flesh-and-blood women to explore the mythical dimensions of a folk belief firmly rooted in real memories, whereas Kateb is content to have retained the mythical figure, ever more out of reach.

Afterword

Having left Tunis for Morocco, Djebar wrote her third novel. *Les enfants du nouveau monde* seemed to be unconditionally on the side of the revolution. In its New World allusion, its hope that this war would, like the American one, usher in a more just society, it presented itself as a rebuke to the First World's paternalistic invention of the Third World. Later, in *Women of Algiers,* she would conceive of the friendship between the Algerian guerrilla woman and the returning Frenchwoman as an inversion of First World maternalistic benevolence. With each new work, her vision was becoming increasingly oppositional.

Although Djebar says that she seldom rereads herself, she claims to "remember with great precision what I set out to do," and so, in flat contradiction to most of her critics, she dismisses theme as the least important aspect of her third novel, preferring to draw attention to the structural challenge she had set up for herself: a new use of time and space, she would come to call architectural. Covering only twenty-four hours, *Les enfants* opens with a tremendously effective scene whose maximum visual impact foreshadowed Djebar's handling of closed and open space in her films to come. From inside the traditional enclosure without a roof, a house courtyard, the women avidly follow the ongoing battle on the mountain above. A literary effect stemming from all-too-real social causes, this binary structuring of two imaginary universes, one male, one female, was deliberate.[20] Motionless, the women can only watch, confined to quarters. Outside, men are fighting, moving, or (to use the term Djebar is so fond of) *circulating,* with its implication of unfettered autonomy of body and mind. To this spatial and kinetic polarity she returns almost obsessively in the present collection, driving the point home with "Forbidden Gaze." If, as critics aver, such

---

20. The binary inside/outside structure was obligingly presented by Djebar herself as the ideological topography of this third novel in most of the interviews she gave regarding this work. Critics have merely followed her lead—most recently, Mildred Mortimer, in *Journeys through the African Novel* (Portsmouth, N.H.: Heinemann, 1990).

Afterword

topography is a constant of the collective imagination in the Maghreb, it is one that Djebar has appropriated in the name of justice. She would take up the cause of Algerian women rather than bemoan, as her writing brothers were wont to do, the plight of sons abandoned to themselves by an absent traitor-father—from Kateb Yacine's 1956 *Nedjma* to Rachid Boudjedra's 1969 *La répudiation* (Repudiation)—or of those abused by an all-too-present father, but one conquered, emasculated, emotionally dead: from Mohammed Dib's 1957 *Le métier à tisser* (The loom), to Nabile Farès's 1970 *Yahia pas de chance* (No-luck Yahia). Nowhere does the binary topography of imaginary space and time, the Bakhtinian "chronotope," appear with more power than in the first short story of the collection, with the description of the forced confinement of a former war heroine by her revolutionary brothers, who no longer know what to do with war heroines now that the war is over.

Djebar returned to Algiers on 30 June 1962, just a few weeks after the publication of *Les enfants*. It was her twenty-sixth birthday and the very eve of independence on 1 July. In the streets of every single Algerian city, the crowds were jubilant, and the mood was one of reconciliation. Within a year, however, the party in power had tried to mold the nation into a unified cultural model. Historian Mostefa Lacheraf, now a member of the government, expounded on the party line by attacking writers who were too bourgeois, and, in fierce public debates, he resurrected the old language question as a test of patriotism.[21] His opening speech to the First Party

---

21. For a succinct, yet accurate assessment of the Maghrebian problem, see Jacqueline Kaye and Abdelhamid Zoubir, *The Ambiguous Compromise: Language, Literature, and National Identity in Algeria and Morocco* (London: Routledge, 1990). Two distinguished thinkers have added their contribution to the larger debate, both from the critic's point of view and from that of the practicing writer: For Africa, Kenyan Ngugi wa Thiong'o, with *Decolonizing the Mind: The Politics of Language in African Literature* (Portsmouth, N.H.: Heinemann, 1986); for the Caribbean, Martinican Edouard Glissant, with *Caribbean Discourse* (Charlottesville: CARAF Books, University Press of Virginia, 1989).

Congress that same year claimed that the new nation must be defined by—and as—a linguistic reterritorialization solidly anchored in Arabic. Quite a few Algerian critics toed the line.

A lecturer at the University of Algiers by then, Djebar began her fourth novel, *Les alouettes naïves,* for catharsis and found herself "blocked." Born female in a patriarchal culture, she was tapping into a suppressed history, *her* story, that she understood, for the first time consciously, to have been repressed by *his* story. If linguistic hegemony was to be enforced, as the new nation would have it, could patriarchal hegemony be far behind? It would take ten years of personal turmoil and the wound of self-enforced silence before she could trust herself to explore the conflict in *Women of Algiers.*

Alouettes was kindly noticed by a few French critics because of its intensely sympathetic portrayal of those who would come to be regarded as "the lost generation," no longer French acculturated but not quite at ease with their new identity. The North African critics, however, were outraged at its sexual frankness. A Western reader must be careful not to misinterpret. As Djebar explains in the 1986 interview for *Contemporary French Civilization,* Islam sees no sin in the act, homage paid by the creature to the Creator. But one cannot help noticing that the just who make it into paradise to be rewarded by eternal delight are men, and heaven's erotic priestesses, the houris, are women. The contravened taboo was in the display of a female pleasure no longer at the service of men. In a long interior monologue, the protagonist discovered that, in the sexual act, she still kept a part of herself inviolate; worse, that her erotic development led to an autonomous sense of self. Without making of Djebar a closet feminist from day one, we can find in her work a steady evolution that would eventually develop into the very strong stand she calls "my own kind of feminism"—in part, due to her encounter with Western feminism, of course; in part, due to her experience with filmmaking; and in part, no doubt, due to her own experience in the refugee camps instead of on the battlefield, because some "apparatchiks" had decided to "get the women out of there" (unp.). Years before *Women of Algiers,* this great turning point in Djebar's career that consecrated her as the *Pasionaria* of the Moslem world, she dared stage a woman as subject rather than object of desire.

With these two war novels, *Enfants* and *Alouettes,* the scope widened. War was supposed to be the great crucible birthing a revolution: new woman, new man, new society. But behind this new social order hid the problematic question of woman's insertion into the new patriarchy that, by any other name, was still a patriarchy. Djebar's off-the-cuff remark about the inflated use of the term *revolution,* "correction, I never use that term; I call it 'the Algerian war,' " marks the distance between the ideal and the reality, between a revolution that never quite bore the fruit of hope, and a war that bore bitter fruit. Stuck at the border, the writer locked horns with the peculiar Marxism of Third World nationalists, who subsume the concept of liberation by reason of sex under that of liberation by reason of race or ethnic group. The American reader may remember that much the same attitude prevailed with the Black Power proponents in this country, some of whom, like Eldrige Cleaver, idolized Fanon to such an extent that they went into exile in Algeria partly to follow in his footsteps.

In the years following the publication of *Alouettes naïves,* critical interest abated. Plunging back into theater work, she adapted several plays for her husband and his crew at the Theâtre de l'Arlequin, a small, experimental stage in Paris, translating and directing at least one, Tom Eyen's *The White Whore and the Bit Player* in 1973. As a meditation on Marilyn Monroe's media cult, it dealt with female desire and its representation, something that would resurface in *Women of Algiers* and take center stage in *L'amour, la fantasia.* That same year an Algerian woman critic published a searing assessment in an Algerian journal, *El Djazairia.* Farah Ziane continued the attack on Djebar's lack of social consciousness, calling her work the perfect example of "marginal literature" on the part of a writer "born in a well-to-do family, of conservative if not puritan bent."[22] These tired arguments *ad feminan*, which Djebar remembers with a matter-of-factness that does not quite conceal her pain ("gut reactions against anything coming from a woman"), were part of a party line on national identity, stiffened by Algeria's self-appointed leading role in the nonaligned summit of that same year that sought to convince the First World that the Third World could stand on its own, politically and culturally. What, then, would constitute an authentically Algerian culture once expression in the French language was removed? The issue was one of political power, and it was enforced by the cultural hegemony of the dominant Arabic-speaking group. As Djebar's contemptuous dismissal of this ongoing Arabization-from-above policy indicates, the issue is far from settled in a country that is, at the very least, multiglossic.[23] Any writer who, after independence, persisted in claiming both her Algerianness and the use of a language other than Arabic was negotiating a minefield.

Djebar is unusual in her defiant embrace of the French language as an instrument of self-liberation. For the generation of writers who reached prominence prior to independence, men all, French had been a problematic oppositional weapon wielded simultaneously to fight the colonizer and to indict the colonized father, who had, if not collaborated in his own defeat, at least been unable to save his son. For Djebar, French gradually became the instrument of a liberation brokered by the bilingual father as an escape from the increasingly restrictive brothers, guardians of the physical and intellectual harem. Witness the emblematic topos she sets up in *L'amour*,

22. Farah Ziane, "Assia Djebar ou la littérature marginale," *El Djazairia* 33 (1973): 38. This is the official publication of the UNFA (Union Nationale des Femmes Algeriennes; National Union of Algerian Women), and it has followed rather narrowly the party line.
23. To simplify: French, classical Arabic on which much of written standard Arabic depends, vernacular Algerian Arabic, Kabyle, Bedouin and assorted tribal languages, as well as other types of Arabic now reaching Algerians through the media (broadcasts from Egypt and the Middle East). The question of language is an old one in colonial and postcolonial literatures.

la fantasia, the openly autobiographical sketch of a little Arab girl going to French school for the first time, "her hand in the father's hand." In a 1985 newspaper article, she went so far as to claim her right to French as "the booty of the colonial war."[24] When Djebar speaks of looting the French language and, in the Overture, of giving a feminist voice to a "language that in turn has taken the veil for so long a time," she is simultaneously appropriating the oppositional tradition and turning it on its head.

Djebar's unusual language so unnerved critics that, as early as *Les enfants du nouveau monde,* some wondered whether her hold on Cartesian French might not be slipping. It was a question that would come back to haunt her, one that Berque's coded praise of her "latinity" still raises.[25] It explains her semifacetious, semi-irritated response regarding her relationship to language in the interview above. This gutting of Cartesian textual order was something that the men had attempted as well (Kateb, for one). But, with Djebar, such stylistics were put at the service of women's justice exclusively. And so, the question of language intersected the structuring of space and, with it, the representation of woman's body.

In the Djebar text, the oppressor's weapon is flooded with Arabic cadences and images, turns of phrase and syntax gradually making their underground presence felt in sinuous arabesques so convoluted that, on occasion, they can become a translator's nightmare.[26] This stylistic signature is quite visible in *Women of Algiers,* particularly in the polyphonic divan of the water-carrier (a traditional poem used to give dignity to the life of an abused woman) in the title story, as well as in the long, dense sentences of the Postface. It figures again in the multivoiced passages from "The Dead Speak," entertwining both the silent and the spoken thoughts of Aïcha, the

24. Assia Djebar, "Du français comme butin," *Quinzaine littéraire* 436 (16–31 March 1985): 25; a special issue on "Ecrire les langues françaises."
25. Berque, "La langue de l'envahisseur," p. 54.
26. McDougal, for instance, simply dropped entire phrases and, on occasion, sentences, when translating the Postface.

repudiated one, with snatches of real conversation and the omniscient narrator's own silent comments to herself. Djebar relies heavily on typography and page makeup for polyphonic effect. The two stories "Women of Algiers" and "The Dead Speak" happen to be among those that do not contain portions borrowed from her previous works and can be said, in this sense, to be new. They show that, by the time she wrote them, the writer was fully conscious of the language question and was eager to connect it to the Woman's question. The reasons were private as well as political: the years of exile and contact with refugees from different linguistic and cultural traditions; the university years in Algiers as a professor of history, where, she remarks in the interview above, "I realize now that I always included oral material, almost without thinking"; the burning question that agitated the new regime eager to establish its authenticity, that of the proper national language in a wildly heteroglossic nation; the avowed party policy that the new nation should be monolingual; and the fact that, for three years in the seventies, she had considered, then discarded, writing in Arabic—she can read classical Arabic, and has gone back to studying it. The question her work posed was: Which (or whose) Arabic?

The film experience in the late seventies, two years of immersion not only in the village life of her home area but in its own languages, changed all that. The film project was triggered as well by months of research at the Algerian institute of musicology and her lasting interest in the variety of distinct vernacular cultures. For instance, Sarah, the young musicologist and authorial alter ego of "Women of Algiers," studies songs from Laghouat, the deep south under the influence of Bedouin desert people, and from Tlemcen, a Berber city to the southwest. Sarah's name is simultaneously a biblical reference and, as a good example of the presence of Arabic in the French text, the short form for Sarahoui, a people who once came from the Saharan south; it also happens to be the name of Djebar's maternal clan through the female line, that of her mother's mother, a descendant of highly revered religious leaders: it is the clan name of the grandmother who became the main model for the central character in "The Dead Speak," Yemma Hedda, and who also gave some of her idiosyncracies (and some of her reminiscences) to the great-grandmother of "Nostalgia of the Horde." In Djebar's writing, no character's name is ever chosen lightly.

As for Tlemcen, a city toward the Moroccan border, it historically also had a strong Jewish community that had preserved the musical treasures brought back from the Spanish exile when Moorish princes in Madrid or Valladollid customarily retained Jewish scholars and artists. Hence, again, the dual connotation of Sarah as a Judeo-Arabic name and the presence, in the first story, "Women of Algiers," of a traditional Jewish singer (the modern Kahina, as it were) that an American reader, used to thinking of Jewish tradition and values as coming primarily from Central Europe, may well find puzzling. Likewise, the title of her first film, *Nouba,* a term that in the vernacular refers to a public celebration, also designates the five movements of an Andalusian type of music, perfected at the Moorish court. On and off in the collection, we stumble upon mentions of the Aurès mountains, a chain to the southeast whose particularly difficult access has long isolated its people from the leveling influence of the central government. The Aurès people were, and have kept the reputation of being, tough, self-sufficient, and not a little savage, with each mountain-crag village an autonomous enclave that has fought off successive waves of invaders—and this includes Arabs pouring into the Maghreb from the east as well as Europeans from the north. The once seminomadic, ruggedly independent Aurès *chaouias* (the term means "shepherds" in their language, a Berber tongue somewhat related to Kabyle), whose women have long thrown off the veil and made decisions for themselves, have kept their ways, their language, and their distinct culture, including the secret craft of weaving the beautiful rugs upon which some of Djebar's characters sleep. It is no accident that drug-addicted, pain-crazed, barren Leila of "Women of Algiers," dreams of running away, a child at the breast, all the way to Lalla Khadidja, the vernacular's affectionate, female nickname for Mount Tamgout. This is the highest peak (close to seven thousand feet) of another mountainous enclave to the north, the Djurdjura mountains of Greater Kabylia, an impassable barrier in the shape of a pyramid. In Djebar's work, Berber and Kabyle cultures and peoples, whose presence in North Africa predates the Roman and Arab invasions, stand for stubbornly individualistic cultural norms and a deeply rooted sense of historical difference; in other words, they constitute an effective human barrier against the juggernaut effect of "Arabization from above." As her last book of the quartet indicates—with Roman mosaics and Libyan statuary rising up from the subterranean void to which the modern sons have consigned their non-Arabic past—Djebar is keenly aware of a blending of cultures on North African soil that goes back well before the Arab invasion of the seventh century.

In turn, this proud sense of the past explains her choice of topic for her upcoming film venture, her third, on the life of a Kabyle woman.[27] The mother of famous poet Jean Amrouche and of novelist and ethnomusicologist Marguerite Taos Amrouche, Fadhma Aïthh Mansour Amrouche was an illegitimate child sent to a Christian school by the local French authorities at the turn of our century. This experience rendered her unfit for village life upon her return. She exiled herself to Tunisia, then to France. Unwanted as a Kabyle Christian convert—who could read and write French but not Arabic, yet was expected by her French teachers to facilitate French encroachment into an Arab-dominant, Moslem culture—she is a good example of the deleterious effect of acculturation, whether one calls it "Arabization" or *mission civilisatrice*. The French "will to civilize" usually resulted only in driving a wedge between various ethnic groups. Gathering all of Djebar's favorite themes—the politics of language, one woman's displacement through two hegemonic and mutually exclusive cultures, the tribes' painful confrontation with modernity, the role of exile and memory—her third film

27. Based on F. A. M. Amrouche's autobiography, *Histoire de ma vie* (Paris: Maspéro, 1969).

promises to be even more controversial than *Nouba*. And the reader who knows Djebar's careful attention to names cannot help noticing that Amrouche's first name, Fadhma, is the Kabyle variation of Fatima, the prophet's favorite daughter, she who says no to Medina (to quote the title of a chapter in *Loin de Médine*). It also happens to be Djebar's own name.

Since it is the women who were able to nurture the old ways, it may well be that in them resides the power to heal a society fractured by multiple conquests: a society that has looked to the West (the memories of the Moors' empire), then to the East (the unfurling of Islamic faith); has suffered through the Turkish occupation, the French colonization, and the subsequent war; and is now going through all the warring discords of the Pan-Arab failure, with its epigone, the swift rise of Islamic fundamentalism. When such a society, oblivious of its past, renews the confinement and abuse of its women, it is practicing a selective and lethal form of amnesia; one that drove Djebar to silence and a "disenchantment . . . akin to despair."

The obsessive urge to break out of cultural confinement was already present in her first two novels, with their precise portrayal of impulsive young girls running away to a radically different universe, French-inspired, and its different cultural and behavioral values. These works were deemed inferior, and their clearly spatial representational semiotics were overlooked. Critics spoke of them as social documents dealing with the typical conflict of colonial literatures, insertion into modernity. I have argued that, correct as this sociological interpretation may be, it is severely limited.[28] The dark underside of the conflict is not the wish to be integrated into a patriarchal society—however strongly the female self may feel its inevitability—but the terror of severance from a primal female bond that, obliterating time and history, transcends the political. These novels constitute Djebar's first, admittedly

28. Clarisse Zimra, "In Her Own Write: The Circular Structures of Linguistic Alienation in Assia Djebar's Early Novels," *Research in African Literatures* 11 (Summer 1980): 206–23.

muted, attempt at an oppositional stance that raises questions of sex and gender, rather than of ethnic group and nation. From these early novels onward, images of genderized space increasingly take center stage in her work, describing the way in which space defines the female body's self-awareness as well as the way the body, in turn, defines itself and moves through such space; hence, in *Women of Algiers*, the intertextual reading between Delacroix's vision and Picasso's. Eventually, such imagery came to dominate the quartet, as in *Ombre sultane*. With its difficult title implying simultaneously the shadow projected by a real sultana (i.e., the sultana's shadow, but not the sultana herself) and the fact of being a shadow to a sultana (i.e., a make-believe sultana but not the real sultana), the 1987 novel claims for its intertextual reference Sheherazade's own story in the Arabian nights, wherein one captive sister functions as the other's self. *Ombre sultane* charts the parallel quests of two women who move about in the streets of a modern Algerian city. One, the traditionally subservient wife, is experimenting with throwing off the veil behind her husband's back and moving about freely outside (again, that most obsessive of Djebar's phrases and figures, "circulating"). The other—Westernized, veil-free, French-educated and that husband's first wife, who divorced him and chose this second wife for him in an ambiguous blend of traditional and nontraditional behavior—now "shadows" this second wife from a distance. By the end of the novel, the liberated first wife—ambivalent about these tentative steps toward freedom—is slowly coming to the decision to go back to her hometown and, if not to a traditional confinement, at least to a less-progressive way of life. Having come full circle from the first two novels about youthful, exuberant runaways, *Ombre sultane* makes the question of genderized boundary breaking, and the psychic of the ensuing freedom, its major theme.

Erotic yet unsexualized (what I have called homoerotic), the women's relationship subverts the patriarchal economy of desire in all of Djebar's novels. It resurfaces in the bond between women that the illiterate wife of *Les enfants du nouveau monde* describes as "thicker than blood" (p. 84), a loyalty that makes her go against her husband's orders at the risk of death. It is at the center of *Les alouettes,* wherein the discovery of female pleasure is brokered and protected by the old grandmother figure. Finally, it structures all of *Women of Algiers,* in defining relationships that will end up forgoing either language—French or Arabic—as the tainted preserve of men.

The most ambitious of Djebar's pre-1980 novels, *Alouettes* expands on this intuition of incompatible male and female universes found in the early novels and hints at the problematic integration of the revolutionary woman in postwar Algeria, where they will be neither whores nor dutiful matrons: "The 'women fighters,' as they are called in the uneasy tones of people baffled by this new species. . . . Apart from the prostitutes, apart from the respectable harems of cloistered wives, where should one put them and, above all, how is one to behave with them?" (*Alouettes,* p. 235). Post-independence Algeria confirmed the uneasy premonitions of *Alouettes.* Those women who would not stay in their place were simply pushed aside, and the new culture reterritorialized according to the old sexualization of male power politics.

The Algerian conflict lasted eight long years, although there had been plenty of warm-up, small-scale rebellions before November 1954. Djebar's casual reference to 8 May 1945 in "The Dead Speak," for example, harks back to a peaceful march of ordinary Moslem civilians in cities of the hinterland, which ended in a bloodbath that spread over several days. No one ever knew who fired the first shot. By the time it was all over, more than one hundred Europeans were dead, and vigilante groups had taken blind revenge on anywhere from six thousand to forty-five thousand Algerians. The repression bought the French ten years of peace, but it also persuaded the Algerians that, sooner or later, they must go to war. The cost of the war was enormous. Over a million Algerians died, which is to say, over ten percent of the population. The French used napalm, large-scale destruction of villages, and the official policy of *regroupements,* so-called regroupings or herding of populations into squalid refugee camps, dubiously called "pacification hamlets"—tactics that the United States would later apply in America's own Vietnam War, under the program of strategic hamlets. Eventually, those French officers traumatized by their own defeat in Vietnam (where many of them had served) and frustrated by the protracted warfare in Algeria came to practice torture. Worse, the government looked the other way.[29]

Women of Algiers starts with a scene of torture. The focus is neither on the barbarity of the French nor even on that of their collaborators, as it had been in the previous war novels, but is exclusively on the Algerians themselves. The collection exhibits a clear steadiness of purpose: these stories are by, for, and about Algerians—hence, the author's lingering puzzlement at their impact outside of Algeria. The only French woman, Anne, is thematically and ideologically a secondary character, whose role is to reinforce the shift in power relations between what colonial administrators used to call the metropolis and its former colony, on the one hand, and, on the other, between women of Islam and their European sisters. Pointedly, Sarah decides not to tell Anne that her "burns" are the result of torture, an implicit comment on the Frenchwoman's dangerous ignorance. The stance is no longer strictly oppositional, Paris versus Algiers, East versus West, which is to say, colonial. In this reshuffling of ideological positioning, Djebar's work is entering a postcolonial phase. It remains, however, in one aspect: that of gender. The torture scene is one practiced by male perpetrators on a female body.

The theme of the battle of the sexes, of which the torture scene is the emblem, marks the continuation from the preceding novel, *Les Alouettes naïves,* to this, her next work, *Women of Algiers,* although more than ten years of silence separate them. The battle no longer unfolds on the ahistorical terrain of erotic exploration; it now permeates all aspects of

29. The best researched and most scholarly source (as well as a "good read") remains Alistair Horne's magnum opus, *A Savage War of Peace: Algeria, 1954–1962* (London: Macmillan, 1977).

life, individual as well as collective, private as well as public. The first story of the collection takes up the question of the "woman fighter," as *Alouettes* had called the baffling new species of nontraditional females (*Alouettes*, p. 235). Leila, who uses heroin for the pains left by war wounds, some of them clearly the result of torture, is kept in solitary confinement by the male doctors of the new, Arab-run, aggressively modern hospital where she may be in the process of losing her mind. This is the new, scientific version of the age-old seraglio: confinement and death of she who will not conform. On the symbolic level, these male doctors are but the transposition of the male attendants presiding at the torture scene that opens "Women of Algiers." Leila is temporarily sprung from her locked hospital room by an artist, himself a homosexual and a former drug addict. Djebar has set out to strip away all social pretenses; she punctures the self-serving hypocrisy of the new order. Broadly sketched in the first story, the allegorical landscape is gradually expanded: this new species, the postrevolution woman, has the choice between death by annihilation to the will of a master (the return to a traditional marriage, devoutedly hoped for in "The Dead Speak," but just as violently shunned in "There Is No Exile") or death by insanity. The addict's refusal of treatment is a rejection of the revolutionary brothers' definition of well and unwell, acceptable and unacceptable, forms of female self-assertion.

The women fighters are also an embarrassment because their female flesh simply won't go away, making a public spectacle out of the breaking of the most powerful taboo in Islam: the denuding or unveiling of woman. The imagery of confinement and the language of the tortured body are intertwined in *Women of Algiers,* subjects that connect the collection to Djebar's preceding works, negative semiotics that implies its reverse: a female body as subject—not only of its own desire (the homoerotic strain persists)—but subject of its own mode of writing, acting out its own textual self-inscription. This process, which in the wake of French theory Djebar calls "scriptive" (unp.) unfolds a series of images that bypass the patriarchal desire wherein the female body can only be a silent object looked at from the outside, the target of a French painter's "forbidden gaze," as is the body stretched on the torture table of the opening scene. It is a body whose blindfolded face "forbids" her to look back. In *Women of Algiers,* every human experience, even the social experience, must be explored through the body. There is simply no other way for women whose society, enforcing female modesty and its corresponding taboo on verbal expression, has denied them access to any language other than that of the flesh. The female flesh has its specific drives as both lived reality and transcendental symbol. It functions as a metaphor for that other, nonsubjugated female self that language, the preserve of men, cannot access. Leila's scarred body is its own hieroglyphic cry for help, as is Sarah's. The only way that Sarah, who's "always had a hard time with words," can respond is by silently disrobing. The Arabic-speaking reader may also hear the silent rustle of the vernacular, as Sarah's garment falls, denuding/unveiling her. In the Algerian vernacular, the woman who goes "unveiled" is said to go "denuded," concepts and ideological consequences on which the Postface, "Forbidden Gaze, Severed Sound," theorizes at length.

The passionate encounter between Sarah and Leila counterbalances man's own encounter with the female body, the torture scene that Sarah's husband dreams night after night. In this nightmarish sequence, man is the director of a film whose sound has been "severed." Although in its use of the passive voice the first story leaves out the culprit, the Postface reminds us that it is men who have purposely obliterated the truth, severed the sound of woman's voice, and sequestered its physical equivalent, woman's body. This cutoff sound stands for man's refusal to acknowledge the physical specificity of the women fighters, the significance of their maimed, naked bodies, a recognition that would integrate them into the new social order by making their physical sacrifice not only acceptable but honorable. Their well-documented tortures included ghastly genital mutilations: for instance, the well-publicized case of Djamila Bouhired, real-life "fire carrier" daughter to

Afterword

Djebar's imaginary "water carrier," who is clearly referred
to in the story of Messaouda in the Postface. As things stand
in "Women of Algiers," the physical signs of the horrors of
war are, on the female body, dishonorable. The female body
is the emblem of a guilt the brothers can escape only by denying its language. Cries Leila: "They are ashamed of me."[30] In
fact, they are ashamed of themselves, of their inability to observe the ancient patriarchal injunction to keep their women
inviolate, untouched—confined. As the silent yet screaming
signifier of their private failure in the midst of a public victory, mutilated female flesh recurs throughout the collection,
in the pummeled face of "The Weeping Woman," as well as
in its doubles, repudiated Aïcha of the unrequited love and
sunken chest in "The Dead Speak" or the old water carrier of
the broken spirit and the broken body in "Women of Algiers."

And yet in this world that, as Djebar concedes in the interview, she may have wished "without men," one is struck by
the compassion that the writer feels for her male characters;
even if, as the interview makes clear, she is not altogether
reconciled to it herself. "The Dead Speak," for instance, is
highly critical of "the little one" who returns as a hero to an
ancestral world he no longer understands, a world that is, for
him, the world of "before"; he will use the silent devotion
of his repudiated cousin in much the same way that he accepted as his due the war sacrifices of his grandmother. The
story juxtaposes quietly but rather effectively images of the
long, traditional wake in honor of Yemma Hadda to the swift
dumping of often nameless bodies of dead guerrilla fighters
in the bush. Hardened by the experience of war, spiritually
anesthetized by its physical horrors against the moral pain of
others (his grandmother, who is barely alive upon his return,
her sharecropper, her repudiated niece), Hassan stands at the

30. A cry eerily echoed by Kateb, during a symposium at Temple University
in March 1988: "There is among us [Algerians] a feeling of guilt toward
women, because we know how much we oppress them" (quoted in Bernard
Aresu's Introduction to Nedjma [Charlottesville: CARAF Books, University
Press of Virginia, 1991], p. xx).

conclusion of the story on the public square, celebrating the first day of independence with the requisite political speech about heroes, as the fashionable white veils of female admirers billow in the summer breeze. We are on the seventh day after his grandmother's funeral, and the detail must be shocking for a devout Moslem. This should be a full day of ritual mourning and prayers over the freshly dug grave of the departed. Pointedly, the story closes with Aïcha, the unwanted one, in silent meditation over Yemma Hadda's burial spot. These two women are the only true, self-sacrificing heroines of a sordid new order.

But the story seizes the returning grandson, a former *willaya* fighter, at the very moment of doubt, poised between two incompatible worlds. The moment of return, the very moment of revolution's triumph is also, for him, a moment of doubt: of himself, of this "revolution" that Djebar, as she reminds us in the interview, has never called by that too-optimistic name. Hassan can no longer feel, but we are made to feel for him, as we are made to feel for the outmoded devotion of the old sharecropper and as we are made to feel for a truer war hero: Ali, the surgeon of "Women of Algiers," likewise so drained by the war that he can respond neither to his wife nor to his son. Yet, in spite of their failing marriage, she defends him against his son's rage at not having a hero for a father. This is Djebar's response to the writers-sons' indictment of the fathers: this refusal to glorify the past, this attempt to see it clearly, may be another, purer form of heroism. In each story, the real tragedy of incommunicability, the real drama of dehumanization wrought by the war, strikes down only the men; for the women, however imperfectly, have each other. They have a history that binds them together because, as the great-grandmother of the "Horde" makes plain, it has come down to them through the centuries of the oral tradition: a chain of women bound by a chain of stories by means of which they resist simultaneously the brothers' amnesia and the conqueror's brutality, through the age-old power of what Djebar calls, in the Overture, their own "underground" voice. For, as she discovered, "woman's memory spans centuries."

Afterword

However, *Women of Algiers* is far from celebrating woman's triumph. "Nostalgia of the Horde" is the transmitter of a subterranean ambivalence, since the great-grandmother's story is one of social integration at the cost of autonomy: the message is one of submission. Should the great-grand-daughters emulate the terrified child bride, or should they resist the father? Freedom from pain, the epiphany of physical and spiritual self-integration, comes but briefly in "Women of Algiers," in the physical contact between Sarah and Leila. It lasts eternally only in the movements of Picasso's dancers; that is to say, it remains an imaginary projection of desire in an ideal female universe. Overture and Postface frame an act of representational ambivalence, a *mise en abyme*—the liter-ary device by which a piece of writing calls attention to the artificiality of the imaginary compact and calls into question the very conditions of its own production.

As *mise-en-abyme* devices for the collection of short stories, Picasso's dancers pose rhetorical and visual questions that cannot find an answer. "Are they *really* speaking *in truth?*" asks Djebar's Overture (my italics). The phrase puns on *vrai-ment,* the French word meaning simultaneously "really" and "truthfully." Is this joyous celebration really happening in the real world? And the short stories proceed to demonstrate that it is not—not yet. Is this celebration happening in truth? And the short stories proceed to show that it is a truth the society refuses to grant. How is one to speak freely with the constant awareness of "the eye through the peephole"—liter-ally, in the original French, the spying eye (*oeil-espion*). The original term evokes simultaneously the attentive "female ser-vant" of the 1832 painting, described in the Postface, whose eyes may indeed be those of a spy, and the spyglass, like the spying hole (peephole) in the door of a seraglio as yet un-opened to the sun. Eventually, spying eye and spyglass become metonyms for the orientalist painter himself. In Delacroix's painting, Djebar draws our attention to the representational symbol of the spying act, the attentive "woman servant" of the Postface, whose attention is simultaneously aural and visual; she is the proxy of the master, as the great-grandmother of

"Nostalgia of the Horde" had been proxy of the father: both servant and great-grandmother are female icons of the law. Picasso's painting says that women must break out into the open, birth themselves by reinventing the language of the body, of the precognitive impulse, the last territory uncharted by Logos. For dance constitutes its own visual language and needs no speech, no words under veils. In Picasso's painting, the women are naked, their language "unveiled," and the spy-servant is no more.

But Picasso's is only an imaginary response to Delacroix, whereas Delacroix's painting had been triggered by "real" Algerian women. Thus, working our way back from Picasso's open space to Delacroix's restrictive enclosure, we move back to a silent painting of silenced women, motionless bodies, "as if surprised in their conversation." The absence of sound is accompanied by the absence of eye contact: severed sound and lost gaze. "Forbidden gaze," because it is taboo for Moslem females to look a man in the eye—and even more so an infidel. "Forbidden" also in the other direction, because the painter should not be there. The year is 1832. The author reminds us: "Only two years earlier, the French painter would have been there at the risk of his life," had he been found there; barely two years, which is to say at the very moment of conquest, when any intruder inside the harem could be killed on sight. The painting thus commemorates simultaneously the colonial aggression and the gendered transgression: male violation of female space in both cases, since woman is Algeria. In this absence of eye contact, the posed women are gazeless, hence voiceless. Other voiceless and gazeless women come back to haunt us, the blindfolded, anonymous woman of Ali's nightmare, sacrificial goat on the altar of the revolution; the shrouded body of Yemma, no less sacrificed by a revolutionary grandson who has forgotten the old ways and the true meaning of *Yemma*—the respectful title for older women and the arabic for "mother." One might say that, in the one hundred and fifty years since the first documented alien gaze invaded the harem's space in Delacroix's painting, nothing has changed. Both really and truthfully.

Afterword

But this first Western look at the other's other, Delacroix's gaze, sees only sumptuously dressed and bejeweled objects offered for contemplation; "posed" statues off which the orientalist's gaze bounces. Inward-looking, the women are very much subjects unto themselves. The gaze that passes between the foregrounded two, clearly subjects to each other for whom the intruding painter is object, triggers their granddaughter's writing, one hundred and forty-four years later. This "world without men" is not necessarily inimical to men, but it has no use for them as long as they insist on limiting the lives of women. Nor does Djebar, in this intertextual rewriting of Delacroix's vision, advocate a Pollyannish crosspollination between Western and non-Western values. She has been battered enough by the postwar politics of her country to have lost her illusions. More modestly, and perhaps more courageously, she speaks for a personal freedom that would liberate women and men from the shackles of tradition, wherever and whenever these features hinder their mental and physical well-being. In so doing, she speaks for us all.[31]

Clarisse Zimra
Southern Illinois University

31. This translation could not have seen completion without the patient forbearance of press editor Cynthia Foote and the generous collaboration of all concerned in solving problems caused by a maddening aspect of Djebar's original style: the swift shifting among language registers, as well as the deliberate use of Arabic vernacular in semitranslation (for example, the habitual use of "my liver"—i.e., my most precious part—for something like "my beloved"). A smooth passage may, now and then, be dotted with little traffic bumps, as it were. Meandering run-on sentences and a swift succession of fragments are also a Djebar feature, as well as highly idiosyncratic punctuation, marking the halting and circling of mental processes.

WORKS IN FRENCH

Novels

La soif. Paris: Julliard, 1957.
Les impatients. Paris: Julliard, 1958.
Les enfants du nouveau monde. Paris: Julliard, 1962.
Les alouettes naïves. Paris: Julliard, 1967.
L'amour, la fantasia. Paris: Jean-Claude Lattès, 1985.
Ombre sultane. Paris: Jean-Claude Lattès, 1987.
Loin de Médine. Paris: Albin Michel, 1991.

Play

Rouge l'aube. Algiers: SNED, 1969.

Poetry

Poèmes pour l'Algérie heureuse. Algiers: SNED, 1969.

Short stories

Femmes d'Alger dans leur appartement. Paris: des femmes, 1980.

Films

La nouba des femmes du Mont Chenoua. 1979.
La zerda et les chants de l'oubli. 1982.

WORKS IN ENGLISH TRANSLATION

The Mischief (La soif). Trans. Frances Frenaye. New York: Simon and Schuster, 1958.
Sister to Sheherazade (Ombre sultane). Trans. Dorothy S. Blair. London: Quartet, 1987.
Fantasia, an Algerian Cavalcade (L'amour, la fantasia). Trans. Dorothy S. Blair. London: Quartet, 1988.

———————

CARAF Books
Caribbean and African Literature
Translated from French

A number of writers from very different cultures in Africa and the Caribbean continue to write in French although their daily communication may be in another language. While this use of French brings their creative vision to a more diverse international public, it inevitably enriches and often deforms the conventions of classical French, producing new regional idioms worthy of notice in their own right. The works of these francophone writers offer valuable insights into a highly varied group of complex and evolving cultures. The CARAF Books series was founded in an effort to make these works available to a public of English-speaking readers.

For students, scholars, and general readers, CARAF offers selected novels, short stories, plays, poetry, and essays that have attracted attention across national boundaries. In most cases the works are published in English for the first time. The specialists presenting the works have often interviewed the author in preparing background materials, and each title includes an original essay situating the work within its own literary and social context and offering a guide to thoughtful reading.

Caraf Books